# Buried Once

## Max Dalman

Originally published 1946
London, U.K.

This edition published 2023 by

OREON

an imprint of

The Oleander Press
16 Orchard Street
Cambridge
CB1 1JT

www.oleanderpress.com

ISBN: 9781915475343

Sign up to our infrequent newsletter
to **receive a free ePub** of
*Fatality in Fleet Street*
by Christopher St John Sprigg and get
news of new titles, discounts and give-aways!

www.oleanderpress.com/golden-age-crime

A CIP catalogue record for the book
is available from the British Library.

Cover design, typesetting & ebook: neorelix

# Contents

# 1

---

# Witching Hour

FOR THE THIRD TIME in half a mile Virginia Blakeney stopped and looked back. Perversely enough, the clouds chose that precise moment to cover the moon, and she could see little enough; but there was no doubt about it. Someone was following her.

For two or three seconds after she herself had come to a halt she could hear the footsteps continuing somewhere in the blackness of the lane. Then came silence. Whoever, or whatever, it might be back there in the shadows was waiting too.

If Virginia had been unduly afflicted by nerves, she would never have chosen to walk the two miles from Utton Road station at midnight. She was used to the country, and to its normal night sounds. When the expected car had failed to arrive to meet her train, she had set off without a qualm, though there was scarcely a house between the station and her home. But there was something a little frightening about this. Why should her follower stop whenever she stopped, and yet hurry whenever she hurried? After her second halt, she had deliberately put on speed to outstrip him; but at the end of a breathless quarter-mile, there he was, if anything closer than ever.

Besides, it was such a queer step. Certainly it was not the ordinary thud of country boots. It was lighter, and yet dragging, suggestive of lameness. It might be only her imagination that detected something stealthy in it. Just for a moment, she seemed to have a vision of an odd, misshapen figure, stumbling and feeling its way behind her, until it came close enough to— But that was silly. She told herself that she was becoming fanciful, and after listening vainly for a moment longer started forward again.

Almost immediately the following step recommenced. She heard it with a feeling almost akin to panic. There was something in the relentless persistency of it which unnerved her. And then, as she remembered the road ahead, the thought came to her that there was a chance of testing it once and for all. Just ahead there was a turning; or rather, the road forked. One branch was the merest track, a grassy accommodation lane along which no one could conceivably have any reason for travelling at that time of night. On the other hand, it was possible, for anyone who knew the country well, to regain the main road across country without any great loss of time. If she were to turn up there, she might throw her pursuer – she was already thinking of the footsteps' owner in that light – off the track completely. Or, if he followed, she would at least know the worst.

At the junction of the two lanes she stopped again. Again the steps continued for a few steps and stopped in their turn. That was enough. She crossed the road to enter the track, and immediately the echoing tread broke out again behind her, evidently hurrying.

She broke into a run as she reached the fork. On the rutted, overgrown surface her feet made scarcely a sound. The shambling steps behind came more distinctly. They could not be twenty yards away. Over the roadway the overhanging boughs of the uncut hazels made a positive tunnel, the floor of which was silvered only in patches by the capricious moonlight. Then the thought crossed her mind that, if there was danger, this was even worse than the lane that she had left—more lonely, more isolated. It was too late to go back. As she reached a bend which would hide the junction from her sight, she glanced back, in the realisation that her pursuer must be reaching the critical point. The action was fatal. Even as she was aware of the dim figure framed in the entrance to the lane, she stumbled in a hidden cart rut and fell headlong. A stone caught her shin. In spite of herself she let out a little cry of pain.

In an instant she was on her feet again, staring at the stranger in something very like terror. What she saw confirmed her most sinister imaginings. He had stopped too, silhouetted against the opening, with the fitful half-light and shadow half revealing and half hiding his shape. And it had all the monstrosity of her fancy. Hugely tall, it was marred by a strangely-formed, enormous hump on the back, and a large, foreign-looking hat gave the head a vast disproportion. That was all she had time to see. At a limping run the figure started forward, coming straight towards her.

Flight was her first impulse. But that was useless. She might hide. The spot where she had fallen was in the deepest shadow, and it was impossible that she could have been seen. On a sudden impulse she dived noiselessly towards the ditch, and lay there panting as the footsteps pounded forward. In her utter panic, she was aware of nothing else, except for the wild beating of her own heart, which it seemed as though the other must hear.

He was coming nearer. He was almost level; in a minute or two he would be past. Then she could make a break for the road. But luck was against her. Perhaps it was the very stone over which she herself had fallen. The stranger also tripped, though without actually losing his balance. She heard a grunt of pain, and he seemed to be exercising a war dance on one leg.

As he finished, he kicked out viciously, and something hard struck her a sharp blow on her injured leg.

Probably she cried out, though she did not know it. She was suddenly aware of a figure looming over her, apparently gazing down. Then she heard a startled exclamation.

"Good heavens! What—?"

In the tone of the voice there was complete reassurance. Her fears vanished like magic. She rose to her feet, conscious in the place of her vanished panic of an anxiety not to appear more ridiculous than was absolutely necessary. Then there was the rattle of matches and a light flared.

Even that feeble flame was enough to show how utterly preposterous her fancies had been. It revealed the lower half of a young good-looking face wearing an expression of mild bewilderment, though the top of it was still hidden by a large, floppy hat of the kind affected by some artists, and by even more people who wish to appear artistic. The light showed also the large canvas rucksack strapped to the broad shoulders covered in a rough tweed coat. Then the match flickered and went out, and as it did so, he spoke.

"I say— I'm fearfully sorry... I'd no idea— Did I hurt you?"

Virginia shook her head, not thinking of the uselessness of that form of reply in the darkness. For the moment she was speechless. She repressed a wild impulse to laugh hysterically, and was conscious of a distinct feeling of gratitude that there was no light for him to see her blushes.

"Are you all right?" the voice came anxiously. "Silly thing to do... Lost my temper... Did it hurt you?"

"It—it's nothing," Virginia stammered, though the throbbing of her leg gave the lie to the answer. "What—what was it?"

"A beastly stone! Caught my pet corn—a recently-acquired pet, I might say. I kicked it and— You see, I never expected—"

Virginia felt, with some embarrassment, the need for giving an explanation of one's presence crouching in a marshy ditch in a remote country lane at midnight. There seemed to be nothing for it but the truth.

"I don't see how you possibly could," she admitted. "You see—I was frightened—a little. I heard you following and couldn't make out who or what it was. There's never anyone about here at this time of night, and I was such an idiot that I imagined—"

"There certainly isn't," the young man interrupted wholeheartedly. "That's why I was following you—and even so I was beginning to think it was a will-o'-the-wisp or somethi ng... But why—?"

"The moonlight made you look so queer," Virginia hurried on. "And I thought you were chasing me. So I hid in the ditch to let you go by."

His voice as he replied was distinctly apologetic.

"I'm fearfully sorry... The fact is, I'd lost my way, and I couldn't see a soul to ask. I knocked at one house—the only one I came across. A chap answered in a Cockney accent from the bedroom window and he told me to go—" He broke off. Well, he suggested a destination which, I hope, is not mine," he paraphrased carefully. "Then I heard you and tried to catch up. But I kept on thinking that I'd lost you. I had to stop and listen—"

"And I stopped to listen for you—and hurried on so as to get away!" Virginia laughed a little shamefacedly; then hurried on. "Where did you want to get to?"

"I don't expect you've ever heard of it. No one has, except one chap, and all his directions were like this: 'Well, zur, you go down Marsh End Lane, and past thicky haystack and through the gap past Thompson's post—' I know I got as far as Marsh End Lane—I found the marsh. That's my last recognisable point."

"But where—?"

"Lower Utton... I suppose there is such a place? The map said so, but—"

"It's about two and a half miles away," Virginia told him. "I'm going near there. If you like—"

"I'd be awfully grateful. Then it's up here?"

"No... Not exactly." Virginia laughed again. "You see, I came up here to put you off the scent... You can't imagine how sinister you looked in the moonlight with that pack... This way."

There was silence for a moment as they started to retrace their footsteps towards the lane. Then the young man heaved an exaggerated sigh.

"That pack—" he said mournfully. "There you put your finger on the crux of the matter... That's why I'm here."

"But—" Virginia began. "But you're not selling something?"

"No. I've been sold—a pup. Doctor's orders. You see, it's like this. Sometimes I work. Really I do—quite hard. Well, not being used to it, of course it gets me down. I'd been over-doing it. The doctor ordered a complete rest and suggested a walking tour!" He laughed hollowly. "As a complete rest—a walking tour!" he repeated. "Just fancy that!"

"I thought you were lame... We turn here."

There was silence again for a little while. In spite of the strangeness of their meeting, Virginia had plenty of other things to think about; and her thoughts had travelled so far from her companion that she came to herself with a start as the flow of conversation recommenced.

"I'd better introduce myself, if I may?... My name's May-field—Tony Mayfield."

He waited as if for her to reciprocate, but she did not.

"I say," he went on, unrebuffed, "I suppose there's a pub at this place—Lower Utton? It's marked on the map. I meant to sleep there."

"What?" Virginia roused herself to answer. "Yes... The Golden Lion... But I'm afraid that Mr. Sidley will be asleep—"

"I'll wake him." There was grim determination in his voice. "You know this place quite well then? You live here?"

"Not exactly at Utton." She was aware that he was fishing for information, and was momentarily tempted for that very reason to refuse it. Then she repented. "Scalford," she confessed. "I turn off soon. But the road's quite plain from where I leave you."

"Scalford?" There was a new interest in his voice. "I say, that's the place the chap disappeared from, isn't it?"

"Disappeared?"

There was nothing in the single word to warn him and he could not see her face. He embarked upon the explanation with enthusiasm.

"Yes... At least, that's what people are saying... Chap of the name of Blakeney—George Blakeney—"

"George—?" This time there was no mistaking the emotion in her voice; though he could not tell precisely what it was. "It—it's not true. It can't be true!"

"Well, you know, that's what they are saying... Went off a few days ago, it appears, in the middle of the night, without a word to anyone. Not been seen since... The family's offering some lame explanation or other that no one believes... Of course, it may be all gossip—"

"But—but why—" With a desperate effort she managed to keep a measure of calmness in her voice. "What happened? Why should he—?"

"There was some talk of his having got into trouble—" Mayfield hesitated. He had a horrible suspicion that he was unintentionally plunging into deeper waters than he liked. "Doing a bolt, you know—"

"Why?" Virginia demanded, and it was impossible to tell from her voice what prompted the question. "What trouble?"

"Really, I don't know exactly—" Mayfield hesitated. "There may be nothing in it—"

"But they said something? What was it?"

There was an urgency in her tone which obviously was not going to accept any denial. Tony lost his head.

"There was some talk of a woman—" he admitted, and wished next moment that he had not. "Of course, I don't know any details... It's simply what people were saying. When I heard the name—"

"What happened to him?"

"They were saying he'd left the country—to South America or somewhere—"

"Who?"

"Oh," Tony said unhappily. "Just some people in a pub... But of course probably there's nothing in it. People will gossip—"

"And repeat gossip." She stopped and faced him, and as the moonlight fell on her face he saw that she was angry. "You say there's nothing in it, and yet you repeat it in casual conversation with someone you don't know—"

"But I didn't mean—" Tony began.

She interrupted him. "You can't miss your way... About a mile straight on—down the hill. The first village you come to... Good night, Mr.—Mr. Mayfield."

Before he could attempt to answer she had crossed the road at a run to a small gate which pierced the high bank on the right. The slam of its closing broke in upon his pleading.

"But, please—I didn't mean—"

She scarcely heard the words. Worry and indignation combined to make her almost unaware of the bumpy pathway along which she was hurrying, and it was only when the first stile barred her way that she glanced back. He had made no attempt to follow. A momentary compunction struck her. Of course, he could not know. But he should not have said it—like that... It could not be true. And yet the certainty that it was grew in her steadily as she hastened on through the dewy grass towards where the church tower showed silvery in the moonlight two hundred yards ahead.

That was the meaning of the message she had received. In spite of the innocence of its wording, it had aroused her alarm sufficiently to make her risk the last train and a doubtful connection rather than wait until the morning. It must be true. George had disappeared. But why? Her anger against Tony Mayfield suddenly revived as she recalled the explanation which he had hesitantly given. That must be gossip—the malicious gossip of villagers or servants who are never at a loss for a discreditable explanation of anything unintelligible. But why could he have gone? Had he really gone? The questions repeated themselves monotonously without finding answers.

The tall stile with its stone steps brought her to her senses again. She realised that she was very tired. There was a sharp pain in her side as she breathed, and her bruised leg throbbed painfully. On the topmost step she paused for a moment to recover her breath, clutching the coping of the wall as a sudden faintness threatened to overwhelm her. With closed eyes she had stood for a couple of minutes when imperceptibly she became conscious of a strange sound.

"Crunch... Thud... Crunch... Thud... Click... Thud—"

Rhythmically, uninterruptedly it went on, the sharp, metallic clicks seeming to punctuate at irregular intervals the normal alternation of the other two sounds. She listened automatically, with growing bewilderment. It came from the churchyard at her side. With an uncomfortable clutch at her heart she turned and looked, and as she did so the noise stopped.

For the time being the clouds had passed over. In the cold, soft light the tombstones shone with a ghastly whiteness, contrasting oddly with the sombre shapes of the tall yew trees and the grey of the dew-soaked grass. Beyond the looming darkness of the trees the shape of the church tower rose blackly against the summer sky, and from the tall ilex trees on the far side came the faintest rustle of sound. Beyond that there was nothing.

She shivered a little as she looked. Upper Utton Church stood remote from such village as existed; and to a great extent the village had ceased to exist. Even in the bright sunlight it was a gloomy place, suggestive of death and decay, and in the moonlight it was pervaded with an appalling loneliness which frightened her. Virginia was not by nature superstitious, but for more human reasons she would never have taken the short cut if her anger had not momentarily made her forget everything. Just beyond the great square-topped tomb of some long-forgotten family, the withering wreaths showed faintly on the grave where her mother had been buried only a few days before. Involuntarily she glanced towards it with a catch in her breath which was almost a sob, and as she did so the noise recommenced.

"Crunch... Thud... Crunch... Thud... Click..."

It sounded from the very corner where the grave lay. And with a thrill of horror it came to her what it was. Someone was digging.

To save her life she could not have moved. "Crunch... Thud ... Crunch... Thud..." and then the click of the spade striking a stone in the sandy soil.

All at once something gleamed in the moonlight, the gleam of polished steel. It flickered and disappeared, to reappear a moment later in conjunction with the rhythmical beat of the digging. It saw the gleam of the moonbeams on a spade. And only then she saw the dark figure below it.

Surely it was not a man. It was much too short. Then she saw the reason. Whatever it was was standing almost up to the shoulders in the grave which had already been half dug out.

The skin prickled on the back of her neck as she stood staring in a stricken fascination. There was a queer story about the churchyard; of the bad old days of body snatching, when a "resurrection man" had been found dead in the grave he had opened, killed by the terror of what he had found there. Now it recurred to her mind in a surge of blind panic. But it must be human. It must. For some unknown reason it must be the old gravedigger engaged on some perfectly legitimate work. Her reason told her that, even though a small voice inside her said that it was absurd... She had half convinced herself, when there was a queer hollow sound as though the spade had struck something wooden. The thuds gave place to a faint scraping sound which sounded eerily in the stillness. It ceased. A tiny light glowed, outlining the oblong of the open excavation. For a moment the oblong patch showed yellow. Then there was only the pallor of the moon.

The digger was clambering out of the grave. She could make out its moving blackness against the pile of excavated earth. The next instant it was standing in full view, though that view permitted her to see no more than a tall dark shape against the dusky stone wall. It had its back towards her; at least there was no pale oblong of a face. She saw its arms raised to the sky in a sudden violent gesture; then it turned. Something seemed to snap in Virginia's brain. Beyond a point terror cannot increase. She had to do something or faint; and she was not the kind of girl who was given to fainting. To her own unutterable amazement she moistened her dry lips with a tongue which was scarcely less parched and called out.

"Who—who's that?" The words sounded quaveringly. "What are—what are you doing?"

There was no reply. Instead, for a second or two the figure hesitated; then with queer, soundless leaps began to cross the tombstones towards her. In her new desperate courage she stood it for half a minute. There was a face. There was a grain of comfort in that; but the head was bent and she could not distinguish it. For a second or two a great flat-topped stone barred its way, and the moonlight fell full upon it raised momentarily to the sky.

With a queer, strangled cry Virginia stumbled down the steps and ran blindly, for the white beams shone on the grinning features of a skull.

# 2

# Distinctly Odd

"It certainly is very odd, Stroud—distinctly odd... Most incomprehensible... I cannot understand—"

Spoken in a mild, cultured accent vaguely reminiscent of Oxford, the words came to the ears of Tony Mayfield as he lay irreverently sprawling on a sun-warmed, moss-grown tomb in Upper Utton churchyard. They awakened him completely, and he opened his eyes and sat up. If there was anything odd and incomprehensible, there was at least a sporting chance that it was his business.

He had been thoroughly tired, after a lazy day which gave him no excuse except the fatigue of the day before. According to his programme he should have left Lower Utton behind him bright and early that morning, and he assured himself that it was the necessity of resting his twin blisters and an active young corn which had made him postpone his departure. That there was any other reason he steadfastly refused to admit. In fact, on that subject he felt distinctly uncomfortable, and he could have blushed at the mere thought. A few innocent, and of course quite purposeless, enquiries had informed him that the inhabitants of Scalford House were John Blakeney, the bedridden squire, Richard and George Blakeney, his sons, and Virginia Blakeney, his daughter. The enormity of his lapse was only too plain.

Besides, in all probability Virginia had been right. The supposed disappearance rested upon the slightest foundation; for the alleged woman in the case there seemed to be no foundation whatever. George was a fairly stiff landlord—for, during his father's illness, he had had the management of the estate; he was a stiff man generally, and like many virtuous souls, was not liked. George had had the temerity to go off unexpectedly, without telling the world in general and the village in particular where and why he had gone. And that was all. He was inclined to dismiss the mysterious disappearance of George as a myth.

There remained Virginia, however, and the two glimpses he had had of her face, by match and moonlight, persisted oddly in his mind. He had spent a large part of the morning trying to arrange an accidental meeting in the vicinity of Scalford House, but without result. Virginia remained invisible; the whole house was blankly unresponsive, and he had seen no living soul but a gardener and a couple of servants. He dared not take the simple course of knocking at the door. If Virginia's mood of the night before persisted, he judged that she would have him thrown out on sight. And so, he had booked rooms at the inn for another night.

Lunchtime, and the dartboard at the inn, had elicited the story of the ghost-struck bodysnatcher; and that was what had brought him to Upper Utton churchyard. Fatigue, disappointment or the unaccustomed midday beer had made him fall asleep on the very grave associated with the legend; and he had slumbered untroubled by ghosts for what must have been a considerable time.

He pricked up his ears as the cultured voice spoke again, coming from just beyond the yew tree which shaded him.

"Are you sure, Stroud," it reasoned, "are you sure that there can be no mistake? Possibly by some inadvertence you left the rake there when the grave was filled in?... It is certainly

distinctly odd... I cannot think that here in our peaceful village—"

Two pairs of trouser legs and boots were all that could
be seen of the speakers. They were standing beside a mound
of fresh earth, and one, Tony judged, was clerical; the other,
sexton.

"How could I now, your Reverence?" demanded another
voice in a tone of injury. "And me using it that same evening
afterwards?... No, Vicar, I tell 'ee she've been dug up! Leastways, the grave have... Look at thick rake, I tell 'ee, sir! Did'n
bury hisself, did'm?"

A gnarled hand came into view with the words. Following
its gesture Tony noticed for the first time the object which it
indicated. There was nothing particularly exciting about it.
An ordinary rounded piece of wood, like the top of a broom
handle, projected two or three feet above the newly-turned
earth. Evidently it was the subject of the dispute, but for the
moment its exact significance escaped him.

"Some foolish joke, perhaps?" the vicar suggested, but
without much hope. "Perhaps it has simply been driven in?
Without, of course, the head attached."

He added the last words hastily with the air of one who
anticipates an objection to an otherwise reasonable theory.

"I've pulled 'en and I've pulled 'en, your Reverence, till I
near pulled my arms out. That there sand wouldn't hold 'en
thicky way... No, sir. Her ladyship have been dug up, that's
what I say... Leastways, the grave have."

He repeated the final words like one who hopes by
mere repetition to convince an exceptionally stupid listener.
Abruptly it came to Tony that he was listening to a private conversation; but there are times, he told himself, when
eavesdropping becomes a positive duty. And besides, it was
all too interesting. In the minute of silence during which the
vicar was pondering his rejoinder, he had suddenly realised
what it was all about. Apparently the vicar also understood.

"It almost seems, Stroud, as if you must be right," came his voice regretfully. "Dear me, what a lamentable incident!... And what do you suggest, Stroud?"

"Why, dig her ladyship up again, and see if she be there, sir—then we'd know for sure." Stroud's voice had the patience of one who points out the obvious. "And I'd get my rake, anyhow!"

"Oh, no... Really. No... I don't think we can do that, Stroud. I believe the Home Secretary—at least the churchwardens—" The voice of the vicar faltered uncertainly. "I have already sent for Mr. Alness and perhaps he can suggest—"

"The Home Secretary, sir?" There was utter contempt for that minister in the sexton's voice. "Why, sir, I mind we applied to he some twenty year back... For ever of questions, and the relative's consent and all... Days it took... And who knows what they'll be doing with her ladyship meanwhile?"

"Really, Stroud," the vicar protested. "Really we have no evidence that the body has been removed. Possibly the grave has been disturbed. Indeed, I think we may say that there are certain indications that this may be the case... But that is all, I trust—I sincerely trust so... I hope—I hope most fervently that her ladyship rests where we laid her."

"Maybe you've never digged a grave, sir?" Stroud demanded almost truculently. "Loose soil it be, I grant you, and dug recent.... But 'twould take me a good three-four hours to empty 'en, and two or three to fill 'en in decent again... Who'd do that for nothing, your Reverence? 'Tisn't in nature, I say... That is, if it be a human being, sir."

The last words were spoken in a tone of such mysterious gloom that their sinister meaning was evident. There was shocked reproof in the vicar's voice as he replied.

"Really, Stroud, these heathen superstitions—" he protested.

"Ah, there's ghosts in the Bible, Vicar," Stroud rejoined. "Not that I'm saying it were ghosts, and not that I'm saying it weren't. But, you see, 'tis like this, your Reverence—"

The sound of rapidly approaching footsteps on the flagged walk broke in on his words, and saved the vicar that argument. Both of them turned to greet the new arrival.

A pair of breeches came into view beneath the leaf-curtain. A new voice sounded, with a pleasant briskness about it.

"Good evening, Vicar... 'Evening, Stroud... What the dev— I mean, what on earth is all this? There must be some mistake—"

"Nothing on earth, sir," Stroud reproved, "and nothing, we hope, to do with the devil—that is, his Reverence says not. But 'tis what's under the earth, sir, or what isn't... The vicar says her ladyship be there, and I says she ben't... Look at thicky rake, then."

The vicar intervened with as much exasperation as his mild nature allowed him to exhibit.

"Just a minute, Stroud... It's like this, Alness—"

In what, for the vicar, was obviously a singularly simple and lucid explanation, Tony heard the main outlines of the conjectures he had built up confirmed. Three days previously, Lady Blakeney's body had been buried; the rake had certainly been at large on the previous day. That afternoon the sexton, going about his lawful occasions in the churchyard, had found the earth of the mound loosened, and the rake buried halfway up its handle. The vicar ended on a note of apologetic appeal.

"What are we to do, Alness? Stroud suggests—"

"Dig her ladyship up, I says," Stroud interrupted. "And if she be there, why, then we don't say nothing to no one. And if she ben't—well, dang me—!"

"Dig up the coffin, eh?" Alness said reflectively. "No... I hardly think that we can do that... Not without authority... I admit that it seems queer. But don't you think we're making too much of it? It's not very likely that the coffin has been tampered with in any way or the body stolen... More probably it's some foolish trick. That rake, now—?" He bent down over the projecting handle and gave a tentative tug. "Seems firm enough, I'll admit... But there must be some explanation—"

"That's just what I was saying," the vicar assented with relief. "The question is, should we inform the police of what has happened. Of course, we don't want any unnecessary scandal—"

"Tell the police and you practically tell the newspapers," Alness averred with a confidence which Tony did not share. "No, we don't want scandal and publicity. And we'd certainly get it. That old resurrectionist story—that and the mystery of the opened grave. What d' you think they'd make of the two combined? A good story for every penny rag in the kingdom, eh?"

"And, of course, there's the family to be considered," the vicar supplied. "The old man—and that poor girl— If publicity can be avoided, it seems to me that we should do everything in our power to do so."

"The fact is, it would just about polish the old man off," Alness said, with a trace of sympathy. "We all know that. Now, we don't know that any harm's been done here... Probably the body's still there—I think the chances are that it's still there. Come to think of it, that rake doesn't go down far enough for a full-depth grave."

"And it ben't full depth," Stroud interrupted. "Hadn't gone five feet, we hadn't, before we struck the coffin. 'Ah,' I says to Henery, 'this be old Grimsby, this be... Always one for making the resurrection easy and saving hisself a bit of sweat, he were....' That's what I says to Henery. So her ladyship, she's got the bare legal minimum, she have. No, sir... That rake be resting right on the coffin top, it be."

"Perhaps," Alness soothed him. "But I'm not building much upon the rake.... Now, if we do tell, there's the scandal, and the unpleasantness for the parish and the suffering for the family—my own family too, I might say.... But if we don't, who'd be worse off?"

"I know, Alness, I know. And yet—" There was an unhappy note in the vicar's voice. He paused, and his next words were definitely an appeal. "What do you think would be the best thing to do, then?"

"I've not a doubt in my own mind. Say nothing. Keep it between the three of us... Stroud wouldn't say anything, I know, if you asked him to be quiet... Maybe when they put up the stone we could satisfy ourselves quietly. That's what I suggest."

"And what about my rake?" Stroud demanded.

"Your rake? I'll tell you what I'd do about your rake. I'd come along quietly tonight with a saw and cut it off level with the ground. That would deal with that. And I'll buy you a new rake tomorrow."

"Then—then you'd say nothing about it to the family?" Obviously the vicar was tempted, but not quite convinced. "Surely, Alness—"

"In some sense, I can say that I represent the family. After all, Vicar, she was my aunt. The whole point, it seems to me, is not to give the family unnecessary pain... That, and the scandal. And there will be one if these reporter fellows get hold of it. They'd sell their souls for a sensation any day. No, if we can avoid it, the Press mustn't know—"

Perhaps it was unwise. But the temptation was strong. Tony rose to his feet and, feeling in his pocket, walked briskly round the yew tree that separated the group from him.

"Good evening," he said politely.

There was no denying the effectiveness of his appearance. For a moment there was dead silence. Tony wished that he had had a camera. The three men before him were so exactly what one would have expected from the parts that he had mentally assigned them. Even without the clerical collar he could have spotted the vicar, elderly, white-haired and benign—the type, Tony thought, who was an expert on obscure and quite unnecessary points of scholarship. Probably he was writing a book on local birds, or theology. The sexton, apple-cheeked, and actually with whiskers, might have stepped straight from a film representation of rural England; the third man, in riding clothes, and actually carrying a crop, was typically the local squire.

Tony scrutinised him a little more carefully than the others. Much as he disapproved of the idea from a newspaper point of view, there was something about the immoral course of action Alness proposed which rather appealed to him. And there was intelligence and decision in the churchwarden's face; though momentarily it expressed principally surprise at Tony's sudden apparition. He was the first to recover himself.

"Who the dev—?" he began, and stopped in time. For a churchwarden, Tony thought, and considering that the vicar was present, he was a little too much inclined, perhaps, to cite the Accuser of Souls, even though he generally managed to stop halfway. "Who are you, sir?" he demanded.

"My card," Tony answered and handed it over. "I'm afraid, Mr. Alness, you're a little too late... The Press is already adequately informed—or one representative of it. Though if you would care to give me a statement, or an interview—"

Alness disregarded him. He was frowning at the card as if he had some difficulty in reading it. The vicar flashed him a mute glance of appeal, and he laughed shortly.

"Anthony E. Mayfield, the *Morning Sun*... A reporter, eh? I've never heard of the rotten rag."

"That," Tony assured him, "is a misfortune which seems likely to be remedied shortly."

"And, to put it bluntly, you've been eavesdropping, eh? I suppose that's your idea of playing the game?... Evidently you heard something. What was it?"

"A most interesting suggestion on the part of a church-warden of Upper Utton Church," Tony said suavely, "that the vicar and he should condone a felony and withhold information from the police. Also the full story of an occurrence which the vicar aptly described as 'distinctly odd.'"

Alness laughed. "That's your line, is it? Well, of course, you can twist it that way... I certainly said that it would be a tragedy for the family, and that I wished it wasn't necessary to raise an unnecessary scandal. There was no suggestion of suppressing anything."

Tony refrained from calling him a liar. That would, no doubt, be his story, and he would stick to it, and it was sufficiently near the truth for it to stand a good chance of being believed. Alness, he decided, was quick-witted. He was on the point of a mildly-cutting retort when the vicar intervened.

"Really, Mr.—Mr. Mayfield," he said placatingly, "I trust there will be no unpleasantness. No doubt you accidentally heard what we were saying. But I am sure we may trust you to make no unfair use of it, or at least to handle it so that—so that—"

"That's no good, Vicar," Alness struck in. "We'd better try him another way... Look here, what's this worth to you? A fiver, maybe?... Now, if you go home and forget it, I'll make you a cheque for ten pounds right away. What do you say?"

There are probably corruptible reporters, as there are corruptible policemen. On a general average attempted bribery is to both a certain method of making sure one will suffer for it more than ever. Tony flushed.

"I shall certainly forget nothing whatever, Mr. Alness," he said. "I shall print the full facts to the best of my ability, and in the full conviction that the facts should be printed. Here is a grave desecrated, possibly a body stolen—certainly a crime committed—"

The discussion had reached a point when the attention of those engaged in it was concentrated entirely on one another. None of the four noticed the two figures approaching over the soft turf until they were right upon them. It was a man and a young woman, and at the sight of her Tony's jaw dropped. It was Virginia Blakeney.

She had not seen him. She was staring down at the mound of earth and there was horror in her eyes. It was the young man who broke out excitedly.

"Then there's something in it, Vicar?" he demanded. "Virginia came home last night absolutely done in and fainted. Couldn't get a sensible word out of her... Then she told an amazing tale of someone digging up a coffin in the churchyard, and chasing her, with a face like a skull. Naturally we thought she'd been seeing things—"

"She actually saw the coffin dug up?" Tony demanded briskly.

The young man eyed him. Facial resemblance alone would have been enough to tell anyone that it was Richard Blakeney.

"Police, eh?" he demanded. "No, she heard the spade ring on the coffin. Then she called out—"

"Just a minute, Dick," Alness snapped. "You're making a mistake. This—this young gentleman is not a policeman. He has the dubious honour to be—" He glanced at the card. "Mr. Anthony E. Mayfield. A reporter, we understand, of that doubtless worthy but unknown paper the *Morning Sun*. And—"

At the sound of Tony's name Virginia had looked up. She gave a little cry as she recognised him, and hastily looked away.

"And," Alness continued relentlessly, "he has just been promising to give us all the publicity he can—"

Dick Blakeney had flushed a deep purple, and there was sheer rage in his eyes, but he spoke quite quietly.

"Then," he said in a low voice, "I think, Mr.—Mr. Sun reporter, you're going to get the hiding of your life—"

He lashed out as he spoke. Tony dodged, and Alness caught his arm. But the vicar effectually intervened by stepping between them.

"Please, Blakeney," he said, and for the first time there was a note in his voice which compelled attention. "I know there's provocation but remember—remember where you stand. Dick, my boy, don't do anything that can only be regretted—"

Dick Blakeney drew a deep breath and subsided trembling. The vicar turned to Tony.

"I am sure, Mr. Mayfield—" he said, and though the words were polite enough there was a cutting undertone in them which made Tony blush more than Alness's calculated contempt—"I am sure you will see the propriety of leaving us at the present time... No doubt you must do what you conceive your duty. I pray that you will do it without malice, and in accordance with your conscience..."

Tony gave one quick glance round. Virginia met his eyes for a moment only, and the expression on her face was one of utter loathing. He set his lips.

"I hope I shall, Vicar," he said. "Good evening."

There was no response to his greeting. In a dead silence he turned and moved towards the gate. Only as he reached it did he glance back towards the group at the grave, though he had felt that their eyes were boring into his back every yard of the way. In fact, four of the five people were no longer visible. Only Stroud stood by the grave, staring gloomily down at his rake handle. Tony set his jaw and stepped out into the lane.

# 3

---

# Strange Encounters

IT WAS BETTER NOT to return to his previous headquarters at the Golden Lion. Tony had made up his mind about that before his temper had had time to subside. As things were, the vicar and Alness would have no option but to inform the police, and it was quite possible that he might find himself bothered by official enquiries and prohibitions which at the moment he was anxious to avoid. A glance at a one-inch ordnance map showed him the existence of another village a bare three miles away, which promised what he was most anxious to get at that moment—a telephone. He set off briskly along the lane in the opposite direction from Lower Utton, and as he went he tried to work things out.

There was certainly a good story there, but the vicar's appeal lingered unpleasantly in his mind. There might be nothing in it which was really serious. He was inclined to agree with Stroud, that the vital question was whether "her ladyship be there or whether she ben't", but that question he had no means of answering. The information which his question had extracted from Dick Blakeney was interesting. The mysterious gravedigger had actually reached the coffin when he was interrupted. Had he done more? It must have required sufficient nerve to fill in the grave after being discovered. Would he have found time to do the additional excavation and opening of the coffin? There was no answering that; but as he thought it over an idea came to him which made him hesitate in his first decision to send off the full story for the next morning's edition.

He pondered on it. It was taking a risk—that the story would leak out to other newspapers if he waited, and that he would be scooped on a story which was at the moment peculiarly exclusive. Had he been in the position of an ordinary reporter, he could certainly never have taken it. As it was, he was tempted from various points of view; though he tried to assure himself that it was purely the interests of the paper which finally influenced him.

A trunk call from the village proved perfectly practicable—unusual, perhaps, as the expression on the postmaster's face showed, but still, it could be done. It was not more than ten minutes before he was through.

"Sun Office... Who is that, please?" an impersonal voice asked.

"Mayfield speaking. Put me through to Mr. Staines immediately."

"Yes, Mr. Mayfield. He's in the office."

There was the click of the connection. Almost at once a new voice spoke in a cheerful, conversational tone which was unmistakable.

"Hull-ullo-ullo!" it said brightly. "Sun Editor's Office, that is.... Who's that?"

The thought crossed Tony's mind that probably Staines would be the last person on the staff to answer a telephone call correctly.

"That you, Brian? Mayfield speaking—"

"Oh, hullo, Tony, old boy! Still alive? How're the old dogs? Try alum, old boy. Wonderful thing for hardening the skin—"

"Shut up!" Tony snapped. "This is serious, Brian. Listen. I think I'm on to something. But I'm not quite sure whether it's to our advantage to publish or to hang on a bit—"

"Always the little busy bee... Paper's blooming, by the way. I've had six complaints this morning—"

"Listen," Tony interrupted. "You take this story. Write it up yourself, and don't let it out to a soul—not even to old Tabley. Keep space for a front page lead—but you must be prepared to fill it up another way. Hold it until the last possible moment, and wait for me to come through. I suppose about three o'clock is the best we can do. If I don't come through, don't print it... Got that?"

"Right-o... Fearfully intricate though, isn't it?... I'll have to collaborate with the Sub., but I needn't tell him why... O.K. it is... Shoot!"

Tony began to dictate, in the excitement of the moment forgetting who was at the other end. A mournful whistle broke in upon the flow.

"Just a minute, old boy... Hold your horses... I say, hadn't I better get a shorthand wallah on to it if you're in a hurry?... That new typist you engaged is an awfully jolly girl, isn't she?"

"In spite of that she can type," Tony said cynically. "No. Don't get her, or anyone. I'll go slowly—"

The dictation proceeded, with a slowness which exasperated Tony to distraction, though Brian had obviously settled seriously to work.

It was not until the very end that the voice at the other end interrupted.

"But, I say, old boy... Hamlet without the Prince of Denmark, what? Don't forget the local angle, above all else. 'One whale in the Thames is worth a hundred in the Atlantic,' you know—"

"Local angle?" Tony queried eagerly. It was the one defect in the story from the point of view of a provincial paper. "There isn't one?"

"Oh, yes... See 'Local Men Make Good. Number thirty-four. John Blakeney—'"

"What?... Don't remember it."

"You wouldn't... I've just finished it... Hot stuff—pure 'John Halifax, Gentleman'... Am I to use that?"

"Yes. Run that, anyhow... Tomorrow."

"About old George—the missing heir. What am I to do with him?"

Tony thought. "It's too risky," he decided. "He's not officially missing, and the family are explaining it away... Don't touch it... And don't let this out to a soul. No one else knows yet—"

"The operator might," Brian suggested. "Of course, she's too nice a girl to listen in, but—"

"If it gets out through anyone, they're sacked," Tony said with ungrammatical grimness.

"And that goes for me too, big boy... O.K... Hear you later. So long."

There was a worried frown on Tony's face as he rang off. The important thing now was to discover what was happening in the village and to do so, if possible, without any unpleasant encounters. But he was hungry, and another half hour might even be to the good from the point of view of seeing how things developed. Besides, he was more than tired of walking. He made his way to the local inn where, over bread and cheese and beer, he successfully negotiated the hire of an ancient bicycle. The landlord was conversational and curious. He eyed Tony speculatively.

"You'd be a reporter, maybe?" he suggested at last, after failing in several attempts to ascertain the reason for his visitor's presence. "Down about that Scalford business?"

Mentally Tony cursed the natural inquisitiveness of country people and the peculiar stamp which some occupations seem to put upon a man.

"Me? I'm just on a walking tour," he evaded. It was a consolation that he was speaking the strict letter of the truth. "What business is that?"

"Walking tour? Now that wouldn't do for me!" The fat man behind the bar laughed wheezily. "You've not heard, then? Oh, it's just what they're saying. Gentleman got into trouble with a woman and ran away... well, we can't all be saints, and he wouldn't do her no harm—not if I know her kind."

Tony pricked up his ears. "You know the woman then?" he asked casually. "Now I come to think of it, I did hear something, but I thought it was just talk."

"Old Crouch was talking to some purpose a couple of nights ago, then," the landlord rejoined. "One or two over the eight he'd had and was shooting off his mouth proper about George Blakeney... It's his sister, he said, and talked of damages and heaven knows what, till Jack Biggs, who works as gamekeeper at the house, threatened to give him a hiding. Then he cleared out."

"Probably your beer's too good for him," Tony suggested with tactful mendacity. "Some people will talk when they've had one."

"It isn't beer he's been drinking lately—it's spirits, and all I'd give him. Must have come into a fortune, or something... Not that anyone knows how he gets a living."

"He's not a local man, then?"

"Local? Him? No!" The landlord emphasised the point by spitting out a stray fragment of tobacco. "He's no good... Proper Cockney, he is. I know them."

"A Cockney?" Tony remembered the man at the cottage window. "Does he live up the road here—about a mile and a half away? Cottage on the left?"

"That's it... Him and his sister... Two or three years ago, they came." He eyed Tony shrewdly. "Know him, then?"

"Knocked him up to ask the way last night," Tony grinned. "He told me to go to Hell!"

"I reckon he could show you the way there... and, Great Scott!" He looked through the window up the street. "Talk of the devil—!"

"What?"

"It's him.... Tanked up already, too. Must keep a bottle at home."

The man who entered and ordered a double whisky had certainly been drinking. Probably, Tony judged, he had been drinking for weeks, and at his present rate could hardly hope for a long life. The landlord eyed him dubiously before he turned to the bottle. Then he winked at Tony.

"Found Mr. Blakeney yet, Jim?" he enquired roguishly. "Gentleman here thinks it's all just talk—"

"Talk?" Crouch glared at Tony with bloodshot eyes. "They'll find out if it's talk—Mr. Richard, and that stuck-up chit of a girl and all of them... Talk? Why did he bolt, then? Why did he run off in the middle of the night without a word to a soul? Talk!"

He gulped from his glass. If there was one thing Tony wanted it was that he should go on talking. He tried to draw him out.

"It's really true he's gone, then?" he said.

"Ah! That's true enough." It was the landlord who answered. "John Smithers saw Mr. Richard driving him to the station—and proper black they both looked, he said. And Coombes, who's courting at the house, he says there's something wrong. Ay, he's gone. But—"

He broke off and shrugged his shoulders. Tony made a mental note of the names. They might come in useful later. But it was Crouch he wanted to encourage.

"You think you've got some claim on him, then?" he asked.

"If there's a law in this land, he'll pay for it yet... All the claim the law can give a woman—" His voice trailed away into a vague mumble, in which Tony could distinguish nothing, except something which sounded like "estate"; then he gulped the last of his whisky, and pushed the glass across the counter. More," he said thickly.

The landlord eyed him as he bent forward, leaning on the bar. "You've had enough, Jim," he said sharply. "And a bit more too... You'll get no more to drink here. I've my licence to think of. You go home and sober up."

"You think I'm drunk?" Crouch roused himself suddenly and assumed a bellicose attitude. "You're a damned liar! For two pins I'd knock you and your twopenny-halfpenny pot-house—!"

There was an unexpected interruption. None of the three had noticed that anyone had come in, and Tony looked round in surprise as a woman's voice sounded behind them.

"That's enough, Jim!" The words were in a marked Cockney accent resembling those of Crouch. "You're going home."

The man positively cringed before her. "I weren't saying nothing," he muttered defensively. "I'd only just come—"

"You're going home." She disregarded him and turned to the landlord. "Give me a double gin, and a bottle of Scotch."

As the landlord obeyed, Tony had leisure to study her, while Crouch waited abjectly. She might once have been pretty in a bold kind of way. That was some years ago. What was obviously dye and make up helped to conceal her age without improving her appearance. She met Tony's eyes, and her lips tightened. The landlord fulfilled the order, Tony thought, just in time. She drank the gin at a draught, picked up the bottle and her change, and stalked out, followed by the man.

"That's her." The landlord jerked his thumb towards them as they vanished. "Nice couple, aren't they?"

"I'd rather you had 'em for neighbours than me." Tony finished his beer with an affectation of leisureliness. "Well, it takes all sorts to make a world... I'll be getting along to make the most of the light, I guess... The bike's in the yard?"

"Yes. I've pumped her up. She'll last you for a bit... But you watch that there brake, sir... Good evening."

It was not only the brake, Tony found, but most of the rest of the machine which wanted watching. Luckily at that moment he had no great occasion for speed. He had changed his mind, and his immediate purpose was to follow the couple who had just left. It was quite possible that they were only going home—and it was certain that the man ought to be there. Still, there was a possibility that he might overhear something, and he was convinced, more by the woman's abruptness than the man's garrulous threats, that there was more in the story than the vapourings of a drunkard.

The man and woman had got a fair start, though Crouch was not making particularly good speed. He was well clear of the village before he sighted them, and then he almost came upon them too suddenly. The lane, too, was awkward, and he was often forced to allow them a bigger margin than he could have wished, but, thanks to the cycle, he was always able to keep them in view. Undoubtedly they were going to the cottage, and as they approached it, the cover was better. He was able to get quite close by the time they turned into the gate.

It was a derelict-looking place—two rooms up and two down, he judged, with a ragged, neglected garden in front, and two or three untidy sheds of the kind which utilise cardboard boxes and corrugated iron to make good structural deficiencies. But what was more important to Tony was that there seemed very little chance of creeping up to investigate as long as the occupants were at home. The bare front afforded no cover, and the most solid and effective part of the whole place was the high fence on the other three sides. Nothing could be done there by daylight, at least, and it seemed as though in all probability he had wasted his time.

The woman produced a key, flung the cottage door open, and almost pushed the man inside. Then, rather to his surprise, he saw her hand over the bottle of whisky. Whatever might be her motive in removing him from the public house, temperance reform was apparently not the reason. Standing on the doorstep with one hand on her hip, she addressed a few parting words.

Tony had not led a particularly sheltered life. He had lived in mining districts where every second word was monotonously unprintable; he had associated with the much-maligned bargee, and lived in the worst slums of London: but he had never met her equal in malediction. By the time she had finished and slammed the door on him, Tony judged that the unfortunate recipient of the remarks would need at least the whole bottle to restore him.

The woman, apparently, was not staying at the house. She had returned only to deliver her brother. She not only closed the door but locked it; then started down the garden path again with a suddenness which almost caught him unawares. He had to pedal hard to get out of sight and find a hiding place before she could command a view of the road, and the hedges were exasperatingly inadequate. He had almost reached the fork which led to Lower Utton before a friendly gate offered itself, and he was able to push the bike inside.

It seemed a long time before the woman came in sight. He was almost afraid he had missed her, though there had been no turning. At last she came, walking purposefully, and rather quickly, like someone who has been unduly delayed. Tony let her pass, watched her turn towards Lower Utton, then followed cautiously. Preoccupied as he was with his task, it was with something of a pang that he recognised the road which he had walked with the girl the previous night, and the gateway leading to the church which had been the scene of their hasty parting. He wondered what the girl was doing then, and still more what she must be thinking of him. That was not a particularly pleasant reflection, and it was a relief when the actions of the woman in front made it necessary for him to concentrate on the chase once more.

She had stopped just short of the first house in the village, a pleasant modern bungalow with a garden which had forced itself upon his notice even as he passed it casually. And her behaviour was unusual. She was peering round the trunk of a convenient elm tree with her eyes fixed upon the front of the house, and plainly anxious to avoid being seen. It was only after a little difficulty that he found a spot from which it was possible to follow her example, and even then he was not much wiser.

Two people were standing on the creeper-shaded verandah of the house, an elderly man in a tweed suit and cap and carrying a stick and a dog lead, and a young girl. At least, at the first glance he had thought she was young. As he watched, he was not so sure. There was a suggestion of unhappy experience in the attractive face, even though at the moment she was smiling cheerfully. The reason for the dog lead was running in eccentric circles round the well-kept lawn, and at intervals emitting protests against the delay of the serious business of going for a walk. Altogether, it was a pleasant little domestic scene, Tony reflected, and one which it was hard to imagine could excite the interest of the harpy beside the tree.

The dog's persuasion at last took effect. The man turned and whistled to it and with a smile at the girl turned down the path and was lost to Tony's sight behind some bushes. Then he heard the closing of a gate and the sound of a whistle receding in the direction of the village.

It seemed to be what the woman had been waiting for. In a moment she had left her hiding place and was making for the gate. After a minute or two, she reappeared, going up towards the verandah where the girl was still standing. A very brief greeting passed between them; with something like a furtive haste the girl ushered the woman inside the house and closed the door.

For half an hour by Tony's watch nothing happened. He was beginning to think that he had better give it up when the woman emerged again. There were the marks of temper on her face; the girl had just as obviously been crying. Tony was still looking at her when the sound of approaching footsteps made him suddenly realise the probability that he would be discovered. He could not possibly get out of sight in time. There was only one thing to do. Mounting the cycle, he pedalled unsteadily to meet her whistling cheerfully and carefully avoiding any more notice of her than a casual glance.

Evidently she was going home. And, on reflection, it seemed the best thing for him to do as well. It was getting late, and a good deal depended on what had happened in the village. Obviously the best place to find that out was the inn. He abandoned all thought of further sleuthing and started down the hill, noting, as he passed the police station, that the local constable was in his front garden, coatless, and apparently engaged in de-caterpillaring cabbages. That did not look like any great excitement. Perhaps the storm had not yet broken.

Undoubtedly he was preoccupied. Otherwise he might have remembered the defective brake. That, and a small but rapid terrier dog in pursuit of a cat, was his undoing. Failing to stop, he tried to swerve, succeeded, and crashed full into the wall. Promptly the front fork collapsed. He tumbled headlong, acquired a few new sore spots, and staggered to his feet, to find himself facing the elderly man whom he had just seen leaving the bungalow.

"You all right?" Tony found himself looking into a grave, pleasant face with kindly eyes, and the voice expressed anxious concern. "I'm afraid that wretched dog of mine—"

"No damage, thanks," Tony answered without strict truth. "It was partly my fault, you know. I ought to have remembered that that beastly brake was no use. They warned me when I hired the thing—"

"I'm afraid the cycle—" The elderly man eyed it. "I doubt if it's repairable... Really, it was my dog's fault. You must let me pay."

"That's absurd... Besides, the market value of the thing can't be ten bob... It's quite all right—"

"You must certainly let me pay... Here's my card... You're staying in the neighbourhood?"

Tony nodded. "For a day or two," he said. The thought occurred to him that originally it had only been for a night, and at the present rate at which things were happening it might be a fortnight. On holiday," he explained to forestall any speculation. "I started on a walking tour. Hence the cycle."

The elderly man smiled. "If you should want to borrow one for future explorations, I have one I could lend you," he suggested. "It's the bungalow just at the top here. Either I or my daughter are generally at home." He glanced at his watch. "I must be getting on. Please come if it would be of service. Good evening."

Whistling to the errant terrier, he started up the hill again. Tony glanced at the card.

"M. L. Newent," he read, "The Bungalow, Lower Utton."

It was a piece of luck, in spite of bruises. So far as cycling was concerned, he was through with it, but all the same to ascertain the name of one of the people who were acting oddly and to obtain an entry into their house was more than he could have hoped. Arranging with a cottager to store the wrecked bike, he pursued his way towards the inn.

All was calm there. There was no hint of graves and worms and epitaphs; no suggestion of stolen corpses. The landlord politely asked if he had enjoyed his walk, told him that he had missed a fine Norman doorway, and suggested a meal which Tony gratefully accepted. As he ate, he tried to work out the probable sequence of events since he had left the group in the churchyard. Obviously, in view of what he had said, they must inform the police in mere self-protection. Then, why was there this beautiful air of peace? He was inclined to think that it was a matter of the cast and outlook of the people concerned. In a matter of that kind, they would not communicate with the local bobby. Quite probably they were on friendly terms with the chief constable. And he might have been the kind of man who would say "Tut-tut! These beastly journalists. Don't worry. Look into it myself."

It was all a matter of might. Of course, more might have happened than appeared, and the remoteness of the church could easily have eluded the village intelligence system. The best thing seemed to be to go and see if anything was happening there. And, in any case, he had intended to go there. There was a point he wished to verify and a half-formed suspicion in his mind which might make more than a casual visit there necessary. Acquiring a key, on the grounds that he wished to study moonlight effects and might be late, he set off.

By the path it was only a short distance to the church, but the last daylight had gone, and the moon was just rising before he reached it. In the daylight the place had seemed pleasant enough—a comfortable spot of shade after the arid lanes he had been walking. Now it seemed very different. The approach on this side was completely overhung by the evergreen oaks, and on the fieldside by an overgrown hedge. It was dark as pitch ahead of him, and the soft carpet of leaves made his footsteps weirdly soundless. He hesitated for a moment before plunging into the shadows, and as he glanced round, noticed the stile beside the church wall. That must have been the way Virginia had come, and perhaps it was his own best way. After all, it was absurd to march up to the front gate with a flourish of drums and trumpets, to be stopped, possibly, by a stolid policeman left on guard. A back entrance, probably via the wall, was the best for his purpose. He mounted the stile and moved along the side of the churchyard, looking for a possible place for climbing. Not until he reached the second stile did he find one, and there, standing in the very spot where Virginia had waited the previous night, he surveyed the ground.

The desolate beauty of the place, barred with the long shadows of the rising moon, did not interest him. What he was looking for was some sign of a watcher, and for some minutes he looked without result, searching the ground faithfully, yard by yard. There seemed to be no one on the main gate; or, if there was, he had the sense to remain under cover. There was no glow of a cigarette; no sign of anyone. Of course, the thick bushes and shadows might conceal an army; the grave itself was in a black oblong cast by a yew tree. But in his experience it was difficult for anyone to remain absolutely still and silent for very long. All he had to do was to wait, and if there was anyone there, he would give himself away. He waited.

Probably it had only been a few minutes, though it seemed an age. Suddenly he heard it, a queer, scraping sound coming from somewhere over in the far corner. He listened to it for a moment, puzzling as to what it could be. And all at once he realised the truth. Whatever the sound was, it came from the desecrated grave. In a moment he was clambering over the wall and had dropped silently on the long grass at the foot.

Stalking was easy. Great tombstones, overgrown bushes, and the black shadows concealed him; thick turf underfoot made his passage soundless. Even observing every precaution, it only took him a minute or two to cross the graveyard and gain the shelter of a huge stone table from which he could peer to see the grave.

There was someone there. And the someone was working on the grave. He could hear the click of stones against an iron tool, and the scraping of something on the hard earth. He could even make out the shadowy movements of someone or something in the darkness, but who or what it might be he could not make out. He had watched for some little time when he looked round startled as a sudden light fell on him. But it was only the rising moon which had just cleared the tree tops. And almost in the same moment the revealing rays caught the figure at work upon the grave. Tony pursed his lips into a soundless whistle. It was Stroud.

# 4

---

# A Fight with Death

FOR A MOMENT TONY felt utterly surprised. And yet there was no reason for it. Of all the people in the country, Stroud was, in one sense, the only one who could legitimately work upon the graves at any time he cared. But at eleven o'clock at night, and in the dark—! The business was still preposterous, and so far as he could see, it could only mean one thing. After all, the vicar, Alness and company had decided to try to keep the matter dark. Stroud had come surreptitiously to tidy up the grave and remove the damning rake handle. And probably, if his paper printed the story, they would all combine to deny it.

What then? Where was his evidence? It all rested on his word about an overheard conversation and a projecting rake handle. The only proof would be to dig up the grave, and he could produce no evidence likely to justify that. And the end, despite the truth, might be a conviction for libel, or an abject withdrawal on the part of the Sun. The thought filled him with a hot anger. He had an impulse to emerge and confront the old gravedigger, and to force the plot out of him. Then he restrained himself. Instead, very cautiously he began to circle his way round to a spot which would bring him near enough to obtain a clearer view.

He reached the tomb which he had marked unobserved. And now the light was better, and he could see exactly what was happening. Stroud was conscientiously raking up the loose earth into the proper pyramidal mound over a new-ly-dug grave, working as methodically and carefully as though it was midday and he was about his lawful business. In the moonlight, his thin face looked ghastly. Tony remembered what Richard had said Virginia saw—someone with a skull for a face. It might easily have looked so... Could it actually have been the sexton? He found himself rejecting the former theory. Alness would have concealed it all; perhaps, for the sake of the family, Richard Blakeney would have done the same. But he could not, under any circumstances, imagine either Virginia or the vicar being a party to such a fraud.

Was the old man mad? That was much more likely. It was quite conceivable that a man might be so affected by such a ghastly trade that his turned brain would drive him to ghoul-ish activities in the hours of darkness. Stroud was muttering to himself as he worked, and Tony strained his ears to listen, but at first could catch nothing. At last a few words louder than the rest reached him, spoken in a tone of injury.

"—no matter what parson says."

The inaudible muttering was resumed. The work was nearly finished before he could distinguish two words spoken in a tone of deep contempt—"Home Secretary!" Obviously Stroud was going over the conversation in the churchyard in his mind. The man must be mad. And then, as he gave the final touch to the mound and straightened his back with a rheumatic groan, he spoke a single sentence quite clearly.

"And her ladyship be there, after all," he said with triumph. "And I've got my rake!"

The truth flashed upon Tony blindingly, and on a sudden impulse he left his hiding place, and stepped forward full into the moonlight.

"Stroud!" he said.

The sexton started round like a frightened rabbit, with a queer little animal cry. Perhaps, in spite of his trade, he was not without his share of superstition. For a few seconds he stared at Tony wild-eyed; then recognition dawned. His lower jaw shot out obstinately.

"The reporter chap!" he repeated to himself. "The reporter chap!" And then with a hint of bullying: "And what be you doing here, zur?"

"I think it's a matter of what you've been doing, Stroud," Tony rejoined. "I've been watching you for some time."

"Well?" Stroud demanded. "Graves be my business, bain't they? Bain't yours, zur."

Tony sighed, and shrugged his shoulders. "Very well, Stroud," he said with an air of resignation. "If you're going to be unreasonable—" He broke off and paused. "Do you know what I'm going to do, Stroud?"

"No, zur." The answer came stoutly enough, but there was just a hint of anxiety in the tone. "Bain't no business of mine, as I can see, zur."

"But I'm afraid it is," Tony said regretfully. "Because I'm just going down to tell the constable that I've seen you engaged in the unauthorised opening of a grave, Stroud. And I expect that'll mean gaol, Stroud. A fine, anyhow... And you're bound to lose your job. Because people simply wouldn't put up with a sexton who went about opening graves in this casual way, Stroud. They wouldn't feel a corpse was safe—"

There is nothing more infuriating than the constant repetition of one's own name. Combined with the threat, it produced the desired result.

"If I bain't allowed to open 'un, who be?" Stroud burst out.

"No one," Tony rejoined with a certainty which he did not feel. "No one by himself, Stroud... Did the vicar give you orders? Or Mr. Richard? Or the police or—"

"Maybe they didn't," Stroud admitted. "Vicar said as he was going to report it to the chief constable. And I knowed what that meant—"

"So you came and did it on your own? And destroyed the evidence of what had been done? Well—!" Tony shrugged his shoulders. "It's your own affair—but if I were you, I'd try and get out of it."

Stroud scowled at him unhappily. "What be I to do, then?" he demanded sulkily.

"Tell me the truth, first... You dug out the grave, didn't you?"

"Saw me, didn't 'ee?... Ay, part of it."

"And then?"

"I got my rake."

Tony suppressed his impatience with an effort. "I mean the body?" he asked. "It was still there?"

"Ay, leastways the coffin hadn't been opened."

"You're sure?"

"Helped screw her down, didn't I? Screws hadn't been turned last night... Earth weren't even loosened round the lid. No, she be there right enough."

Tony decided to accept the expert's opinion. "It was your own idea?" he asked.

"Surely. Vicar and the rest, they said, 'Wait for the police.' I says, 'Better find out and get it over.' So I dug 'un."

It was a beautifully simple point of view. So simple, Tony reflected, that there seemed to be absolutely nothing more he could hope to find out. Besides, there was no saying that someone else would not come along. The sooner the gruesome dialogue came to an end the better. He thought for a moment.

"What be I to do, then?" Stroud appealed.

Tony considered. "Well, the rake's out... You'll have to admit that. But you needn't say you opened the grave—"

"And how else could I get 'un?"

"Wriggled it out gradually... Oh, I don't say it could be done," he hurried on as he saw the objection coming. "But they won't know that... They'll call you a fool for doing it, but that's better than the other... Don't say anything about the grave, or the coffin not having been opened—or about meeting me... They wouldn't accept your word about the coffin, anyhow, if they decide to do anything about it."

"Maybe 'tis best," Stroud said dubiously, and thought. "Ay, zur, 'tis best," he added more confidently. "That be what I'll do, zur... And thank 'ee, zur."

"Don't mention it... And now, don't you think we'd better be getting on. If anyone found us here—"

"I'll put my tools away, zur." He was gathering them together. "And, anyway, zur, I got my rake!"

As he waited for the sexton to reappear, Tony reflected how circumstances alter cases. He had just been guilty of doing exactly what he had accused Alness of doing, and he was not in the least ashamed of it. The sexton rejoined him, and they walked to the gate in silence. Then a point occurred to the reporter.

"You must have started pretty soon to get it done," he suggested, "and worked hard."

"Started as soon as they'd gone, zur... But I be a terrible strong man for digging, zur."

"Shouldn't have thought you had much practice here... People look as though they live for ever."

"Well, zur, I go round the three parishes... Two we had last week, zur. Lady Blakeney and Mr. Cobham, next to hers."

"Two?" Tony echoed idly, and then a thought occurred to him. "And the graves were next to each other?" he asked, trying to keep the eagerness out of his voice.

"Almost, zur... Bentley's be in between, but that be an old grave, and full. You see, zur, that be the only part of the old yard where yee can bury a corpse, and all old graves."

They had reached the stile leading to the field path. Tony made up his mind quickly.

"I'll turn off here," he said. "So I'll wish you good night... Mind, I'll say nothing if you don't—"

"Good night to 'ee, zur... And thank 'ee."

Reaching the second stile, Tony passed it, waited only until he was positively sure that the sexton had really gone down the lane, and had not tried to spy upon him; then he was over the wall, and making his way through the tombstones again. Two fresh graves! That offered a new possibility. He had come to the graveyard on the vague off-chance that the digger, interrupted in his work by Virginia, had filled in the grave without opening the coffin, and might try again if no alarm seemed to have been given. But this offered a new possibility. Suppose in fact the unknown had opened the wrong grave? It would explain all his actions as Virginia had seen them. He had excavated the coffin just so far as to be able to read the plate, and found his mistake. And the chances of his returning were more than doubled.

No one in the village knew what had happened. He might easily think that whoever had called out had accepted the supernatural explanation and fled. The matter must be desperately important for him to have tackled it at all—unless, indeed, it was the work of a madman. He might try again. At least it was worth waiting to see.

There were the two graves, as Stroud had said, with only Bentley's between them. But Bentley's was a massive monument, with two overgrown rose trees on it, and it was impossible to see one from the other. What was more interesting still was that the grave on the other side of Bentley's was, in the half-light, distinctly similar. A mistake, he decided, was certainly possible, especially assuming that the person concerned was not in a calm frame of mind. He looked around for a good hiding place, found a secure nook beside some bushes, and settled himself as comfortably as possible, determined to maintain an alertness which nothing could escape.

Excellent as was his intention, its performance was difficult. Twice in the first half hour he found himself dozing and had to force himself awake by sheer willpower. His sleep the night before had been short; he had been taking a quite unaccustomed amount of exercise. Reluctantly he cut his period of watching down from three to two hours. If nothing happened by two—

He must have dozed off completely. Suddenly he was awake, with the moonlight shining on his face. He sat up, with the dazed feeling of someone who wakes in unexpected surroundings. For a moment he could not imagine where he was, or why he was there. Then it came back to him—and in the same instant he heard the noise.

"Crunch—thud—"

Wide awake in a moment, he peered through the leaves which sheltered him. His guess had been right. The mysterious digger was again at work, this time upon the other grave, and only a few yards away from him. And yet at first he could see very little of him. The shadow of the trees had moved round, and now, whereas he himself was in the light the grave was in black shadow, and seemed all the darker because of a staring white angel on the tomb just behind it.

But there was the man—if it was a man. Although he had come there prepared, and in a mood of complete scepticism so far as ghosts were concerned, Tony felt a slightly eerie twinge as he watched the dark figure bending and lifting itself to the rhythm of the spade. It had its back towards him, and he could see little but the shadowy outline, and the large hat which covered the head; but it seemed to him to be dressed completely in black from head to foot, and even the hands which held the spade. The shade of the trees was not quite complete. Occasional stray flecks of moonlight filtered through, giving an oddly chequered effect which deceived the eyes rather than aided them, and yet they seemed to reveal to Tony one queer thing which affected him unpleasantly. The back and arms of the figure seemed to glisten, like the moist skin of a toad. In spite of himself the idea sent a slight shiver down the reporter's spine.

Was it a man, after all? He put the doubt from him. It could be nothing else. And either it had been working very hard or he had slept for some time, for considerable progress had already been made on the excavation of the grave. The hole was over two feet deep over the whole area, and deepening every minute, for the black figure was working with a furious precision. Tony watched it in fascination, wondering what he was to do.

Obviously the soundest plan was to let the work continue. Then he would know what the intention behind it was. He tried to work out the possibilities. The obvious thing was that a body was to be stolen, and until that moment he had scarcely considered anything else. But there were other possibilities. He recalled a story in which a fresh grave had been used for the disposal of a murdered body. It might be desired to put something into the coffin, or to take something out. Tony gave it up, and settled himself down to wait.

Twice the figure paused and straightened its back as if to take breath, but still without turning round; then it resumed work again. Tony found himself dreading the moment when it should turn. Was the face really a skull? He was conscious of an almost overwhelming desire to bring things to an issue immediately; and yet he knew that his decision had been right. It was better to wait and see—

The matter was unexpectedly taken out of his hands. Though the night was fine, it was still too early in the summer to sleep out of doors without covering, and for some time he had been feeling distinctly chilly. All at once he felt as if he wished to sneeze. He fought it by every means he could think of but it persisted. And just as he believed he had beaten it, it came without warning. He sneezed.

The figure whirled in a flash, and though he was prepared for what he saw, an exclamation of horror burst from him.

"Good heavens! What—!"

It was more horrible than he could have imagined. There was the skull face, and though it was not illuminated by the moon it glowed with an infernal fire of its own. For a moment it robbed him of the power of movement, and the two stood facing each other. His courage returned. Anger at his own lack of nerve made him throw caution to the winds. He sprang straight at it, reaching for a hold about the waist. His tackle missed by a fraction as his adversary dodged; but he caught an arm, only to find that another unpleasant surprise was in store for him. His clutching hands could not hold it. The skin slipped greasily from between his fingers, and he heard a queer, mocking laugh. Then, before he could recover, two leathery hands closed about his throat, and he was fighting for his life.

He felt himself choking; and the shining skull face of his enemy shone through a red mist which was overwhelming everything. And as he fruitlessly tugged at the strangling hands trying to break their grip a queer lucidity came over his mind. Of course it was all a trick. The death's head which shone before him was only a painted mask; the greasy body an old trick of Indian thieves; the hands—

His senses were leaving him. In the very last few seconds there flashed into his mind a piece of information he had learnt years before from a friend who was interested in tricks of self-defence. Releasing his useless grip on the wrists, he crossed his hands and struck outwards. The next instant he was free and staggered back, gulping in deep gasps of air.

But the other was at him immediately. With a desperate effort he struck out, and by good luck rather than judgment the blow landed. His opponent gave a coughing grunt and backed away with one hand to his throat.

Tony himself was too far gone to follow up his advantage. He could only lean gasping against the tombstone upon which he had come to rest and try to collect his strength for another effort. Then suddenly his enemy stooped. As he rose, Tony saw the outline of the uplifted spade against the stars. Instinctively he put up his hand to ward off the blow. There was a fierce pain in his arm, a great flash of light, and he knew no more.

# 5

## First with the News

It was just three weeks later that Tony Mayfield entered the editor's office of the *Morning Sun* for the first time since his unfortunate holiday. The intervening period he had spent principally in a nursing home recovering from the effects of concussion and a badly-injured arm; to which a chaste black sling and an unaccustomed pallor still bore witness. Strictly speaking, his absence should have continued for at least another fortnight; but in spite of the journalistic dictum that no one is indispensable, his presence at the editor's desk was at least highly desirable from several points of view.

Many people had said he was extremely lucky to become editor and virtual owner of a morning paper at the age of thirty-two; those who knew the circumstances were less sure. In a town of that size, a morning paper was a wild speculation which might, if its capital held out, become a commercial success. Founded by his uncle in a moment of beautiful optimism, the *Sun* was still in the stage when it was spending money rather than earning it, and, except for backing horses or staging plays, there are few better ways of losing a lot of money than on a newspaper that fails. And having conducted his offspring to the precise stage when it was a toss up what would happen, his uncle had unfortunately died, leaving his newspaper interest to his nephew largely because there was no one else.

Tony was grimly determined that it should succeed; and on the staff which his masterful uncle had accumulated, there was no efficient directing substitute. That was partly why he had returned at the first available opportunity; but there was another reason. It was contained in the page proof which he had just finished reading, and the proof, more than the precarious position of the paper, accounted for the frown which creased his forehead. He had taken it up again for another glance when a brisk knock sounded on the door.

It was the commissionaire who entered, bearing a visiting card.

"Inspector Dunster would be grateful if you could see him as soon as possible, sir," he announced.

"Dunster?" Tony knew both the town and the county police, but the name was new to him. He glanced at the card, and raised his eyebrows a little. "Scotland Yard," he said thoughtfully, and paused. "Very well, Sergeant. Show him in at once."

"Very good, sir."

Tony was always expecting the commissionaire to forget himself and salute, but so far he had been disappointed. He sat frowning for a moment; then folded over the proof in front of him, seized a sheet of paper, and when the inspector entered was feverishly scribbling notes for a slashing article on the local sewage.

Perhaps the inspector was accustomed to this type of subterfuge, for there was the faintest smile on his face, which faded instantly as Tony looked up with the air of a busy man who has momentarily forgotten the reason for a visitor's presence. There was nothing of the bull-necked, wall-eyed, wooden-faced type about him. In appearance, at least, he was hardly older than Tony himself; though, like most things about his appearance, that was deceptive. A pleasantly-humorous mouth and a pair of innocent blue eyes somehow combined to put people at their ease, and he had always found it far more useful than any official bullying.

"Oh, sit down, Inspector," Tony invited. "I shan't be a moment."

He scribbled the words "Scandalous inaction on the part of the town council," crossed out the word "the," and pushed the paper from him, too unpleasantly aware of the mild interest in the other's eyes to carry the game any further. Then he pulled the telephone towards him.

"Just a moment," he apologised and lifted the receiver. "Sub-editors, please... Chief Sub-editor... Oh, hullo. That proof is all right... Yes. As soon as you can."

The inspector was still watching him with polite attention. He gave the impression that if Tony had liked to chat with the entire office staff individually and write the next week's leaders, it would be a matter of indifference to him.

"And now, Inspector?" Tony asked briskly. "Sorry to have kept you waiting—"

"Not at all—sir." There was only the slightest pause between the first part of the sentence and the respectful monosyllable, but Tony felt the inspector said it with an effort, as Sergeant Watson avoided saluting. "Perhaps you can guess why I've come, sir?"

Tony raised his left eyebrow only and looked blank.

"I'm afraid not," he said briefly.

The inspector glanced at the sling on Tony's left arm.

"And yet, sir, you can't have had much chance to forget," he observed pleasantly. "It is about what happened at Upper Utton three weeks ago."

Tony's eyebrow rose a fraction higher.

"Really?" he said. "But I understood that matter was settled."

"Hardly." The inspector smiled. "Otherwise they would scarcely have gone to the expense of calling us in... Local councils really hate it, you know."

Tony did not respond. "It indicates," he said acidly, "a remarkable change of attitude on the part of the local police. In my last interview with them I gathered that the affair of the rake and the ghost seen by Miss—Miss Blakeney must be a stupid hoax, the authors of which it was impossible, and not very necessary, to find; that my own experiences were faked by me with a view to a journalistic sensation—though I overdid the part by falling and injuring myself on a spade, probably because I was drunk. Also, that I was lucky to escape being charged."

Dunster sighed. He had not been unprepared for some such attitude.

"I don't think that was said, sir," he corrected mildly.

"It was certainly conveyed... Further, having promised to deliver a message to my deputy editor, and to inform him what had happened, they took advantage of my being unconscious to do neither, and merely said that I had had an accident."

The inspector had been studying the pattern of the carpet. Now he looked up quickly.

"And yet, you didn't print anything about it!" he said. "That's what particularly strikes me." He paused. "You see," he went on with a smile, "until I'd seen you, I couldn't be sure you weren't a cautious type of person who might prefer to avoid any threatened legal trouble even at the cost of a good story. Now I must say I should like to know why."

This time Tony did smile, but there was no good humour in it.

"The reason—" he began, and corrected himself. "One reason, at least, may very soon become apparent. Beyond that, I don't feel inclined to explain."

The inspector inclined his head in assent. "What I came for, sir," he said, "since we have been called in and I am in charge of the case, was to ask you if you would mind repeating your evidence to me and answering a few questions—"

Tony hardly let him finish. "No," he said. "Under the circumstances, I don't think I should at present. Certainly not except under legal advice, and with a lawyer present, in view of the suggestions that have been made. The police have already got all the information I can give." He stopped. The inspector was rising from his chair when he went on: "Unless you can explain why they have changed their minds."

"For publication?" Dunster queried.

"Not necessarily—if you can show me it's not in the public interest. I won't bind myself."

The inspector thought for a moment. "The fact is," he said slowly, as though speaking his thoughts aloud, "that I shouldn't be justified in telling you in the ordinary way, but it's been done so thoroughly that it's bound to come out very soon. The wonder is that it isn't in print already... Yes... I think I can tell you."

"Well?"

"Strictly speaking," the inspector said slowly, "our being called in has no direct connection with what happened to you at all... It is simply this. Scotland Yard, the local chief constable, and various influential people have all received anonymous letters making a very remarkable suggestion. Briefly, it is that George Blakeney"—Tony started a little at the name—"that George Blakeney did not run away; that he was murdered; and that the murderer was his brother Richard." He smiled. "I can safely tell you that last part," he said. "I don't think the libel laws would let you print it."

"Murdered—" Tony repeated blankly. "By Richard?... But surely that's obvious nonsense? Isn't it the usual cranky kind of letter you get if anything happens that people are inclined to gossip about?"

"Perhaps... But, as it happens, in this case there are a few pieces of confirmatory evidence. I'm putting myself rather in your hands by telling you all this. I'm doing it because I don't think you were very well treated, and I'm really amazed at your moderation." He smiled. "The official family explanation is that George got fed up with things, became a victim of the wanderlust, and, despite his family's entreaties, thought he'd travel... I don't know if you realise just how out of character that was, but still, people do odd things—"

"Not much more out of character," Tony suggested, "than the locally accepted story that he bolted because of a woman. By all accounts he was a perfect misogynist."

"It isn't locally accepted any more. The truth is, that the murder theory is so generally accepted locally that Mr. Richard dare hardly show his face in public. However... persuasion proving of no avail, Mr. Richard drove him to the station and, having an engagement (unspecified), left him there to wait for the train... Perhaps you don't know Utton Road? It's not a station, but a halt. It has no permanent staff on duty at night. George was left alone on the station by Richard, and that was the last seen of him."

"That's hardly grounds for suggesting murder."

"No. Though Richard has a motive. The father, as you know, is on the point of death. The estate is entailed. If George died, Richard would inherit the lot. In addition, there has already been some dispute about the management of the property... All the same, as you say, it wouldn't be any reason by itself for expecting murder. But when we came to look into the matter of these letters we discovered all kinds of confirmatory details."

"Such as?"

Dunster hesitated for quite a long time. "I'm afraid I can't go quite so far except under promise of secrecy." He smiled apologetically. "You'll understand—"

"I don't think—" Tony hesitated in turn. "I don't feel justified in giving it... Perhaps I can suggest a few you might have come across... You've interviewed the guard of the train and found that he did not in fact pick up anyone corresponding to George at Utton Road Halt... You've looked into possible steamship sailings, and failed to find anyone corresponding to George in name or description on their lists... Perhaps you have witnesses to a quarrel? Perhaps George has been unduly agitated? Perhaps—"

He broke off. Dunster had been listening with polite, but impassive attention. Now he ventured to prompt.

"Perhaps—?" he suggested.

"I don't think I want to go on at present." Tony grinned. "Am I right?"

Inspector Dunster only smiled.

"Of course, a good deal of that any decent reporter could find out for himself... In any case, I fail to see the connection with the grave business."

"There are points which connect. For example, the first grave to be opened was Lady Blakeney's—"

"They do believe it was opened now?" Tony asked with a trace of sarcasm.

"They know it was... The first witness to the gravedigging was Virginia Blakeney... And the mere fact that anyone is digging graves when there's a suspicion of murder is itself a link."

"I don't see much sense in it," said Tony, with a denseness which was assumed.

"There doesn't seem to be any... But there might be insanity. Suppose Richard's story is true. Suppose that his mother's death had unbalanced George's mind; that when Richard left him alone at the station he went completely off his head, and started opening graves and so on, hiding somewhere in the neighbourhood—"

"Found any traces?" Tony asked innocently.

Inspector Dunster gave another charming smile. "We've only just been called in, sir," he evaded.

"And that's the theory you're working on?"

"It's a theory."

"I don't think much of it. Plausible up to a point—but I don't think it deals with this mystification of painted skulls and so on. A madman wouldn't do that."

"It's hard to say what a madman would do."

"I don't believe George could remain hidden in the district so long. Everyone knows him. He'd have to feed and so on. He would need a confederate... No, I don't think it's likely."

"Perhaps you've a better one?"

"I hardly know enough to form one," Tony countered. "It's just as likely that George was murdered by Richard; that Richard is a student of fiction and knew the best place to hide a body is in a graveyard. That would explain why he didn't chase the girl."

"But why choose his mother's grave? A little ghoulish, don't you think?"

"That was a mistake. And so he tried the following night—"

"And still didn't bury the body?"

"I interrupted him." Tony frowned. "The main point seems to me to be, were the coffins tampered with or not?" he said. "We know, according to Miss Blakeney's story, that he'd actually reached the coffin when he chased her... Did he look inside? Did he take anything from it—not necessarily the body? Again, I suppose I was knocked out at about three in the morning. Unfortunately I don't know exactly how long I'd been asleep. But I wasn't found until six—and then the grave was neatly filled in again. My point is, was a body stolen or not?"

"It was not."

"How do you know?"

"I may as well tell you," Dunster said slowly, "because it actually tends to kill the news story rather than otherwise. We got an exhumation order and looked to see if the bodies were still there. They were. Neither coffin had been tampered with in any way." He shrugged his shoulders. "And that does seem sheer nonsense. Imagine anyone doing several hours' really hard work and taking all that risk with nothing to show for it. There's no sense in it—"

"He was interrupted the first two times—" Tony suggested.

"But there were only two—"

"There may be more." Tony smiled curiously. "However, it's certain that, so far, there are no bodies missing?"

"Certain. Of course if—"

From somewhere underneath an unmistakable musical roar interrupted him. The machines were running off an edition of the paper, and a slight frown creased the inspector's face for a moment. The hour was unusual. There was an enigmatic look on the young editor's face.

"What do you think," he said after quite a long pause, "about my idea that the opening of the first grave was a mistake?"

"It's worth looking into," Dunster conceded. "And now—"

"Another thing I thought of—that old Stroud, the sexton, might have gone off his head." There was something in the journalist's manner which puzzled the inspector. He seemed almost to be making conversation, waiting for something to happen. "I gave that up, though, after I'd been laid out. I don't think he'd have had the strength, mad or sane."

"Probably not." Dunster waited. "Anything else?"

"Aren't you rejecting this woman story—the explanation given before the murder story ever came up at all—a little too easily. I made a few enquiries myself, and there is a man—"

"I've interviewed him... He simply broke down and admitted it was all nonsense. He's just an old drunkard. There's not a shred of evidence to connect George with the sister. I don't know if you've seen her. But I ask you if it's likely—"

"Not now... She may have been good looking in a way a few years ago. I think— Ah!"

There was the sound of approaching footsteps. A sharp rap sounded on the door. Without waiting for permission, a small office boy entered and with an unusual air of importance he handed to Tony a paper still wet from the press.

"Special edition, sir!" he announced unnecessarily.

"Thank you, Tommy." He accepted the sheet, glanced at the front-page headlines, and waited until the door closed again. "Perhaps you'd like to see the paper, Inspector?" he asked innocently.

"Thank you, but I've seen—" Dunster began. Then, as his eyes caught the headline, he broke off. "Good heavens!" he exclaimed, and snatched it.

With startled eyes he glanced along the print, muttering to himself as he read.

"Body-snatching Mystery. Skull-faced ghost at work. Three graves desecrated—"

He stared at the sheet; then looked up at Tony.

"Three?" he said simply.

"Another last night." Tony smiled. "As a matter of fact I rather thought there might be. That's why I've had a man down there watching... In the next village this time. A middle-aged agricultural labourer—"

"And the body's stolen?"

"I'm afraid I can't say. The grave's disturbed... As a matter of fact, I was only waiting for the edition before I went down myself. Perhaps I could give you a lift?"

Inspector Dunster nodded dumbly.

# 6

## Encounters

PERHAPS THE SHOCK OF the journalist's revelation had been too much for the inspector; perhaps he was merely biding his time. At least on the way down he had contented himself with a bare minimum of perfunctory questions, and at their arrival in the village took his leave with a brief word of thanks as if only anxious to get away.

Tony was not particularly sorry to see him go. Seated by the window of the inn parlour, he looked out over a pleasant prospect of thatched roofs and apple orchards while he tried to work out a plan of campaign. It might have been a form of reaction after his triumph which made him all too conscious of the difficulties. There were many lines of approach, but most of them seemed closed to him. Interviews with any members of the Blakeney family were obviously hopeless. He had not so far found a copy of the anonymous letter to which he could obtain access. The grave itself was not likely to tell him much, and in any case the reporter who had sent the news could be relied upon to watch that.

In all of these the police had obvious advantages, and judging by his past experiences they were not likely to be helpful. On the whole, his best chance seemed to be to concentrate on the one piece of information which he alone possessed, the woman's mysterious visit to Newent's bungalow, and he had almost made up his mind when the sound of someone talking in the passage outside made him turn towards the half-open door.

"Mr. Mayfield is in the parlour, you say? That's all right. I can find my way—"

There was something vaguely familiar in the voice. He was trying to place it when the door was pushed open and the speaker entered. In spite of himself he gave a little start of surprise. It was Alness.

Tony had risen to his feet, and for a moment the two men stood facing each other. Then Alness smiled, an unexpected, deprecating smile, and closed the door gently.

"Good afternoon, Mr. Mayfield," he said.

"Good afternoon, Mr.—Mr. Alness, isn't it?" Tony rejoined, and waited.

"I'm glad I found you in," Alness said politely, and hesitated. "I haven't long to spare, but I wanted a word with you... If I might sit down—"

He crossed the room and took the chair on the other side of the window. Tony followed his example in silence. He was completely puzzled by the visit, and until he knew more about the reason for it, his best line seemed to be not to commit himself. Apparently Alness himself found some difficulty in coming to the point. Tony met the scrutiny of the keen blue eyes studying him, and the thought crossed his mind that perhaps he had misjudged the man. There was an attractive firmness in the strong, clean-shaven face, and the rather full, humorous lips which suggested qualities he had not previously associated with his opponent of the churchyard. At last Alness broke the silence.

"I expect you're surprised to see me, Mr. Mayfield," he said. "I'll come to the point at once. In the first place, I want to offer you an apology."

"An apology?" Tony raised his eyebrows, and left it at that. His manner was not encouraging, but Alness was not to be deterred.

"Yes. I'm afraid at our last meeting I offended your professional feelings severely by my offer of—shall we say, compensation? Since then the enormity of my offence has been brought home to me. I understand that my suggestion was as though you offered me a tip in my capacity as a J.P. to alter my decision in a case... I can only plead the Johnsonian excuse of pure ignorance—and say that I'm sorry... Am I forgiven?"

He smiled conciliatingly, and Tony responded. He was never a man to bear malice. Besides, the thought flashed through his mind that, if Alness for some reason of his own wished to hold out the olive branch, it was hardly in his interests to refuse it.

"Of course," he said. "Really, I ought to do the same. The circumstances were—well, unusual, and I don't expect my own manner was all one could wish... Cigarette?"

Alness accepted, lit it, and again seemed momentarily at a loss. He glanced at his watch, and seemed to make up his mind.

"I'm glad that's settled," he said with a slightly crooked smile. "It was a necessary preliminary, and I haven't much time. As you may have guessed, I have an ulterior motive for this visit... From the fact that you're here at all, I suppose that you know the latest developments?"

"The grave—?"

"Partly. I didn't actually mean that. You've heard, I mean, of these anonymous letters, and, since you travelled down with the inspector, I can assume that you know Scotland Yard has been called in."

Tony inclined his head in assent. "I know a little," he admitted. "I'm anxious to know more."

"We'll go into details later," Alness said rather surprisingly, and paused for a moment. "Anyhow, you know what is being said about my cousins. That George Blakeney is dead, and that Richard murdered him?"

"Well, yes," Tony admitted. "Of course, gossip like that—"

"Is extremely unpleasant, believe me. Even if that was all, it's got to the stage when we should have to do something about it. But it's more than unpleasant... Mr. Mayfield, I'm getting a bit scared by it."

Tony raised his eyebrows. Alness did not look a man to trouble himself unnecessarily.

"Scotland Yard is here," Alness resumed. "Why?"

"I suppose to find the writer of the anonymous letters," Tony suggested a little doubtfully. "And, of course, this grave business. When the local authorities found it couldn't be kept quiet, they probably thought it was a bit beyond their depth."

Alness shook his head slowly but with decision.

"No," he said at last. "Or rather, that's only part of it. The real reason for the presence of Inspector Dunster is that they believe the letters. They're trying to pin a murder charge on Richard Blakeney."

"What?" Tony demanded. "But that's impossible... There can't be a murder charge. There isn't a body. There's not the faintest proof that George is dead at all."

Alness puffed at his cigarette and frowned for a second or two. Then he looked up.

"Suppose there was?" he demanded.

Tony was startled. "You don't mean—" he began, and broke off.

"No. I don't mean that I've found the body or anything of that kind. I only want you to consider my cousin's position if George's murdered body was found. What would the police evidence be against Richard?"

"Well," Tony considered. "I can tell you what I've heard in that connection. It's said that Richard and George had quarrelled; that Richard benefits by George's death— By the way, is that a fact? Under George's will?"

"The property's entailed in the heirs male, or the bulk of it... Yes?"

"They'd say, naturally, that Richard was the last person to be seen with his cousin... That they drove to the station together, but apparently never arrived there—"

"In fact, that so far as can be checked, Richard has given an account which the facts contradict. They'd certainly say he was lying about what happened... And the worst of it is, I'm pretty sure they'd be right."

"You mean—? But if so—"

"Even if it's so, of course it doesn't mean that Richard killed George. But he did lie about what happened, I'm fairly certain. They could find a little more than that, I think. For example, wouldn't you say on your own experience that Richard was a man of hasty temper? And might be provoked to a violent attack?... And if the letters are to be relied upon, there might be more than that—if the body's found." He paused. "Well, Mr. Mayfield. Imagine yourself a member of the jury. What would your verdict be? Short of an eyewitness, what more evidence could you hope for? At least, you can see there's a case to go for trial, and, in view of the old man's health, even that would be fatal. And that's why I've come to you. I want your help."

"My help?" Tony echoed.

"Yes. At our first meeting, Mr. Mayfield—" He smiled a little wryly. "At our first meeting, I admit that I was in favour of hushing up an unpleasant affair. Things have got beyond that. There's only one thing to do now, and that is to find out the whole truth—to explode the case against Richard before it can come to a trial." He glanced at his watch again. "That's where I think we might work together... I've no time to go into it now. Suppose you came up to see me tonight... Say half-past eight. I shall be out until then. We could talk things over—and perhaps I could show you a copy of the letter... You'll come?"

He had risen to his feet to go. Tony rose too. He was feeling distinctly puzzled by the whole affair, and more than a little inclined to be suspicious of his visitor's intentions. But it was hard to see how any such interview could be to his disadvantage. It was, in fact, precisely what he had been wishing for, and thinking impossible, a few minutes before. He nodded.

"I'll come," he said with a trace of hesitation. "At least we can discuss things—"

"Good. That's all I ask. Till tonight, then... Good day, Mr. Mayfield."

Tony stood there for a moment as the door closed behind his visitor; then turning to the window watched Alness as he made his way briskly down the village street. The whole affair was sufficiently mysterious, and he was more than a little inclined to think that there must be something more behind it. But at least it could do no harm, and might clear his way a good deal. In the meantime, he was still where he was, and, failing anything better, he decided to carry out his original plan of claiming acquaintance with Newent by borrowing the promised bicycle, and perhaps paying a visit to the cottage where Crouch and his sister lived.

But, in fact, he had no very definite plans in his mind as he started up the street, conscious of the curious glances which were turned upon him as he passed. Keenly alert to atmosphere, he could sense the change of attitude of the village. His dramatic departure in an ambulance, and his reappearance in the company of a Scotland Yard inspector had abolished any chance of posing as a casual tourist this time; and the mere fact that Alness had found him at the inn showed how quickly the news had spread.

That might have its disadvantages, but he had to make the best of it. Without stopping, he nodded a cheerful recognition once or twice to people to whom he had spoken on his previous visit. And then suddenly his heart seemed to miss a beat. Coming down the road towards him was a figure he could not fail to recognise, though he had met her only twice, and once in the darkness. It was Virginia Blakeney.

For an instant something very like panic overwhelmed him, and if there had been a chance of escape he would have turned and run for it. But in the same moment she saw him. She gave a little start and flushed, hesitated a second, and then crossed the road straight towards him.

"Good—good afternoon, Mr. Mayfield." Her voice faltered a little and it seemed to him that there was something rather pathetically brave in her smile. "I—I hope you're better—"

"Oh—yes. Yes, of course." Tony stood there dumbly struggling for words. "Quite all right. It was nothing, really—"

He felt that he was talking like a fool, but if she noticed she disregarded it.

"I—I've been wanting to see you, Mr. Mayfield," she said in a low voice, and looked round, almost guiltily. They were beyond the main area of the houses, and for the moment out of view of curious eyes. "I wanted to thank you—and to tell you I was sorry—"

Apologies seemed to be the order of the day. Alness's had stuck in his throat a little, but this was worse than ever.

"Really, you've nothing to apologise for," he said warmly. "I don't blame you in the least if you were angry—in fact, I'm ashamed of myself. Of course, it was my business to find out for my paper—"

"But you didn't," she said quickly. "I mean, you didn't print anything about it—in spite of all that happened. After we'd been so rude to you—"

In this respect, Tony was all too conscious of his lack of merit. He felt impelled to tell the truth at all risks.

"Miss—Miss Blakeney," he said a little hesitantly. "I don't deserve this... I ought to tell you. My paper printed the full story this morning, and I was personally responsible for the whole thing."

The news did not seem to change her attitude, though she winced a little at it.

"I knew that it had to come," she said in a low voice. "Besides, everyone knows. Everyone's talking about it. And they all think—" She glanced round again, as though afraid of being overheard; then glanced at him appealingly. "Mr. Mayfield," she pleaded, "I've been wanting to talk with you... Could you walk a little way with me—towards the Hall? Where they can't see us—" The colour flamed in her cheeks. "Oh, I expect you think I'm being silly, but you can't imagine what it's been like. Everyone looking, and talking behind my back... I can hardly bear to come down into the village any more; but they'd think I was afraid—"

Tony fell into step beside her, and for a few yards they walked in silence. He stole a glance or two at the chin defiantly raised, and the sight of a tear trembling on her eyelash filled him with an impulse to massacre the entire village which was the cause of it. She herself stared straight ahead, and they were some distance from the road along the track leading to the Hall before she spoke.

"I suppose—I suppose you've heard everything," she said at last.

"That's why I'm here," Tony said bluntly, and felt next instant that he had merely been brutal. "I mean, this last grave affair—"

"I meant the letters," she said. "What—what they're saying, about George—and—and Richard—"

"Yes," Tony admitted. "I had heard something—"

"They all believe it... But it's not true... Oh I don't know what has been happening, but it isn't—it can't be that... After all, they're my brothers—"

At that precise moment, the relationship seemed to Tony a perfect reason why no one should murder George and why Richard in particular could not have done. He made a desperate attempt to comfort her.

"Really, Miss Blakeney, you mustn't worry," he said. "It's just some lunatic or other... This kind of thing crops up from time to time—slanderous letters and so on. The police will get the writer sooner or later—"

"The police—" she said, and stopped. "But you don't understand. They believe the letters. They're trying to prove—to prove Richard guilty—"

The thought crossed Tony's mind that, if the police really thought Richard guilty, they must have been singularly clumsy in revealing their suspicions. He was inclined to suspect some heavy work on the part of the local police before Inspector Dunster arrived on the scene.

"You mustn't think that," he said firmly. "Naturally, the police have to make all sorts of enquiries. I expect they have been asking some idiotic questions. But if your brother is innocent—"

"He is!" she burst out; then she drew her breath in sharply. "He can't have done anything," she said, and it seemed to him with less conviction. "But—but—"

She stopped again. They were in sight of the Hall, and Tony felt that his time was drawing short.

"Look here," he said at last. "Of course, there's no reason why you should give me your confidence at all. In fact, I suppose it's quite the other way. Only—only if there's any way I could help you I'd be glad to do anything I can."

"I know," she said quite simply. "But—but it's hard to explain. I know Richard couldn't have done that. And yet there is something. They're not the same, neither my father nor Richard."

"And Mr. Alness?" Tony asked without quite knowing why.

"Oh, he's the same as ever. Though I think he's noticed something too. He's offered to help me. I think he is trying. But I don't feel—"

She broke off with a quick blush which was very enlightening to Tony. Alness, no doubt, had excellent reasons for wanting to help the girl; no doubt that desire had prompted his own visit to Tony. But somehow it was a relief that the girl apparently had no desire to accept help from him.

"As a matter of fact, I've just seen Mr. Alness," he blurted out. "He wanted me to talk things over. I was going to see him tonight."

He waited for her to approve or reject the interview; but she did neither.

"He's been very kind," she said without enthusiasm, and suddenly seemed to realise how near they were to the house. "You—you mustn't come any farther," she said urgently. "My brother—I'm afraid he wouldn't understand... Thank you for—for listening to all this... And now, goodbye."

But Tony could not take leave like that. She was turning towards the gateway when he spoke.

"Miss Blakeney," he said, and as she turned to look at him found difficulty in going on. "I say, I hope you won't think— Well, I'm staying at the inn in the village for a day or two. If there's anything I could do at any time to help—"

"Thank you," she said in a low voice. "And now, goodbye."

He stood watching her until she disappeared round a bend in the drive, and it was only as he turned away that the unprofessional nature of his conduct occurred to him. Instead of finding an exciting story, he was practically committed, between Alness and the girl, to proving the innocence of a young man in whom the police were distinctly interested, if what the girl and her cousin believed was true; and who, in fact, only awaited the appearance of a corpse to be charged with murder. He smiled a little at that as he turned away, thought of a headline or two which would certainly have landed him in legal difficulties, and was starting back along the lane when the sight of a man emerging from a gateway in the wall just ahead made him stop short. It was Richard Blakeney.

Luckily, Tony was still just within the drive entrance, almost hidden by the massive gatepost. It would have taken a more careful look backwards than Richard apparently had time to give to have noticed him. Instead, he merely glanced with a quick, furtive motion up and down the lane, closed the gate gently behind him and started along the road in the direction from which Tony and the girl had just come.

Tony hesitated only for an instant. In the young man's movements there had been a suggestion of stealth which would have excited his curiosity, and as he had looked round, Tony had seen his face. Unless he was very much mistaken, the prevailing emotion in Richard Blakeney's mind was fear, or fear and hate mingled. Tony hesitated only for a moment; then his scruples vanished in the excitement of the chase. As Richard turned abruptly and disappeared over a gateway leading to the fields, he started forward to follow him.

# 7

# Quiet and Peaceful

WITHOUT THE FAINTEST ENTHUSIASM, Inspector Dunster stood contemplating the newly-turned pile of damp earth which was the immediate reason for his hurried return. Undoubtedly it was a grave; no doubt it had recently been disturbed, as Stroud had just finished explaining with considerable emphasis and at great length. But beyond that it told him nothing whatever.

Apparently it had the same depressing effect upon the local superintendent, who had been dragged out of bed at an unwontedly early hour by the sexton's inopportune discovery, and had since been aggravating a tendency to rheumatism by standing about in the damp and missing meals.

"Well, there you are," he observed without hope. "And I suppose we'll have to dig it up to see... Only, you know, the other two were quite all right—"

"All the same, I'm afraid we must make sure," Dunster answered. "Stroud seems certain that it's been interfered with somehow... And no one saw or heard anything?"

"No one." The superintendent lapsed into heavy sarcasm. "You might think in a dead-alive place like this the local inhabitants would cheer themselves up after a hard day's work by sitting about on the tombstones in the small hours of the morning. Oddly enough, they don't. Even this grave business doesn't seem to have stimulated a proper interest in church-yards by moonlight. In fact, some of 'em will walk a mile round to dodge one. So, as it happens, no one was here the night before last—or the night before that, or whenever it happened."

"We can't even settle that?"

"Well, it didn't happen last night, because it's been rained on, and there's been no rain since yesterday afternoon. And it can't be more than a week ago, because it's only a week since the grave was dug. That's as near as we can go."

"And whoever it was just used the tools in the shed there—which isn't even locked. And the rain must have washed out any tracks—if there were any; and there's no earthly reason why there should have been... No. It's not exactly promising."

The superintendent sighed. "All the same, if the papers get hold of it—" he began.

"They have," Dunster informed him, and produced from his pocket the paper with which Tony had kindly presented him. "Here is the first effort."

The superintendent glanced at it, and a dull red flush spread round his collar. Strictly within the limits of the law, Tony had contrived to be fairly scathing on the subject of the police efforts.

"I'd like to meet the chap who wrote that," he said at last, grimly.

"You can," Dunster assured him. "He's staying at the Golden Lion. You may remember him, I think. His name's Mayfield."

The superintendent grunted. Actually he had had nothing to do with the rather dubious handling of Tony's midnight assault, but he might be held responsible. His eagerness to meet the journalist vanished.

"I wonder what the devil he wants us to do?" he said almost pathetically. "We can't watch all the churchyards for miles around all the time—"

"It may come to that," Dunster said seriously. "But I admit it will be a pretty big job. At any rate, we'd better have them inspected—say in a radius of ten miles or so. And in the meantime—"

He broke off, frowning thoughtfully down at the grave.

"I suppose this isn't, strictly speaking, your pigeon, any-how," the superintendent suggested. "Unless you think it has some connection with the letters, and Blakeney's vanishing?"

"I do," Dunster assured him. "It's supremely unlikely that one should have two lunatics in a place like this—or crimi-nals."

"You don't know them as I do," his colleague said bitterly. "Well, where do we go from here?"

"I think," Dunster said slowly like a man considering, "we could do with a drink."

"I'm darned sure we could," the superintendent assented, and his face brightened a little. "But—"

"And I think the handiest place would be the pub that chap goes to—Crouch, you know. It's not far from here?"

The superintendent shook his head, and led the way to the waiting car. They were dodging along the winding lane before he put the question which was in his mind.

"But what's the idea?" he demanded. "I thought you'd finished with that chap?"

"Just an attempt to combine business with pleasure." Dunster smiled. "We could do with a drink—or at least, I could. And it might be a good thing to find out if Crouch has been saying his piece again... You see, the great advantage of a chap like that is that when he gets enough he's almost bound to talk, if his life depended upon it. So, if he does know anything about this grave business, he may have said something."

In one respect they were doomed to disappointment. The fat landlord was positive, and his wife confirmed him, that neither Crouch nor his sister had been near the inn since their questioning by the police. Nor, in fact, had Crouch been seen abroad in that time, though he had been heard by passers-by apparently inside the cottage, and in what seemed to be his normal condition.

The superintendent shrugged. "D.T.s," he suggested. "I'm not surprised."

"I'm not so sure," Dunster said thoughtfully. "In fact, I rather think that his not having been here is really interesting. D'you think his sister has enough influence over him to keep him at home?"

"Influence? He's scared to death of her. He'd sign the pledge if she told him—but she doesn't."

"Hm... I think another interview with him is indicated some time soon. And perhaps—"

The landlord had unsuccessfully been trying to catch what they were saying. He abandoned the attempt, and leaned forward over the bar.

"Excuse me, Inspector," he wheezed, "there's something else I meant to tell you... You were asking, weren't you, if anyone had seen Mr. George just before he left? Well, there's a chap comes in here sometimes—Saturday nights regular, that is. A gamekeeper, name of Bere... And that's a funny thing, because he won't touch anything but cider... Well, I heard him saying something the other evening about having seen Mr. George the day he left, and Mr. George having told him that he was going away for a bit... That's what he said, sir."

"Bere?" the superintendent repeated reflectively. "Seem to know the name... Ah! Two brothers, aren't there? Twins or something. Live at the West Lodge, don't they?"

"That's them... Never married, neither of 'em, and won't have a woman near the place. Steady-going chaps and keep themselves to themselves in a general way. But last Saturday there was a bit of talk, you know, and someone was saying it was funny Mr. George hadn't mentioned to anyone that he was going, and Joe—that's the one without the gold tooth, sir—it's the only way, almost, you can tell 'em apart—he fires up and says: 'You're a liar then,' he says right out, 'for Master George told me himself he were going, and the very day he left, too.'"

"And that was all?"

"That was all, sir... You see, the others were kind of surprised, not being used to Joe going off like that, so they dried up, and Joe seemed put out at having spoken, so he finished his cider and went out. And that was all."

"Thanks," Dunster said casually. "Of course, I don't suppose it's of any great importance. We might have a word with him some time if we're passing. Well—" He finished his beer and sighed. "I suppose it's back to work... Good day."

The superintendent followed him reluctantly, and there was a resigned expression on his face as he slumped into the car seat.

"And I suppose we 'happen to be passing' now," he suggested. "It's only about a mile and a half over a beastly road in the wrong direction."

"Might as well," Dunster said. "Of course, it's clutching at a straw. Probably he can't tell us anything worth hearing. And yet it's interesting in a way to hear that there was someone outside the family who knew about it. It depends what time of day it was whether it's important any other way... Incidentally, how did you come to know him?"

"Oh, there was quite a case about six months ago. The Blakeneys and a neighbour—new arrival called da Vargas or something. They went at it hammer and tongs—trespass, damages, assault, and heaven knows what. The two Beres were witnesses. For the Blakeneys, of course. They haven't an idea between them apart from the family."

"How did it end? The case against what's-his-name?"

"It didn't, really. That kind of thing never does... Sort of dragged on with applications for injunctions and appeals and so on. I expect they're still at it now. Only it's not happened to come up locally just lately."

"And what sort of a man is this neighbour?"

"Nasty bit of work. Complete bounder, rolling in cash. Wanted to get into local society, and they weren't having any. Don't blame 'em. So he turned nasty, you see."

Dunster nodded thoughtfully. It was unlikely enough that a neighbour's quarrel six months ago could have anything to do with the present business, but he docketed the information tidily in his mind. One advantage of the country as opposed to the town, he reflected, was the way in which everyone knows everyone else's business. The disadvantage was that they so frequently expected you to know too. He had asked most carefully and repeatedly for anyone with a possible grudge against the Blakeneys, and now such a promising candidate as this man cropped up quite casually.

Apparently the superintendent thought that the subject was exhausted. He had lapsed into silence. They had left the main road, and, from the way in which the car was bumping over the ruts, seemed to be going down something like an occupation lane. Then he had a glimpse of the Hall, and knew that they must be getting near to their destination. A minute later the car lurched to a stop opposite a neat cottage standing in a little clearing in the woods and they got out.

"There's one of 'em," the superintendent said. "Don't know if we're lucky. Can't tell till I see his tooth... Hullo!"

The man who had been bending over his fork in the potato patch straightened his back and looked towards them; then he dropped his fork and hurried forward. Dunster placed his age at anything over fifty. He was the type which, beyond a certain point in life, seems unaffected by age, and the grey eyes which scrutinised them from the browned and wrinkled face might have been those of a boy.

"Good day, Superintendent," he greeted them as he opened the gate. "It's you again then... You've not brought the doctor?"

His eyes turned to Dunster, and something like disappointment showed in his face as he quite obviously rejected the inspector's claim to medical qualifications.

"This is Inspector Dunster from Scotland Yard," the superintendent introduced with something of an air. "What's that about doctors—er—Jim? Didn't know that you troubled 'em."

"It's not me—it's Joe." Dunster gathered that his colleague had been successful in obtaining a glimpse of the vital tooth. "The old trouble, you know. But he's been proper bad this time. So I asked Robinson's lad just to drop word to Doctor Staithes. When the car stopped I thought 'twas him."

"Sorry to hear that... As a matter of fact, it was Joe we wanted to see. He could manage a few minutes, couldn't he? We shan't keep him long—"

The man was obviously reluctant. "Wouldn't I do, sir?" he suggested. "You see, Joe's been proper bad, and he's just gone off to sleep... He's better, generally, that way. I'd rather you didn't disturb him."

"Well—" The superintendent looked at Dunster. "I don't know—"

"We don't want to trouble him if we can help it," Dunster said. "Perhaps you could tell us... Were you at the pub last Saturday when a chap said something about Mr. Blakeney—"

"No, I weren't there." The gamekeeper's jaw set formidably. "But I heard... Ay, Joe was real angry about that. If he hadn't gone, he'd have hit him, he said—and Joe's not a man to quarrel—"

"Probably it's not very important. But we've been told he said something about Mr. George Blakeney—that he'd met him the day he was going, and he'd said he was going abroad—"

"Ay?" There was suspicion in the countryman's voice. "And why would you want to know about that?"

"I should think it's plain enough. You know what people are saying—that his going away is just a put-up yarn invented by his family. Obviously if he'd seen someone else and told him that would help to put an end to that."

Jim considered; then nodded slowly. "I hadn't thought of that," he said. "Ay, Joe told me about it. He up and told them right out that he'd seen the young master the very day he left—"

"Did you see him?" Dunster asked.

"No," the gamekeeper admitted reluctantly. "I didn't see him myself. But Joe told me—"

"Did he happen to mention what time of day it was when they met?"

"No, he didn't... Not then. But it must have been pretty early in the morning, if he were out that way. Ay, not later than seven, I'd say."

"How do you know?"

"Why, sir, it's a funny thing, we were talking about it not an hour ago... You see, Joe started to get bad as usual—megrims, the doctor calls it, or something like that, sir—and he pulls a little box out of his pocket with some sort of jelly things in it. I was surprised, and I says, 'I thought you didn't hold with chemists' stuff... That's not the doctor's.' And he says, 'No. The young master gave me 'em when I met him up by the Round Copse. Said they'd do me a lot of good.' Not that they have done as I can see, sir—though he is asleep now—"

"But the time?" Dunster demanded. "How could you tell that?

"Well, sir, I knows he hadn't met Mr. George but the once, because he was saying so the other day. And if he met him up by the Round Copse it couldn't have been any time but between six and seven on the Thursday morning, because that's the time Joe would be there—"

"Thursday?" Dunster broke in sharply. "Wednesday, you mean?"

"Thursday I says and Thursday I meant, sir," Jim persisted. "Ay, it was Thursday—"

"But—Great Scott!" the superintendent burst out as it dawned upon him. "According to all accounts, George Blakeney had left by the night train on the Wednesday!"

"Thursday it must have been, sir," Jim rejoined immovably. "It were Thursday Joe goes to the Round Copse—"

"Look here, this may be important. I'm afraid we must settle this somehow... We'll have to trouble your brother. "It may be most vital—for Mr. Blakeney—"

Dunster added his last words, guessing rightly that it was the one argument which would prevail. The gamekeeper was obviously reluctant; but at last he nodded his head slowly.

"If you must, sir—" he assented. "Come in, then—"

Dunster caught the superintendent's eyes as they followed their guide up the path, and shrugged his shoulders. Probably it was a mare's nest, and yet if George had been at the Hall a good ten hours after he was supposed to have gone it might have some vital bearing on the case. It all depended on how far the man Joe was to be relied upon. They would see that soon enough.

Jim pushed the door open gently and peered inside; then he beckoned them forward as he went in.

"He's asleep, sir," he whispered. "Proper quiet, too... I suppose you couldn't come back, sir? He was that bad—"

Dunster hesitated, following the direction of the other's eyes. On an old-fashioned couch in the corner of the bare but spotless room a man was lying, who might have been a duplicate of Jim. The likeness was positively uncanny, and they were even dressed the same, for the man on the couch had contented himself with removing his coat only before lying down. It hung on the back of the chair beside him, on the seat of which a pill-box and a glass of water lay within the sleeping man's reach.

So much Dunster had taken in at a glance; but the fascination of the remarkable resemblance made him look, perhaps, a little more closely than he would otherwise have done. Then he started. For a minute he stood staring; then he crossed the room in two strides.

"Steady, sir—" Jim whispered indignantly. "You don't want for to wake him sudden—"

But Dunster was bending over the man on the couch. There was no need for him to touch the sunburnt hand, which somehow looked curiously unlifelike, to know that there was no risk of that. He drew in his breath sharply as he straightened himself.

"Can't you leave him be, sir," Jim pleaded. "He's so quiet and peaceful, sir—"

"Yes... He's quiet—" Dunster said, and something in his voice made a suspicion of the truth come to his hearers. Jim started forward.

"He's not—you can't mean, sir—not Joe—!"

Dunster nodded. "He's dead," he said in a low voice. The sound of a car outside broke the silence which followed. It galvanised Jim to life.

"The doctor—" he said, and made for the door. "Joe—there's a chance—there must be a chance—"

Dunster met the superintendent's questioning look, and shook his head with decision.

"He's been dead some time," he said. "And, what's more—" He paused, and pointed with his finger. "He's been poisoned... Look at those eyes!"

# 8

# Ending in Smoke

TONY DID NOT KNOW precisely why he was following Richard Blakeney. He had started upon the impulse of the moment, because of something furtive in the young man's general movements; and every yard they went confirmed his suspicion that wherever Richard was going, he wanted to go there without being seen.

Tony had several narrow shaves. Richard had an awkward way of pausing to glance back at unexpected moments, and several times the journalist had to dive hurriedly into the hedge and wait, thinking that he must have been seen. But he was lucky. Richard went on his way, about a hundred yards ahead, and after the first two or three fields seemed to gain confidence. He looked back less frequently, and Tony found it easier going.

He could make no guess at their destination. They were not following a regular footpath, merely dodging through and over a succession of gaps and gates which might be used by farm-workers but which apparently led nowhere in particular. Their general route was at a slight angle to the road, missing the village on their right, and aiming for the lake which gleamed through the woods below them.

Unexpectedly they reached another road. Tony remembered the lane which turned off below the inn, just near the post office. Though he had never had occasion to take it, he guessed that this must be the one; and immediately opposite two cart-tracks branched off at different angles, one continuing along the hillside, and the other descending steeply to the water-level.

He looked up and down the road. It was visible for a quarter of a mile in each direction, and there was no sign of anyone. Obviously Richard had taken one of the tracks; but both of them bent almost immediately and there seemed to be no means of telling which. It was the soft mud at the top of the one leading down the hill which solved the problem. Someone had certainly trodden it very recently—so recently that the water was only just beginning to trickle down into the prints. That someone, Tony decided, could only be Richard; and he started down it hopefully.

A gate at the bottom, leading into the wood which fringed the lake, raised his doubts, and he had recourse to the mud again. Luckily it was thicker than ever. It showed quite clearly that Richard had not deserted the lane, but had followed it where it turned sharply to the left, and, hurrying a little to get within view again, Tony set off once more.

As he went he noticed something else. There were plenty of tracks, obviously not because the lane was much used, but because the stiff clay retained any impression made in it for weeks if the weather was suitable. And as he picked his way carefully, it became clear that the shoes which he was identifying with Richard had gone that way before. There were prints both going and returning at least once, and probably not more than a week old.

For the rest, the marks were much as one might expect, hob-nails and gum-boots, no doubt belonging to farm-workers using the lane. Faintly, and apparently before the last rainstorm, a cycle-track wound its way dangerously over the more solid bits; and not very long before someone had actually driven a car that way. Perhaps it was still there, as the condition of the lane seemed to promise, for there were no signs of returning wheels.

That was not surprising; for Tony's own attention was too much occupied by dodging the stickier patches to deal properly with the business in hand. The lane had been bending continually; then a sudden turn, sharper than the rest, revealed a straighter stretch, and Richard Blakeney only just ahead.

If he had looked round just at that minute, nothing could have saved Tony, but he seemed to have lost some of his earlier apprehension, and was now hurrying along quite briskly. He did look round a minute later, when he stopped by the gate of a tumbledown cottage which was the one building in sight; but by that time Tony was on his guard again, and safely hidden by a patch of willows. Richard stood for a moment looking up and down the lane, then he pushed the gate open and slipped inside, closing it behind him.

Tony crept nearer. It was a risk, for there was no cover just there except the ditch, and, if Richard had suddenly emerged, it might have been difficult to explain what he was doing grovelling in the mud. But Richard did not emerge. In fact, when Tony at last reached a point from which he could peer into the neglected garden, Richard had vanished altogether.

Obviously he had either gone inside the house, or was somewhere round at the back; and, improbable as it seemed, this ruin must have been his destination. The more Tony looked at it, the less likely it appeared that anyone would want to go there for any reason whatever.

The four stone walls still stood, but the thatched roof was almost overgrown, and in one part had already fallen away. The lower windows were boarded up, the upper ones gaped empty of glass with a forbidding blank stare. Perhaps once it had been a pleasant enough cottage; now it had a most depressing air of having come down in the world and of being disreputable—an architectural tramp, Tony thought.

Apparently, though not occupied, it was still used. There were wisps of straw protruding through the cracks of the front door, and the marks of an iron-tyred vehicle of some kind in the mud outside. Probably it acted as a store-house for some local farmer. But the mystery of why Richard Blakeney should go there remained.

Then, as he waited, he noticed something else. It seemed as though the solitary car had also visited that particular spot, for there were the marks of its wheels, and a discoloured oily patch on the grass as though it had been standing there for some time. There was no sign of it now. Clearly its owner, after having done whatever he intended at that lonely spot, had driven out the other way, in the direction from which the farm vehicle had come.

It seemed to Tony that he had been waiting hours, though a glance at his watch showed that he had been there only five minutes. The water was seeping uncomfortably into his shoes, and there was no sign either of Richard or the reason for his visit. The journalist was just contemplating a nearer approach, or at least a detour via the fields, so that he could obtain a view of the back of the building, when his period of watching was suddenly ended.

Richard came unheralded round the corner of the building, and he was in a great hurry. Tony had just time to flop flat among the meadow-sweet and wild mint when the gate was flung open and footsteps thudded past him. Through the foliage, Tony stole a look at the young man as he fled. If the expression on his face had excited curiosity before, now it was startling. His cheeks were as white as paper, and his eyes seemed almost starting from his head. Evidently he thought of nothing but flight, and luckily he had no glance for the spot where Tony lay. The footsteps thudded and squelched down the lane, gradually growing fainter. As they receded in the direction of the bend, Tony raised himself cautiously.

There seemed to be no point in following Richard. Unless he was very much mistaken, Richard was on his way back home, and by the shortest route. There remained the house, and any clue it might have to offer to the puzzle of Richard's presence there and his hurried flight.

Emerging from his hiding-place, with a glance down the lane to make sure, Tony slipped through the gate and stood looking the place over. From the front, it seemed impregnable. Though the paint had blistered from the door, the timber seemed sound enough and a strong padlock held it firm. The windows were blocked completely, with hardly a crack big enough to peep through; and the glimpse he obtained through the one to the right of the door revealed nothing but a heap of straw in one corner of the derelict room. Without a ladder to tackle the upper windows, which yawned so invitingly, there was no getting in that way. Tony moved round to the back.

The garden was an overgrown wilderness. Nettles, brambles and the straggling rose-bushes, which somehow managed to continue the struggle, had encroached even over the flagged path, which came to a dead end in an open-fronted shed. A glance was enough to show that no one could possibly have forced a way through that jungle and departed the same way without leaving traces of his passage. Then, if Richard had come there to meet someone, whoever it was must still be in the house, since Tony had been watching the only way out. But that he had come to meet anyone was mere supposition. He might have come there to get something, or to hide something. Still, Tony was prepared for anything as he turned his attention to the back entrances to the ruin.

Like the front, the back door was padlocked. The lower windows too were similarly shut, and for the first time it occurred to Tony as odd that anyone should go to such trouble to prevent access to a place only used as a barn. If all that trouble had been taken to prevent anyone getting in, he reasoned, there must be something worthwhile inside. But, without tools to force an entrance, there seemed to be no prospect of finding what it might be.

In mere desperation he seized the edge of the shutter and gave it an experimental tug. It yielded scarcely at all, and sprang back immediately to its place with a sharp creak. Then he gave a start and stood listening. It seemed as though the creak had been answered from somewhere inside the building.

There was no doubt about it. Putting his ear to the woodwork he could hear something distinctly—not exactly a creak, but a tapping, a pattering. Somehow neither of them quite described it. He told himself that it must be rats, but he bent again to listen. Now it was louder than ever—a continuous rustling and crackling, and a sound like a high wind.

For a second he was puzzled, then through the crack came a whiff of something which gave the clue. It was the smell of smoke. The place was on fire.

He started back and looked up. There was smoke coming from the chimney, but there was also smoke, and much more of it, coming from behind the chimney. The fire must be in front. He hurried round the corner of the house just as a yellow tongue of flame licked out round the edge of the broken thatch.

He stared in amazement. Smoke and sparks were pouring out of the upper windows, and an orange flicker lit up the grimy walls. The whole place must be ablaze. Whatever had been stored there must have been extraordinarily inflammable for the fire to have gained such a hold in the few minutes during which he had been at the back. It simply shouted incendiarism, and the thought flashed through his mind that the one person who must have been responsible for lighting it was Richard Blakeney.

There was nothing to be done; the fire must simply take its course, and there would be very little of the cottage left by the time it had finished. He had just reached that conclusion when a muffled boom from behind the boarded windows, like the sound of a drum, came to his ears. He stepped back with an instinctive distrust, and that action saved his life.

Next second an inferno broke loose. He never heard the bang. Unexpectedly the heavy shutter flew gaily forward into the roadway, followed by a rush of flame. He found himself on his back, wondering how he got there.

Half-stunned, he staggered to his feet. The very violence of the explosion had momentarily extinguished the fire in the front room, and had at the same time largely cleared the obscuring haze. Hardly conscious of what he was doing, he stumbled forward and looked in.

The ceiling had fallen; in the centre of the room the flooring of the room above had been blown anyhow. The resulting debris had to a great extent covered the miscellaneous rubbish which seemed to be all the room contained, though he could make out the shape of a large oil-drum which might explain the boom and the explosion. Time was short, for the blaze was just creeping back in the direction of the heap, and there was a smell of petrol which was sufficient warning of what might happen. He was just on the point of giving up when the outline of something in one corner caught his attention. It looked like an old boot flung carelessly among the rubbish, and yet—?

Exasperatingly the smoke rolled forward, momentarily obstructing his view. In his eagerness, he forgot all about the danger. He was actually clambering into the window when he felt his legs gripped strongly from behind.

# 9

---

# Unexpected Visit

Dr. Staithes was large, firm and efficient, with a magnificent walrus moustache. He exercised naturally an air of authority which in childhood had caused considerable trouble to his nurse, and which had been increased rather than diminished by a prolonged residence among a docile rural population. He took charge of everything at once, and even the superintendent's rather portly figure seemed to wane and diminish in his presence. Dunster watched with secret amusement, and quite genuine admiration, and took advantage of the fact that he himself seemed to have been left out of the scheme of things to take a quiet look round the cottage.

He found nothing; nor had he had any great hope that he would do. Everything material to the death was on the chair by the bedside, and upon the box and tumbler Dr. Staithes had temporarily placed his embargo. Unless one were to believe that the brother was guilty of murder, or the equally unlikely idea that the dead man had deliberately committed suicide, it seemed tolerably plain that he had died as a result of the capsules, and, if Jim's account were to be believed and Joe had told the truth to Jim, the capsules had come to him from George Blakeney.

In any event it was improbable that the cottage would furnish any evidence, but Dunster believed in making sure, and while Dr. Staithes bent over the still figure on the bed, and the superintendent hovered in attendance, he contrived to go over it very thoroughly.

Jim neither helped nor hindered. The doctor's confirmation of the news seemed to have stunned him and he had subsided into the chair by the fire and sat gazing as if stupefied at the glowing embers of the logs. For the moment Dunster left him alone, and awaited the verdict of the doctor.

It was not long delayed. Staithes had dealt with the corpse and disposed it decently; he had examined the glass, holding it gingerly with his handkerchief, smelt at its contents, tipped out the capsules and counted them, scrutinised each one and the box critically and was apparently on the point of finishing, for he replaced the capsules in the box and the lid on it and cleared his throat in preparation.

"Er-hm," he said, and fixed his eye upon the waiting superintendent. "There must be a post-mortem, of course. But there's no doubt. No doubt at all. The man died of belladonna poisoning, and he's been gone about half an hour. That's certain at any rate."

"Belladonna?" the superintendent echoed respectfully. "That's the stuff the opticians use, isn't it, Doctor?"

"It is used by opticians to dilate the pupils of the eyes... But there are other uses—in medicine, for example."

"You think it was an overdose of his medicine—?"

"His medicine? Humph!" The doctor snorted. "I don't know where he got this stuff, but it's certainly nothing that I prescribed for him."

"You think he was poisoned by the capsules, Doctor?"

"Of course, it's impossible to answer that until after the analysis and a post-mortem. But there are certain very suspicious circumstances. You may have noticed them?"

The two detectives refrained from saying that since his taking charge there had been very little opportunity for anyone to notice anything about the box or capsules.

"What, Doctor?" the superintendent asked in a docile tone.

"Well, first of all, this box. It's mine. That is to say, it's one sent out from my surgery in the past three months. I had a new lot in then, different from the kind I had been using. This is one of them."

The doctor was rather inclined to be too positive, Dunster thought. He ventured an objection.

"But I suppose the same type of box would be sent to other doctors and chemists, and probably in this area?"

"No doubt... But you see this mark?" He pointed to a minute, hardly-legible letter "S" pencilled on the box bottom. "Since I first started practice, I've checked every item dispensed in my surgery; a system of my own. This box certainly came from my surgery. But—" He paused, and raised it in a significant gesture. "But when it came from my surgery, it certainly didn't come here, and it didn't contain capsules."

"How do you know that, Doctor?"

"In the first place, I don't believe in capsules. Pills or bottles, I say. But if I have to use capsules, I shouldn't use that sort. And in the second place, I haven't prescribed any but liquid medicine for Bere."

"Then someone, perhaps one of your patients—certainly someone who could obtain a box dispensed to one—must have put the capsules in, perhaps pretending they came from you?"

"At least it seems probable... But that's not all. Look at the capsules." He tipped one out into his palm and held it, pointing to the little ridge formed by the join. "I should say that it's pretty certain that isn't the work of any regular dispenser. Thoroughly botched, as you see. No, what must have happened is that someone has obtained some harmless capsules from a chemist—quinine, I should say—emptied them, put in the belladonna, and resealed them."

"Would that be difficult?"

"Not particularly... I should imagine that after a few trials anyone of moderate intelligence could do it well enough."

"The belladonna? That would be difficult to get hold of?"

"Ordinarily, of course, if the chemist would supply it, he'd make anyone sign the poison book. But—" He made another dramatic pause, "I suggest that, supposing the murderer had any sense, the very use of belladonna shows that it wasn't necessary for him to get it specially, but that he had some available."

"Why?"

"Because the symptoms are so obvious—and quite well known—in fact, you yourself, Inspector, had no difficulty in guessing at it after a mere glance. His one good reason for using it was that, in all probability, he had a supply on hand, and needn't invite attention to himself by buying any."

Dunster nodded acquiescence. Dr. Staithes, he reflected, might be a little pompous and over-certain, but he was by no means a fool.

"Practically, then, that rules out accident?" he said.

"Practically—yes. It's just conceivable that someone, for a mysterious but innocent purpose, filled these capsules with a poisonous dose of belladonna and disguised them in a box from my surgery." The doctor was heavily sarcastic. "It's possible that he gave them by mistake to Bere, meaning to give him something else; or that Bere picked them up in the road and just thought he'd try a few. But it's hardly likely."

"A few? How many would it need?"

"That's impossible to say, without knowing the strength of the solution. They're large capsules. Probably two would be enough—perhaps one."

"How about suicide?"

"Absurd. The man's been my patient fifteen years. Not the type at all."

Dunster thought that that was dismissing it a little airily, but there were other and obvious objections.

"Then the circumstances suggest murder?"

"The circumstances are certainly compatible with murder. I should imagine that, whoever murdered the poor fellow, would go about it something like this. He would know, of course, that Joe suffered from these periodic attacks—"

"What was the matter with him, exactly?"

"A kind of migraine—sick headache. Not particularly serious, but beastly while it lasts... Well, he'd give him the capsules, telling him that they'd do him good. It might be weeks, but sooner or later he'd have an attack, take them according to directions, and there you are."

Dunster considered. "There's a certain risk," he said. "Suppose he'd told someone who gave him the stuff—"

"Not likely. He wasn't a talkative sort. In any case, it would be secondhand evidence—what someone said a dead man said. I believe he'd be safe enough."

It was all very glib. Almost too glib, Dunster thought. The monstrous suspicion even crossed his mind that Dr. Staithes might have worked on some very similar lines himself; that, having arrived too late, by the merest accident, to retrieve the incriminating box, he had faced up to things boldly by giving a theory which was bound to be put forward sooner or later. Then he remembered what Jim had reported of his conversation.

"Well, he might not talk in the ordinary way, Doctor," he said deliberately, "but, in this case, as it happened, he did. He told his brother who gave him the stuff."

"What?" The doctor was certainly startled; whether it was anything more, the inspector could not decide. In any case, Staithes made a quick recovery. "Good heavens," he said. "I suppose I ought not to ask—"

"There's no reason why you shouldn't know," Dunster said slowly. "As a matter of fact, I was going to make a few enquiries from you about it."

Staithes had completely recovered. He met Dunster's eyes unwaveringly.

"Well?" he snapped.

"Jim says that his brother told him they were given to him by Mr. Blakeney—"

"Absurd!" Staithes positively exploded. He flushed angrily. "And let me tell you, Inspector, it's of a piece with the rest of the police proceedings... Abominable! You come down here to find a wretched anonymous letter-writer who's plaguing everyone in the place, and instead of getting on with the job you make a lot of accusations against a decent family that have not the ghost of a foundation. I must warn you, Inspector, that you're rather exhausting people's patience—"

Dunster had let him run on, wondering at the reason for this sudden heat. He interposed gently.

"Of course, it would have come out at the inquest in any case, Doctor," he said mildly. "I thought you might like to know beforehand... Is Mr. Blakeney a patient of yours?"

The doctor hesitated. He was regaining a measure of self-control.

"Well, yes—" he admitted. "Of course, I'm the family doctor... But, Inspector, there must be some mistake. I should look into it pretty carefully, if I were you... What earthly motive—"

"I need hardly say, sir, we shall take every care. And of course I rely on you not to mention it at all... we may hope, sir, that the coroner will adjourn the inquest after formal evidence. So that it may not be necessary to make anything public—at least, just yet... But as to motive, perhaps you could help us. I believe you've known the dead man a long time. Can you suggest any reason why he should be—" He lowered his voice, with a glance at the fireside. "Any reason why he should be murdered?"

"How on earth could I? It's the last thing I should have expected. He was an ordinary, decent gamekeeper who did his job and kept to himself... I don't say there may not have been a few who owed him a grudge, in the way of business, but poachers don't use belladonna."

"Perhaps not," Dunster agreed. Well, Doctor, we'll let you know about the post-mortem and the inquest—"

"I shall see the coroner myself, Inspector." There was almost a suggestion of a threat in the words. "There's nothing more I can do here... Good day."

The superintendent made a grimace as the door closed behind him.

"That shook him," Dunster said almost to himself. "About Blakeney... I wonder why?"

"Friendly with the family, perhaps," the superintendent said with resignation. "That's the worst of a country district like this. You never know whose corns you're treading on—"

"If you'll excuse me, sir, it be a lie!"

They had almost forgotten Jim. Both turned abruptly, to find that he had risen from his seat by the fire. His lips were set, and his jaw protruded in an unshakable determination.

"It were a lie, sir," he repeated. "Leastways, I must have made a mistake. You see, sir, when my brother'd been talking about Mr. George, and then went on to say a chap had given him them things, I must have mixed them up. Mr. George couldn't have done it, sir."

"Now, look here, my man," the superintendent said sternly, "not half an hour ago you said quite definitely that it was Mr. George who gave him them. You told us what was said at the time."

"I was confused like... Mr. George couldn't have done... Why, didn't the young master say he'd left on the Wednesday? Then of course I was mixed up. It were some other chap—and if I could find him—"

"Well, think it over." Dunster soothed him. "We know how attached you were to your brother. If there was any way you could help catch his murderer—"

"If I catch 'un, he won't need hanging," Jim broke out fiercely. "I'll—"

"Come, my man, none of that—" the superintendent began sharply, but Jim did not wait to hear him. Cramming his cap on his head, he plunged for the door. The superintendent made a move to stop him, but Dunster put out a restraining hand.

"Let him go... He'll cool off outside, and that's the best that could happen. At the moment, he'd go to the stake before he'd admit it was Blakeney who gave his brother the stuff. You see, he's torn between his affection to his brother and his duty to the family. When he's had time to think things out—"

"Well, it's your funeral." The superintendent shrugged. Evidently he did not appreciate this little psychological lecture. "I only hope it's no one else's!"

"Why?"

"Only, if he just happened to meet Richard Blakeney—well, he was talking about taking the law into his own hands, wasn't he? And his duty to the family might not be uppermost at the moment. That's all."

"Good heavens, I never thought—" Dunster admitted, and hurried to the door. He was back in a moment, looking distinctly uncomfortable. "Out of sight," he said. "I wonder—"

"Oh, I expect it's all right," the superintendent said comfortingly. "Matter of fact, I think you're right. He's not the sort of chap to do anything in a hurry... Might save a lot of trouble if he did."

"Why?"

"Well, it's plain enough... Didn't it occur to you just now? They obviously called both of the brothers 'the young master.' There's been a mix up all right."

"I don't quite see—"

"Wouldn't it, link up this way? Suppose Richard had killed George. There's no reason for George to have killed Joe that we know of; but there might have been for Richard. Because

Joe had met and talked with George just before he'd disappeared. Well, it wasn't George that Joe Bere met by the Round Copse on Thursday. It's pretty certain that George vanished on Wednesday. It was the other young master, Richard—and Jim mixed 'em up. And Richard believed he knew something—and thought him best out of the way."

Dunster considered it. It was a minute or two before he spoke.

"Well, it might fit," he admitted. "But it's all supposition, of course. And it doesn't explain the anonymous letters, or the digging up of the graves—"

"As for the graves, there may be no connection. I still think that's probably some looney or other. But the letters— They were in an uneducated hand, weren't they?"

"We thought that was probably faked—"

"There's no proof it was. Suppose Joe had reason to think Richard killed his brother? Suppose he couldn't bring himself to make the accusation against 'the young master,' but couldn't let it rest? Mightn't he have done just that—written the letters to put us on the track?"

"It certainly hangs together," Dunster said doubtfully. "Better than anything yet... And you're right about 'the young master.' He did apply the words to both—or rather, he made his brother apply them to George and used them himself of Richard. If George's body was found—"

He broke off and turned with a start as the door burst open.

"Hullo, Joe," a girl's voice called. "Better? May we come in?"

And the next moment Virginia Blakeney entered, with Alness at her heels.

# 10

# Amateur Burglar

INSTINCTIVELY TONY KICKED OUT. For a moment he struggled fruitlessly, gripping the edge of the window as though his life depended upon it. Then the smoke billowed towards him, and left him gasping. His hold relaxed suddenly, and he and his captor, whoever it was, slumped backwards on to the ground.

He rubbed his eyes and looked. So far as the tears allowed him to see at all, the other man had already regained his feet; and he rose too. The smart was beginning to ease a little, and he could make out the man who had gripped him—a well-built, thick-set man in a bowler hat whom, so far as he knew, he had never seen before. Tony was on the point of saying something not particularly polite when the other woke to violent activity.

"Look out!" he shouted unexpectedly. "Look—!"

Before he had finished the words, he had bounded forward, pushing Tony in the chest with a force which sent him staggering back. It was only with difficulty that he kept his feet at all, and, half-choked and blinded as he was, he could neither understand what was happening nor prevent it. The man stopped pushing and stood back. Tony recovered his balance and rubbed his eyes again; then faced the other belligerently.

"Look here—" he began.

A crash behind interrupted him, and he turned, to see a perfect cascade of glowing thatch and smoking timbers falling from the roof on to the spot which he had just unwillingly vacated.

"Thought it was going," his late assailant said phlegmatically. "Just in time—"

"I say—" It dawned upon Tony as he gazed at the smoking pile that he had not been the victim of an unprovoked assault. The man had probably saved his life. "Thank you," he said rather sheepishly. "I'm afraid I didn't understand—"

"That's all right," the other assured him. "Pretty good blaze, eh?"

If anything it was an understatement. Tony stood staring at the conflagration; then with a sudden horror he remembered.

"I say!" he broke out. "Come and help! We must do something—"

"There's nothing we can do," the other assured him with perfect calm. "Nearest fire brigade's four miles away. It'll be pretty well out before they get here. The old place isn't worth twopence, anyway."

All that was perfectly true. But the sight of that boot lingered in Tony's mind. Probably it was just an old boot. And yet—

"But if there's anyone inside—" he broke out.

"No one's any business inside," the man rejoined imperturbably. "But if there is anyone inside, sir, he's dead. No reason why you and I should be."

The logic of this was so faultless that it left Tony for the moment without an adequate reply. The boom of another bursting can, and a second explosion which sent a wave of fire and smoke towards them and brought a part of the wall down with a rattle, added force to the argument.

"Must be something exploding." Tony's rescuer lapsed into the obvious. "Petrol, I expect... Why should there be anyone inside, sir?"

Tony hesitated. There was something unusual about his questioner, something familiar about the sound of the last words or the way in which they were spoken.

"Dash it all, someone must have lit it," he prevaricated.

"Tramp, maybe? You didn't see anyone, sir?"

The man's eyes were on him keenly, and once again the chord of memory half stirred.

"I'd only just come," Tony evaded, and then something else struck him. It did not seem to have occurred to the man for a single moment that he himself might have been responsible in any way. That was odd, if he had only just arrived on the scene in time to stop Tony's entrance. He was puzzled, and felt moved to an explanation. "I was just having a look at the place, and I smelt the smoke," he said almost defensively. "Then I came round to the front and it was all ablaze."

The man seemed to accept that without comment. "Ah. It spread pretty quick," he ruminated.

"Look here, we'd better tell the police, or something," Tony said. "Or—or who owns the place—?"

"I expect the police know by now."

The faint glimmer of a smile which accompanied the words puzzled Tony for a moment; then it brought a sudden illumination. That was it. The man was a policeman in plain clothes. That was what he remembered about the authoritative, but respectful manner of address; and, even including the bowler hat, everything fitted in with the idea. And if he was, what was he doing there? It was not, perhaps, surprising that a detective should be wandering in the district in view of all that had happened in the village. What interested Tony was how he had come to be at that particular place; and the obvious explanation was that he had been following Richard or himself.

That might be awkward. Presumably he would be questioned; in fact, he seemed to see the words trembling on the other's lips. He would have to decide whether or not to tell the truth, or how much of it, and he was hastily trying to make up his mind when a most amazing bellow sounded from the other side of the hedge.

"Hi-urr! What be 'ee doing there?"

With a crackling of twigs the branches parted, and a curious apparition burst into the lane. From the boots, leggings and breeches of the lower part of his dress one might guess that the newcomer was a farmer; from the facts that he was still in his shirt-sleeves and without braces, and that one purple side of his face was clean shaven and the other covered with lather, through which a two or three days' growth protruded like rushes through the snow, it appeared that he had been interrupted while making his toilet. His left hand sustained the breeches; his right flourished a hay-fork; and as he glared furiously from one to the other Tony almost thought he was going to use it.

"What be 'ee doing here?" he repeated. "Which of 'ee done it?"

Tony was never lacking in presence of mind. The detective's imperturbability might have carried the day, but Tony was the more like a gentleman in appearance; and he spoke first.

"I'm afraid I have no idea," he said with his best air. "I think this gentleman could explain."

The farmer's eye focussed on the man in the bowler hat. He clenched the fork more tightly in his hand and raised it.

"What did 'ee go to do it for?" he demanded. "I'll learn you to go about—"

"Here, now. None of that. Put that down!"

The words came in a tone of majestic command which, in a London slum, might have cowed a tougher customer; but on the irate farmer they produced an opposite effect. The handle of the fork certainly descended, but unpacifically. It struck with considerable force the crown of the bowler hat, and the next moment the two men closed.

Tony's mind worked quickly. Shouts came from down the lane. Two men dressed as labourers were pounding towards them. Tony waved furiously and rushed to meet them.

"Burnt the place down!" he said dramatically as he came up to them. "Farmer's got him... Get the police—"

He ran on. A glance back showed that the men had apparently accepted his explanation, and were starting forward again. Actually, whether the farmer had got the detective or vice versa was a moot point; though the former, somewhat at the expense of decency, had called his left hand into play, and was certainly holding his own. A last glance back at the bend of the lane showed an expanse of white pants uppermost, with the labourers on the point of taking a hand. Tony did not stop running. If the detective was tailing him, it seemed an excellent chance of shaking him off. To three other mixed rural personalities whom he met he repeated a formula which seemed to meet the situation.

"Cottage on fire! Get help—"

He reached the road, and, halfway across, halted in momentary indecision. Here all was peace, except for a distant shouting and a white column of smoke rising above the trees. The question was, what should he do next? In his early days as a junior reporter, Tony had had it well instilled into him that a good journalist, no matter what else may intervene, always comes back with the story on which he is sent out. It seemed to him that the rule held. There was nothing in what had just occurred to alter his original decision to look up the Newents; in fact, things might be all the better if allowed to cool down. He had almost made up his mind when his thoughts were rudely interrupted.

It was the frenzied screech of brakes which first made him aware of the presence of the car, and the next moment it had stopped within a foot of him. Only as he jumped back did he realise his escape.

"What the—!"

The uniformed driver's head appeared through the window. Tony accepted the reproof humbly. As a motorist himself, he had suffered sufficiently often himself from the thoughtless eccentricities of the human species on foot to be moved to an apology. After all, he had been day-dreaming in the middle of the road on a blind curve.

"Sorry," he said with contrition. "I'm afraid I wasn't thinking about—"

But the driver was apparently in a hurry. With a vicious jerk he let in the clutch. Tony caught an odd phrase "— looney" as the car started forward; then, as it passed him, he glimpsed the occupants of the rear seat. He stared in disbelief. There was no mistake. The passengers were Crouch and his sister.

The car was out of sight before he had recovered from the shock. There was nothing he could do about it, anyhow. But wasn't there? It had been a hired car, and he seemed to remember quite a pile of luggage on the grid. It looked as if the two were bolting. At least they were probably going away for some time. And that would leave the cottage empty. It was too golden an opportunity to miss.

The village was a danger point, and it would be better to miss it, in case some chance encounter might set the inspector wondering why he had lost his shadow. On the other hand, the way across the fields by which Richard had unwittingly guided him, was certainly a short cut. Though there was the risk of meeting Richard, he chose the gateway, and started off, trying as he went to work out what was happening.

Certainly there was plenty to think about. It was difficult to realise that only an hour or two had passed since his arrival. In that time, Alness had effected a reconciliation and arranged an interview; Richard had paid a mysterious visit to an abandoned cottage, and perhaps indulged in a little mild incendiarism; Crouch had bolted. And he had spoken to Virginia. The last fact, perhaps, interfered with any logical and impartial consideration of the others; and he was no nearer making a coherent whole of them by the time he reached his destination.

The cottage had every appearance of being deserted. For a while he studied it carefully and unobtrusively. The shutters were closed on the lower windows—shutters, he thought, seemed regrettably common in this out-of-the-way spot, from the point of view of one who was contemplating a little housebreaking. The door was shut. There was no smoke from the chimney, no sign of movement. Not a soul had met him on the way there, no one was in sight. He decided to risk it, and pushed the gate open.

Of course, it was always possible that there was someone in the house. For that reason, his best course seemed a pretence that his visit was harmless and above board; and for that reason he went boldly up to the front door and knocked thunderously. The echoes died away inside without reply. All must be safe. With a quick glance towards the road, he moved round the house towards the back.

Here he was safe from observation, unless anyone should actually come into the garden. The high fence which had discouraged him on his previous visit acted as a perfect shield on three sides, with the house itself on the fourth, and he was able to devote his whole attention to the problem of effecting an entry without fear of being disturbed.

It proved to be easier than he had anticipated in view of the impregnable condition of the front. At one time the windows had been similarly defended to those he had seen, but in the rear the general decay of the premises had proceeded further. It was a window into what proved to be an untidy kitchen from which one leaf of the shutter was missing to which he turned his attention, and an examination of it was distinctly hopeful. The fastening seemed to consist only of a single rusty catch which ought to have yielded to treatment easily enough. It proved to be tougher than he had anticipated, however, and after breaking the blade of his pen-knife, he was forced to resort to mere violence with the aid of a broken spade which lay among the rubbish near the fence. Slipping the blade between the woodwork he pressed gently on the end.

There was a rending crash as it gave with unexpected ease and a tinkle of falling glass. Tony contemplated the result ruefully. It was not the catch which had given but the rotten frame itself, leaving a messy result which there could be no disguising. For a moment he hung back, with doubts reviving in his mind about the usefulness of an inspection of the cottage; then he took the plunge. The damage was done now. He might as well derive from it any advantage there might be. He scrambled over the low sill and dropped inside.

A heavy mixed smell of stale food greeted him. As he had already observed, the room was the kitchen, and a door off it revealed an untidy pantry with an extraordinary number of empty bottles. Even a glance was enough to show that there was nothing to be learnt there, and after stopping to listen a moment he moved towards the inner door leading to the front room.

It opened into semi-darkness which, after the bright sun outside, for a few seconds allowed him to see nothing. As his eyes became accustomed to the gloom, he was able to make out the outlines of the furniture by the light which filtered in through the cracks of the closely-fitting shutters and from the door by which he had entered.

For the most part the room was poorly furnished. A deal table and two old-fashioned armchairs, a couch beneath the window and a bookcase with a few tattered paperbacks and ornaments seemed to offer little enough that might be of any interest. The sole remaining hope was the sideboard which occupied most of one wall; and he moved across to examine it. His eyes were now more used to the dim light, and he could distinguish it fairly well. To his surprise, in spite of obvious marks of misuse, it was a reasonably good piece of furniture, though of a style more popular twenty years before. The double-doored cupboard which occupied most of the body opened easily enough, but revealed nothing more exciting than a collection of crockery and dingy plate, and he transferred his attention to the twin drawers above it.

That on the left was locked, and short of calling the spade into action again, there was nothing he could do with it. The other yielded a little, then stuck. He tugged at it, but it still resisted, then unexpectedly gave way. With a crash which sounded thunderously in the silent house, he fell backwards against the table pulling the drawer with him.

He scrambled to his feet and stood listening. The noise had been enough to wake the dead, and he thought that it might even have been heard in the lane outside, if anyone had been passing. For a moment he was half inclined to give up the whole affair; then his resolution returned. After all, it was a sufficiently unlikely chance that anyone should be going that way or have noticed the sound from inside while knowing that Crouch and his sister were away. The drawer lay on the floor beside him, with some of its contents scattered near it, and he turned his attention to this.

There was little enough to reward him, and the only document of any kind was the folded copy of what was apparently a suburban newspaper. He stuffed it into his pocket on the chance that it would repay further examination, at least in giving a hint where the couple had come from, picked up the various oddments from the floor and was on the point of replacing the drawer when his eyes caught a glimpse of something white in the back of the space from which the drawer had come. He reached out a hand and pulled it out. Apparently it was a photograph of some kind, a postcard size group, and after pushing back the drawer he carried it over for further study to the cracks of light which came through the shutters. Then as he bent to peer at it he started up. Suddenly a heavy knocking sounded on the front door.

# 11

## Gone Away

Alness and the girl had stopped dead just inside the room and for a few seconds they stood staring at each other. Dunster was almost certain that the emotion on their faces was only surprise. That, after all, was natural enough. The girl was the first to speak.

"Why, it's the superintendent!" she exclaimed. "And—and Inspector—"

"Dunster, miss," the detective supplied, and waited; but Alness spoke first.

"Good afternoon, Superintendent," he said easily. "You're before us, then... And from the fact that you're here at all, I can only suppose you've heard all about it—"

The inspector glanced meaningly at his colleague, and it was the inspector who replied.

"Heard what, sir?" he enquired.

"Why, the story that brought us here—that Joe Bere had been talking about my cousin's going. It occurred to me as soon as I heard it that if it was true it would go a long way to put an end to all this nonsense once and for all. I mean these silly accusations—"

"Accusations, sir?" Dunster echoed.

Alness smiled. "Oh, I know the police haven't made any charges. In fact, as a magistrate, I can guess that you're not in a position to make any. But I don't suppose you'd deny, Inspector, that you've been investigating the story the letters tell as well as the letters?"

"Well, sir—" Dunster temporised. "We've made some general enquiries, of course—"

"Of course you have... As I say, when I heard that Joe Bere had seen George just before he left, and that George had actually told him he was going away, I realised the importance of having an independent witness to that, and so we came round to see him at once—"

"Instead of to us, sir?"

"We only had it at secondhand. There might have been nothing in it... Is it true? Or haven't you seen him yet?"

Dunster did not answer the question. He was doing some quick thinking. From where the two stood, it was impossible for them to see the couch. They might be speaking the truth. On the other hand, he recalled his own words of a few minutes before. They might have come to remove vital evidence. In that case, he could only admire their nerve—if they knew or guessed what was in the room.

"Perhaps you could tell me what precisely you have heard, sir?" he suggested.

"Why—" Alness began; but Virginia Blakeney intervened.

"Really it was I who heard, Inspector," she said. "You see, the maid told me. Just that someone had heard Joe say that he'd seen my brother, and that he'd told him he was going abroad—"

"What day was that, Miss Blakeney?" Dunster interposed.

"Why—the day he left—Wednesday—"

"The day was actually named?"

"No. But—it must have been—"

"Did you hear anything else he said to Joe Bere?"

"No. Mary just said—well, what I've told you."

"Was any mention made of illness? Or of his giving Joe anything?"

The girl looked at him in bewilderment and shook her head. Alness intervened with a suggestion of impatience in his manner.

"Really, Inspector, wouldn't it be simpler to ask Joe Bere all this? I gather that he must be out and that you haven't been able to question him yet, but—"

"We haven't been able to question him," Dunster said with a significance which apparently escaped his two hearers.

"Then surely you'd better find him—"

"We have found him, sir," Dunster said quietly. He had decided to take the plunge. "He's here."

He turned and pointed as he spoke. Alness and the girl stepped forward, following the direction of his gesture. There was only bewilderment in their faces.

"Asleep?" Alness demanded. "Well, you can wake him—"

"We can't wake him."

It was the girl who first understood the grim meaning of the words: She stared for a second towards the couch; then started forward with a cry.

"He—he's not—? You can't mean—?"

"Great Scott, you mean he's dead?" Alness finished the sentence for her. "But that's impossible. I saw him, only this morning, and he was perfectly fit—"

Dunster studied him. "He is dead, sir," he said after a slight pause. "About half an hour ago."

"But—what happened? An accident—?"

"No, sir... We don't think it was an accident," Dunster said deliberately. "There are good grounds, sir, for believing that it is murder."

Dunster had exploded his bombshell. The results were far from satisfactory. The girl drew a quick, shuddering breath; Alness merely stared incredulously.

"Absurd," he said. "Excuse me, Inspector... There must be some mistake. Who would want to murder Joe?"

"That's what we're trying to find out, sir."

"But—but how did it happen?" Virginia Blakeney burst out. "Are you sure—"

Dunster had decided on a policy of blunt truth and it seemed to him that he might as well carry it a little further, disappointing though the reactions had been.

"We think that he was poisoned by those capsules," he said. "It was almost certainly murder—probably by belladonna."

This time there was no doubt of the effect of the last word upon the girl. She had been pale before; now she was dead white. Her hand went to her throat.

"Belladonna?" Alness echoed deliberately, but there seemed to be a suspicion of a tremble in his voice. "Who on earth—?"

"That—that's the stuff they use in liniments, isn't it?" Virginia Blakeney said surprisingly. "But it's poison, then—"

Dunster's ideas about the use of belladonna were of the haziest, but he inclined his head in assent.

"I believe so, miss," he said. "Among other things—"

"The capsules?" Alness demanded. "Who gave him them?"

"We hope to find that out, sir," Dunster evaded. "But I'd like to get back to that other point—about Mr. George's going away. You see, miss, we heard from Jim Bere what Joe was supposed to have said, and according to him, Joe didn't allude to Mr. George Blakeney by name. He only said he met 'the young master.' What we'd like to know is whether by 'the young master' he could have meant Mr. Richard."

Looking at the girl's face, Superintendent Stockton was conscious of a certain compunction. She was, of course, unaware of the trap the question contained, and her eyes, as they searched the inspector's face as though trying to find the right answer there, affected him unpleasantly. From an official, and even a moral point of view, no doubt the girl ought to tell the simple truth, however it might affect her brother; from a human side, he could not blame her if she was inclined to give the more favourable interpretation to doubtful facts.

"I—I don't understand—" she faltered; and then Alness apparently came, as he believed, to the rescue.

"I don't quite see the point of this, Inspector," he said with the air of a man who points out an obvious fact. "If he said 'the young master' was going away, it obviously refers to George. That's plain enough, surely?"

"Yes, sir," Dunster agreed respectfully. "But you see, in the account Jim has given us so far, there's a good deal that's vague, and in one or two points a definite conflict of evidence. It's a question of whether there was one interview or two—and whether they were both with the same person."

Alness wrinkled his brows and eyed Dunster. It was evident that he guessed there was some vital point in the question, and wanted to find out what it was.

"I don't quite understand, Inspector," he said. "Perhaps you could explain?"

Dunster was only too anxious to do so. No doubt he was being unscrupulous, but he had now got the conversation to precisely the point at which he had been aiming.

"It's like this, miss," he said, concentrating on Virginia. "Joe seems to have heard from Jim that he'd met 'the young master' and that 'the young master' had said he was going abroad for a time... But he seems to have had further conversation with whoever he met, or it may have been another conversation. From this it appears that he definitely met 'the young master' on the Thursday morning early. Now, on Mr. Richard's evidence we know that Mr. George had left the previous night. In that case, it rather looks as though 'the young master' might have meant Mr. Richard."

He paused. Alness's keen eyes were on him appraisingly.

"In fact," he said, "it boils down to this. If by 'the young master' he meant George, his story can't be true, because George had gone before Thursday morning. If 'the young master' could mean both, he might have met George on the Wednesday and Richard on the Thursday... Is that what you're getting at?"

"Something like it, sir... Of course, it depends on whether Mr. Richard was out, or could have been out, on the Thursday morning. No doubt we can ascertain that—"

"But my brother goes out nearly every morning," the girl supplied quickly. "I mean Richard does. It might be hard to find out whether he was out on that particular day—but he generally is."

At that moment, Superintendent Stockton almost hated the inspector. For a policeman, he had a sympathetic heart; and the way in which Dunster, helped by Alness, had lured Virginia Blakeney into giving an answer which might go a long way to hang her brother, struck him as being distinctly dirty work.

"But I expect Mr. George went out too?" Dunster said innocently.

"No. Hardly ever," Virginia said quickly. "I know that he hasn't for weeks—"

Superintendent Stockton felt bound to intervene, in the interests of justice.

"But as I understand it, miss," he said heavily. "You were away on that day. You can't, in fact, say positively whether Mr. George went out or not."

"I—I can't of course." Virginia hesitated. "But, you see, he never does—"

Stockton found he had only made things worse. And, after all, it was a choice of brothers.

"He might have done," he said with the obstinacy of a defending counsel who has failed to get the right answer, and left it at that.

"So the probabilities are," Alness summed up, "that it was Richard he met the second time—that is, if 'the young master' could mean Richard? Well, I don't think there's much doubt about that... I'm pretty certain it might refer to either. Eh, Virginia?"

"Oh yes, of course it might." There was a pathetic eagerness in her voice. "I'm sure either Jim or Joe thought of both Richard and George as such."

The superintendent positively scowled at the glance Dunster gave him. Perhaps Alness noticed it too, for he seemed anxious to steer the conversation away from the point.

"Aren't we rather wasting time, Inspector?" he demanded. "After all, though I'm anxious to get it settled, those silly accusations against my cousin can wait... As I understand it you've got a murder here, and I for one won't rest until we find out who killed Joe." His voice was grim, and his jaw set obstinately as he looked towards the couch. His action seemed to recall to the girl what lay there. She cast a quick look towards the still figure and averted her eyes; then covered her face with her hands. Alness gave her a quick look, and there seemed to be more than sympathy in it.

"The point you've got to find out," he proceeded, "is who gave him the capsules? And why should he be murdered? That is, of course, if you're sure the capsules did it."

"Well, sir, we've secondhand evidence on that point," Dunster said dubiously. "Jim says Joe told him who gave him the capsules—if he's to be relied upon."

"Absolutely, I should say." Alness glanced at the girl who nodded dumbly. "Neither of them are—were—gossips, you know... I suppose I mustn't ask who it was?"

"There's no reason why I shouldn't tell you," Dunster said slowly. "Jim said that Joe told him—" He paused exasperatingly.

"Well, what?" Alness snapped.

"That it was 'the young master,'" Dunster said. "And that it must have been on Thursday morning."

Alness stared for a moment uncomprehendingly; then a look of horror which changed to anger came on his face. In the same moment, the significance of the last words seemed to come home to Virginia. She gave a queer low moan, and Alness just caught her as she swayed on her feet.

"You swine!" he snapped savagely at Dunster, and bent over her. "Virginia! Virginia! It's all right. That doesn't mean anything... Come along. We must see about it—"

Virginia's eyes opened, and she stared at him for a moment.

"We must see Richard," Alness said urgently. "Get a lawyer—Virginia!"

With an effort she stood upright. Alness's arm supported her as they moved towards the doorway, and Alness gave a single furious glance over his shoulder as they disappeared. The superintendent turned to his colleague.

"Well, I suppose you're satisfied," he grated. "You've trapped them into saying what you wanted... And now, seems to me, you've sent 'em off to warn Richard, and he'll probably bolt or kill himself or something."

Dunster had found a cigarette. He lit it deliberately and drew deeply at it once or twice. His face was absolutely expressionless.

"Perhaps I wanted Richard warned," he said slowly. "And, as for the rest, it was Alness who did most of it."

"You would have done," Stockton said, and it was almost an accusation. "I could see all the time where you were going—"

"Apparently Alness couldn't." Dunster smiled, a brief, crooked smile. "You must admit it's settled two vital points. And, after all, we should never have got the truth if we'd said: 'Joe died of the capsules. The young master gave him them. Could that have been Richard, and was he likely to be out?'"

"But you practically held out an inducement the other way," Stockton persisted. "You suggested it would prove Richard innocent if—"

"But assuming they told the truth, it doesn't matter," Dunster pointed out. "And if they didn't—"

"Well, I don't like it—" Stockton began.

There was another interruption. This time the door positively burst open, and the man who entered was into the room before they saw him. Dunster's eyebrows rose as he recognised him.

"Why, Sergeant—" he began, and then noticed a left eye which was already blackening. "What's up? You've been in the wars—?"

"That was an accident—a mistake, sir." Sergeant Comfrey coloured perceptibly in spite of the natural ruddiness of his face. "But I must speak to you, sir—"

He cast a glance at Jim who had retired into the background and stood waiting.

"That's all right," Dunster assured him. "What is it, Sergeant?"

"He's gone, sir—Mr. Blakeney." The sergeant wiped a perspiring brow and his voice was lugubrious. "And if you ask me, he's bolted, sir."

# 12

## Revelations

TONY'S FIRST FEELING WAS one of sheer panic. Then, as the knocking died away, he regained his nerve. In all probability it was only some accidental caller, who would be content with knocking and, on receiving no answer, go away again. No one, after all, could tell from the shuttered front of the house that it contained an amateur burglar. Only if the visitor went round to the back, where the shattered window gave all too obvious evidence, would he realise that anything was wrong. And even so—

The knocking sounded again, more loudly than ever. There was another pause. Tony could hear feet shifting on the stone step outside. Then the latch rose, and the door creaked as pressure was exerted upon it. The latch fell into its place again. Then, in the silence which followed, Tony heard what he dreaded. Footsteps moved along the front of the house towards the corner, and a shadow crossed the streaks of light in the shutter. The visitor was going round to the back.

He had a matter of seconds to make up his mind what to do. He could not get out. The door was not only bolted but locked, and the key was missing. Even if he had been able to open them at all he had no time to undo the shutters. A quick glance round assured him that the bare room was absolutely devoid of hiding-places. Then his eye fell on the staircase. As he crossed the room in two strides towards it, he fancied he heard a muffled exclamation from the back, as though the visitor had found the broken window.

At the top of the staircase a choice of two doors confronted him. He took the one on the left, mainly because it was ajar, and slipped noiselessly inside, just as the sound of a stealthy tread in the sitting room informed him that the visitor had entered.

Probably he was searching in the semi-darkness below; for there was a pause. Tony had a moment in which to take in his surroundings. Obviously it was Crouch's bedroom that he had chosen, for various articles of male dress lay scattered on the chair and on the floor beside an open trunk. From the point of view of concealment, it was almost worse than the sitting room. There was only the hackneyed possibility of the bed, and even that was devoid of concealing counterpane. But as his eyes lighted on the window, he felt a sudden hope. It might be a way out. After all, the cottage was low. If he let himself down to the full extent of his arms, the drop would be trifling. And whoever it might be downstairs would have no chance of getting out in time to catch him, or even to see him, before he was out of the garden. He tiptoed across the room.

The descent was perfectly practicable. The casement was not secured in any way, and he had pushed it open before he saw the car which was standing outside the front gate. It was a consolation, perhaps, that it was not the car by which Crouch had left. Presumably, then, it was not Crouch and his sister coming back. But who was it? And with the question, curiosity overcame his fear of discovery. He must find out.

A quick glance through the window showed that there was no one else outside. The way was clear, then, if he wished to take it; but he did not. Instead, he tiptoed back towards the door and opened it the merest crack.

Sounds came from below, and they were puzzling. The unknown seemed to be searching, but he could hardly be searching for him. There was a clink of china, a drawer opened and shut—presumably that which he himself had examined. Rustlings and movements which he could not place reached him exasperatingly, and a fantastic suspicion crossed his mind. He, as an amateur burglar, had been trapped by a real one. He dismissed that almost at once. Burglars who arrived by car did not choose places like Crouch's cottage, or leave their cars standing in full view outside the gate. But his curiosity increased. He must find out somehow. Pulling the door open a little more widely, he put his head round and looked down the stairs.

The moment was an unfortunate one, the precise time, apparently, at which the man below had finished whatever he was doing and decided to come upstairs. At least Tony had a glimpse of a vague figure actually on the bottom step before he slammed the door hurriedly as a shout echoed from below.

There was no bolt. He must be out of the window before the other was upstairs. He darted across the room, caught his toe in one of Crouch's scattered garments, and fell headlong when safety seemed in his reach.

Feet pounded on the uncarpeted steps. As he struggled to his feet the door opened. With the realisation that it was too late, he turned to face his discoverer. Then an involuntary exclamation escaped him.

"Great Scott!... Newent!"

The artist had recognised him in the same moment. For a few seconds they stood staring at each other. Then Newent advanced into the room.

"Good evening, Mr.—Mr. Mayfield, I think... We seem fated to meet under unconventional circumstances... It would be trite to say this is an unexpected pleasure."

Tony managed a smile. He must put the best face on it that he could. He played for time as he sought for a reasonable explanation of his presence there.

"The pleasure's mutual, Mr. Newent," he said. "How's the dog?'

"Well, thank you... And I suppose I should ask about your cycle, and how your walking tour is progressing... But, instead, Mr. Mayfield, I really think under the circumstances I ought to ask how you got here?"

Ruefully Tony felt that he had let the other get in the first blow. He parried it as well as he could.

"I think I might ask you the same question, Mr. Newent."

"By all means. I had some business with Crouch. When I knocked and couldn't get an answer, I went round to see if he was busy at the back. Noticing that a window had been broken, I thought I had better investigate, to see if by any chance the burglar was still inside. So I looked round downstairs, and failed to find anyone—"

"Not even in the drawers," Tony intervened suavely. "You must have looked very conscientiously, Mr. Newent."

"The drawers?" Newent's eyebrows rose. "I'm afraid I don't follow."

"It certainly seemed to me," Tony said mildly, "that I heard you opening and shutting the drawers—"

"Some strange mistake, Mr. Mayfield," Newent said imperturbably. "A burglar would hardly be in the drawers—"

"Not a full-sized one," Tony said gravely. "And, of course, Mr. Newent, my explanation is precisely the same as your own... I happened to have business with Crouch. After knocking and failing to get an answer, I went round to the back to see if I could find anyone. Noticing the broken window, etc... What do you say to that, Mr. Newent?"

"I should say it was a stalemate, Mr. Mayfield—though I am in the stronger position. For example, I am a well-known and respectable citizen here, and it is known that I have employed Crouch for odd jobs before now. You, if you will pardon me, are a comparative stranger, and here for a purpose which might induce you, through an excess of zeal, to force an entry into a private house. That is clear enough to me, and I think it will be to the police. The only question is, why you should have any interest in Crouch's house?"

"And I think your own knowledge might supply that, Mr. Newent... The circumstance that Crouch's sister is black-mailing your daughter—"

Tony had risked an attack. The results of it were all he could desire. Newent's face flamed; then paled. He crossed the room at a bound, and before Tony knew what was happening he found himself gripped by the throat.

"You know—you know that—" Newent only muttered the words, but with a ferocity greater than if he had shouted them. "You—you're with them. You—"

Tony made a quick movement. Nothing is easier than to break a stranglehold on the throat if you know how, and Tony did. He jumped back, gained the other side of the bed, and faced his opponent.

"That's enough, Mr. Newent," he warned. "If we come to rough stuff, may I point out I'm younger and stronger than you are. And that I know ju-jitsu? So, on the whole—"

The rage died out of Newent's face and he regained some measure of self-control, though his hands trembled and twitched queerly. He moistened his lips with his tongue and spoke in almost a normal voice.

"I'm afraid I owe you an apology, Mr. Mayfield," he said. "You took me by surprise... May I repeat my question? How do you know—why do you think that?"

Tony eyed him warily. "I didn't know," he admitted. "But I do now, Mr. Newent."

"Mr. Mayfield," Newent's voice was pleading, "you've got to tell me... Of course, what I thought was absurd. I'm sorry. But if you can guess, perhaps other people can guess... Mr.

Mayfield, my daughter is all I have in the world. I'd stop at nothing to save her from trouble... You must tell me—"

"I certainly think we'd better talk," Tony agreed. "But I hardly think this is the place... You see, some other innocent passer-by might come along and, noticing the broken window— Well, Mr. Newent, I think it's possible the police would accept your explanation. But would Crouch?"

Newent eyed him for a moment; then inclined his head in assent.

"My bungalow—" he suggested. "We should be undisturbed there... Come, Mr. Mayfield."

Tony emerged from behind the bed and followed him, but did not accept the politeness of going first through the door. Newent's change of mind seemed complete, but he was not disposed to go first downstairs in front of a man who had so recently made a murderous attack upon him. Not a word was spoken until they were standing in the yard outside. Then Tony stopped Newent as he was on the point of turning the corner.

"Just a minute," he suggested. "Better make sure the coast is clear... After all, Crouch might be coming back. Or some passer-by—and however innocent our intentions, Mr. Newent, since we're not going to the police just now, it might be better if we weren't seen—"

But the way was open. So far as Tony could tell, they gained the car unobserved, and with a sigh of relief Tony took a last look at the cottage as they rounded the bend.

Newent drove for a minute in silence. They had half completed their journey before he spoke abruptly.

"I've an idea we might be allies," he said. "You see, I know a certain amount about newspapers, Mr. Mayfield. I know that there are some things they don't publish—and some they daren't. I wonder if you'd care to tell me just exactly how much you do know... I'll reciprocate later—"

Tony had already made up his mind on that point. Newent listened in silence to the few brief facts he had to give, and made no comment until he ushered him into the comfortably furnished study of the bungalow.

"My turn now, Mr. Mayfield," he said. "Cigarette?... Perhaps a whisky and soda. I'm not so young as I was—"

Tony accepted the drink, but watched his host carefully as he poured it, and even then waited until the other had taken a gulp before he himself followed the example. Newent finished his drink before he spoke again.

"And now it's my turn," he said with a distinct effort, and paused. "I'm afraid you'll be disappointed, Mr. Mayfield. The truth is, I know a little more than you do about this—but not much."

He paused, and seemed to be seeking for words.

"You were quite right," he went on at last. "It is blackmail, and Crouch, or rather his sister, is responsible... But you've no idea of the reason?"

Tony shook his head. "I've told you all I know," he said, and waited.

"Well—I hardly know myself. That is, I'm not positively sure of all the facts... It's a matter in which I am not in my daughter's confidence." His face momentarily contracted a little. "In fact, Mr. Mayfield, I only got to know about it very much as you did—only as it happened I was able to overhear a certain amount. The fact seems to be, Mr. Mayfield, that my daughter has contracted a bigamous marriage... I mean, rather, that she has been the innocent victim of one."

Tony nodded and felt prompted to a question. "With whom?" he asked. "And how long ago?"

"That's just what I can't tell you—the man's name, I mean. What seems to have happened is something like this. The man married that woman—"

"Crouch's sister?"

"Yes. He married her very young, in London. Then they parted. Probably the fault was on her side, but I don't know. In any case, they were never divorced, and years afterwards he had what seemed to be convincing proof that she was dead. At the time he seems to have been feeling so thoroughly fed up with women in general that he didn't care whether she was dead or alive... And then a little while ago, he met my daughter, and they fell in love."

"When was this?" Tony asked again.

"I can't say precisely, but I can guess when it must have been... I was away on the continent for a few weeks a little more than a year ago. It was when I came back that I noticed the change in her. At first she was brighter and more cheerful. Then suddenly all that changed. I knew she was in some kind of trouble, and she wouldn't tell me. And I finally found out merely by chance."

"Then you think this man deceived her into a secret marriage?"

"I think that there was a secret marriage. I don't think there was any deception at all. At any rate, from what I heard, he seems to have told her everything, and not to have been in any doubt that his first wife was dead. But the marriage was kept quiet—"

"Why?"

"I understand that there was some kind of family obstacle. His parents would object or something. However, my daughter knew all about that at the time; and at least he made her happy. And then the first wife turned up here."

"Crouch's sister?"

"Yes. And she seems to have started immediately, blackmailing him at first, and later my daughter. That was when I overheard what was happening... My daughter won't tell me anything about it. I had some kind of desperate idea of going to see the Crouches myself, and forcing or bribing them to go away, or get a divorce or something. That was how I came to the cottage this evening."

The last words suddenly roused Tony to some idea of the passage of time. He glanced at the clock. It was actually nearly seven o'clock.

"Then you didn't know that they'd gone away?" he asked.

"Gone away?"

"I believe so. I saw them driving off in a car, with a good deal of luggage. It looked as if they'd be gone for some time. That was why I went to the house. I thought it would be safe to have a look round."

"But," Newent said thoughtfully, "I don't quite see what you expected to find."

"I hardly know myself. Something incriminating, I suppose. Or something to connect them up with this grave business or the letters, which is why I am really here."

"You found nothing?"

"No. At least—" All at once Tony remembered the piece of card which he had taken from the sideboard. "At least I expect that it's nothing—" he said, and pulled it out.

As he had guessed, it was a photograph, an old, faded photograph bearing the name of a London photographer. It was, apparently, a wedding-group, and at the sight of the bride, his eyebrows rose. The girl in the white dress and veil was pretty in her own way, but the face was unmistakable. It was Crouch's sister.

"What is it?" Newent demanded.

"I hardly know. An old photograph I found in a drawer there. A wedding-group— By George! It must be her wedding-group. She's in it—as the bride. Then this chap—"

Newent rose from his chair and went behind him to peer over his shoulder. And suddenly he gave a startled exclamation.

"Good Heavens!"

Tony looked round quickly. "Know him?" he demanded.

"Can't you see?" Newent snapped. "Of course, he's twenty years or more younger. But he's not—?"

"But who is it?" Tony demanded. The fact that there was something vaguely familiar about the face added to his irritation. He could not place the likeness, but it was certainly there. "Who is it?"

Newent tapped the photograph significantly with his forefinger before he spoke.

"I'd take my oath," he said slowly, "that the bridegroom is George Blakeney."

# 13

## Visit

Richard Blakeney, Dunster reckoned, had had some half to three-quarters of an hour's start. At the very most he might have gone forty or fifty miles before the police message which had been sent out circulated the number and description of his car. Although they did not know the direction in which he had started, if all went well they should have news of him pretty soon.

And yet the inspector was not sure. Richard Blakeney was not a professional criminal, and in all probability would not be prepared with the tricks an expert might have used; but there are times when blind luck and inexperience are more awkward to deal with than knowledge, and Dunster knew that there were always gaps. Still, that was just a matter of waiting and hoping for the best. Another problem troubled him more.

"The point is," he said to the superintendent, "if we do find him, what do we do about it? What's the charge?"

Stockton stared at him. "Murder of Joe Bere," he said, like a man who points out the obvious.

"Not if I can help it. Although the doctor says so, we've no guarantee until the post-mortem that Bere died of the belladonna at all. He might have had a dose which was not a fatal dose and died from natural causes—"

The superintendent made an obscure noise indicating his belief in the remoteness of this.

"Well, it's possible... But if he was murdered, and if it was the belladonna that did it, we're still a long way from a case against Richard. We don't know that Richard gave him the capsules—"

"Jim Bere's evidence—"

"I think it's very likely that Jim, if we get him into the box, will deny everything in that conversation likely to incriminate Richard. And then a judge and jury would only have as proof that we say that Jim says that Joe said that a dubious person called 'the young master,' who might be one of at least two people, gave him the stuff, apparently quite openly and innocently... Do you see yourself getting away with that?"

"But still—" Stockton objected, but Dunster disregarded him.

"We've no real motive... Yes, I know we think that Joe might have known something about the murder of George which might have made it desirable for Richard to dispose of him. But we don't know it, and can't prove it. In any case, it rests entirely on the murder or disappearance of George about which we still know nothing. We haven't even proved yet that Richard was out that way that morning. I admit that Richard's bolting—if he has bolted, which we don't know yet—has a suspicious look, but that's all."

"Then you mean we can't arrest him?"

"I mean we shan't unless we've no other course open to us... It's just possible, of course, that Richard will break down and give himself away; but unless he does, we've no case for a magistrate's court, let alone a judge."

"You've forgotten the burnt cottage."

"Well? What earthly connection that we can see has the burnt cottage got with the murder of Bere or the disappearance of George? The evidence that Richard did even that is merely circumstantial, and if he did he could plead that it was an accident, and that he got scared and bolted. By the way, where is the sergeant? I'd like to hear a bit more from him about what happened."

But the sergeant, who entered penitent and holding a piece of raw beef to his damaged eye, had little enough that was helpful to add. His struggle with the farmer had been the last of a chapter of accidents for which he seemed very little to blame.

"You see, sir, I thought it was too risky to follow Richard Blakeney right behind. So when he left the house, I kept an eye on him all right, but I followed the hedges a field or so away, and wasn't very close. Well, when he turned down the lane, it was plain enough to anyone with any eye for country that it went in a big curve, so I cut across the fields, getting a sight of him every now and again, and meaning to come out near the cottage. I was getting closer when I saw him go round to the back; then I had some bad luck with a ditch—" He glanced ruefully down at his mud-stained trousers. "But it wasn't more than two or three minutes, sir, and I thought I'd pick him up easily enough... Well, I was getting pretty close when I saw him, as I thought, coming round the cottage again, and just then I saw the smoke. I lost sight of him for a minute again and got out to the front of the house, and there I saw a pair of legs sticking through the window. I didn't know what he was after, but it was pretty plain the place was dangerous, so I grabbed him. And it was only then I realised they were the wrong legs—"

"Then you hadn't seen Mayfield before?"

"No... That is, I suppose it must have been him I saw coming round the house. And then that fool of a farmer went for me, and when I got back to the house I found Richard Blakeney had gone."

Dunster considered gloomily. After all, there was little enough about the sergeant's conduct which could be blamed, except perhaps his excessive caution in keeping Richard at too great a distance. But his evidence was on the whole extraordinarily unhelpful.

"Maybe Mayfield can tell us more," the superintendent suggested. "It rather looks as if he must have been following Richard for reasons of his own, and he was on the scene before the sergeant."

The inspector nodded. "Perhaps. If he'll tell us... But, unfortunately, he himself seems to have vanished into thin air. We've been to the pub to ask already."

"Gone after Richard?"

"Perhaps. I doubt it. I mean, I don't think that, by the time he'd finished trying to get himself burnt to death and so on, he'd have time to catch Richard before he set out. But the fact remains that no one seems to have set eyes on him since—"

"You don't think—?" Stockton began with a suggestion of anxiety in his voice; and then broke off as a policeman entered. "Well? What is it?"

"Gentleman to see you, sir... Says he's got some information he thinks you ought to have... Name of Vargas, sir..."

"Da Vargas?" Dunster asked quickly. "Show him in... That's the chap you were talking about—the one the Blakeneys quarrelled with?"

"Seems like it. One consolation, if he's got anything on Richard, he won't keep it back—"

Almost the first glance at their visitor was enough to tell Dunster that, whatever the reason for his visit, it was certainly not any piece of Christian charity or forgiveness. Stockton had called him "a nasty piece of work," and the description was apt. Dark-haired, yellow-faced, and rather over-dressed, he would not have made a favourable impression even apart from his expression. It only needed the little glittering eyes and sneering mouth to complete his general unpleasantness. He bowed ceremoniously and seated himself in response to the inspector's invitation.

"I have come, Inspector, because I felt it my duty," he said in a rather high-pitched voice which somehow had an oily quality in it. "Naturally I am reluctant to be forced to say anything against a neighbour... But I feel that you are probably interested in the doings of Mr. Richard Blakeney—"

Perhaps Dunster's automatic dislike had something to do with his reception of this. He eyed his visitor stonily.

"Why should we be, sir?" he countered.

"Well, I thought—I certainly understood—that the police—" Apparently this reception had slightly disconcerted da Vargas. "I understood, at least, that there were matters the police were investigating with which Mr. Richard Blakeney might be connected... For example, I myself received a letter making certain accusations—"

"And you didn't communicate with us?" Dunster interposed.

"At the time—no. I fear I did not appreciate its importance. I tear it up. I fling it in the fire. But now—"

Normally, Dunster noticed, his English was good, though with a foreign intonation, but as his excitement grew it became more and more broken. Dunster studied him for a moment. Objectionable he might be, but he might conceivably have something to tell them.

"Well, sir?" he prompted.

"Today I hear that Mr. Richard Blakeney is—what you call it? An arsonist. That he has burnt the house down, and fled—the house of the good Farmer Chilworthy. I come to tell you."

"It is true that a house has been burnt down," Dunster said non-committally. "If you know anything about it—"

"About the burning—no! But how should it be if Mr. Richard Blakeney had been there before, and at night? How should it be if I had seen him enter? Did the good Mr. Chilworthy give him the permission? I know not. But what did he there?"

Dunster sighed. That was precisely the question he wanted answered.

"Perhaps it would be better if you told us exactly what you did see, sir," he suggested. "We shall then be able to tell whether it has any bearing on our investigations."

"It was two-three-four weeks ago—" da Vargas went on, but Dunster checked him.

"Do you mean it was two, or three, or four, sir?" he asked. "We should like the exact date."

"That I cannot give... But yes. It was two days after we hear that his brother, Mr. George Blakeney, have so mysteriously vanished. The Friday—you know it?"

Dunster nodded. "Well?" he encouraged.

"I was out walking on my land. There have been thieves and robbers after my fowls. I was near the place—"

"You'd been having hens stolen?" Stockton asked. "You didn't report it, sir."

"But no. Not the hen, but the pheasant cock. I was out in the darkness. I was behind a hedge. I creep... And then I see him."

He paused dramatically. Dunster translated. "You mean, sir, that you were out after poachers, and consequently were in a place of concealment near the cottage; and that you saw Mr. Richard Blakeney. Is that correct?"

"But yes... I say, 'Ha, here is my poaching friend.' I follow him. Then I see he have no gun. So I am brave—yes? But there are other ways of catching the pheasant cock. I follow. I track him to the small house. He is at the door. He stoops. He shows a light—and I see it is Mr. Blakeney!"

"You saw a man whom you believed to be a poacher, although he had no gun. You followed him. He went to the door of the cottage. When he showed a light you saw that it was Mr. Blakeney... At which door was this?"

"At the hinder part—the rear. He has a key. He unfastens the padlock. He goes in. A minute—two minutes—three minutes. He comes out. He locks the door. He goes away. I follow. He goes home... That is all."

"Mr. Richard Blakeney produced a key and unlocked the rear door of the cottage. He went inside and remained there a minute or two. He came out, relocked the door and went home... That is all you can tell us?"

"But yes. Is it not enough?"

"Hardly, sir... Did you believe at the time that Mr. Richard Blakeney's entry into the cottage was unauthorised?"

"But yes. Assuredly."

"Why?"

"He looks here—and there. He peeps, he listens. He has the air of guilt—"

"His actions appeared stealthy?... Then, if you had reason to believe that anything was wrong, why did you not inform the police?"

"I do not know. I think. I am uncertain... I am new. I am strange. Is it not so? If I go to the police and say, 'Your Mr. Richard Blakeney, son of your magistrate, of your ancient squires, he is a robber and a burglar. He break into the cottage of Mr. Chilworthy the farmer'... What say they?"

"But as I understand it, sir, he didn't break in, but let himself in with a key; and so far as you know he stole nothing. That is correct, isn't it?"

Da Vargas made a gesture. "These are words," he said magnificently. "But listen... It is the next day when I see the good farmer in his arables. He is scattering the muck. I shout. I hail him. He comes."

"Next day you saw Mr. Chilworthy in a ploughed field spreading manure. You called to him and he came over. Yes?"

"I tell him all. I see the rage flash in his eyes. I think, 'Ha. It is with Mr. Richard that he is in fury!' But he tell me not to speak the damn nonsense. He say I am a dirty little foreigner. He beg me to mind my own business... I go."

"I see. You notified the owner of the property, who disregarded your warning. You therefore took no further action." Dunster thought for a moment. At least the last part of this statement could be checked. Obviously they must see Chilworthy. "Then that is all you can tell us, sir?" he asked. "About the fire itself you know nothing?"

"No," da Vargas admitted reluctantly. "But is it not plain that he do it?"

"I shouldn't say so if I were you, sir. It might get you into trouble... Thank you very much, sir. Yes, if there's anything, we know where to find you—"

The superintendent raised an eyebrow as the door closed behind their visitor. Dunster nodded.

"Yes. I believe him. Though he is a nasty piece of work, and quite obviously prompted by animosity. Well, if what he says is true, it means—"

"It means for one thing that, if we catch him we should have a fair case against him for burning the cottage, at least."

"Perhaps. That might be handy. But it also means that he was behaving queerly shortly after his brother vanished, and it might mean— I think we'll go over the ruins of that cottage pretty carefully as soon as they cool down."

"And in the meantime, we could verify Vargas's story—"

"By seeing Chilworthy? Yes. That would be a nice job for the sergeant." He laughed at the expression on Comfrey's face. "No. We'll all go. Safety in numbers—"

It was only a few minutes' drive to the farm. Mr. Chilworthy was in the yard as they drove up, and exchanged with the sergeant the kind of look bestowed by one tom-cat on another after an interrupted argument. But he knew the superintendent and received them at least civilly.

"Ay, he come to me," he admitted in answer to Dunster's questions. "And I couldn't understand a half of his talk. But he said something about Mr. Richard and the cottage. That's true enough, if he never speaks truth again."

"But you thought there was nothing in it?"

"I thought that he was a dirty little foreigner that shoots foxes, and if Mr. Richard had wanted to go to the cottage, it wasn't my business. His father's been my landlord for years—"

"So you didn't bother to investigate? I mean, you didn't go to the cottage?"

"Well, maybe I did... But it was all right. And what I'd like to know, Superintendent, is when you're going to gaol the tramp that burnt it down—if it was a tramp." He cast a look at the sergeant which was not without suspicion. "You've not got him yet?"

"We hope to soon," Dunster pacified him. "By the way, it seems to have burnt pretty quickly. Had you some petrol there or anything?"

"Ay, maybe there was a drop. Seeing it's handy for the tractors... Ah, it were a bit of a blaze... Haven't seen a better one since Thomson's barn went up... But it was insured—"

"You think the place would have burnt like that if anyone had accidentally dropped a light?"

"Well, 'tis hard to say, sir. These old places be like tinder. Ay, I think it might."

"And when you inspected it after your conversation with Mr. da Vargas, you saw nothing wrong?"

"Nothing, sir... Not then, anyhow."

"Then you did notice something?"

"Well, not exactly, sir... It was two days ago William comes to me and says, 'I see you've got a new lock on the cottage, then.' And I thought he was talking daft, and asked what he meant, and he says he wasn't sure but it looked new-like to him. And I was going to have a look, but there 'tis."

"You mean that William—? By the way, who's he?"

"He be the tractor-driver. You see, we never used the back door, the front being handier. But it just happened that he walked round there that day. And so he saw the lock."

"We'll see William... In any case, the padlock won't have been burnt. I expect you could recognise it, if it were the old one—" He broke off, glancing towards the road. "Who's that? Someone looking for us? I wonder if—"

He left the sentence unfinished and hurried over to the uniformed officer whose motorcycle had just halted at the gate.

# 14

## In the Ruins

It was already growing dusk by the time that Tony Mayfield finished his talk with Newent, and he realised that if he was to keep his appointment with Alness on time he would have to hurry. His discussion with the artist had lasted longer than he had intended, and without progressing very materially; but Tony had lingered on in the hope of getting a glimpse of the daughter, who was so vitally concerned. In that he had been disappointed, and Newent had been adamant in forbidding any direct questioning.

Still, he had made a distinct advance, and at last something concrete had emerged from the mass of vague rumours. The scandal which George Blakeney had feared was the bigamous marriage, which was also behind the blackmail. That might easily account for his flight, or proposed flight, and for the quarrel with his family. But then, had he really gone? And, if so, who was the writer of the anonymous letters? Hardly the blackmailer, who could not risk spoiling the game by a police investigation. And what was the reason for Richard's visit to the cottage and for burning it down? In spite of his promise to Virginia, he could not help feeling that things looked distinctly black for Richard, if anything had happened to his brother. Finally, there was the beginning of the whole business, the digging up of the graves, and try as he would, that refused to fit into place anywhere.

Luckily the artist had been sufficiently hospitable to offer an irregular kind of meal, for it was all too obvious that he would have to miss, or at least postpone, the excellent joint of beef which he knew to be awaiting him at the inn. It was only then that he remembered that he had arranged to share that meal with the reporter who had first discovered the latest desecration and with something of a shock he realised that he had completely forgotten the sordid necessity of sending a message to his paper. The worst of it was that so far he had found very little to send. He might do something with the cottage; though, since he could hardly imply Richard's responsibility, it would need a good deal of dressing up. From all points of view, the blackmail business must be taboo. His best hope seemed to be to trust to Alness and the anonymous letter, which would still be in plenty of time for the editions.

He decided once again to dodge the village, the more so as the alternative route would take him past the burnt-out cottage. It was an idle enough curiosity, he thought, for the place would still be too hot for any investigation; besides, there would in all probability be a mass of sightseers lingering round the ruins and possibly even a police guard. It all depended what view the inspector took of the fire, and that, in turn, on whether the plain-clothes man who had rescued him at the cottage had been interested in Richard or in himself. Either was possible. If the police suspected Richard, it would be elementary to keep an eye on him. On the other hand, Dunster might have thought it worthwhile to see what Tony himself was doing, and perhaps take advantage of any discoveries he might make.

A slow drizzle was beginning to fall as he entered the lane, and it was getting distinctly dark and unpleasant. Halfway to the cottage he passed an excited, talkative group of small boys, apparently on their way home, and the meeting encouraged him to believe that perhaps any crowd would have vanished. The rain was steadily increasing in volume, and if it continued would, by morning, have effectually quenched anything that remained of the fire. In the meantime, it made the lane more like a quagmire than ever, and he was not at all sorry to reach the bend, from which, he seemed to remember, the surface became more solid.

He stopped at the corner looking up the hill towards the place where the cottage had stood. There was still enough light to distinguish the hedges and trees gradually fading into obscurity, and, if it had been there, perhaps the outline of the cottage itself. But instead of its solid bulk, there was a queer, moving whiteness just discernible—evidently the steam produced by the rain on the hot stones.

There seemed to be no one about. He waited for a moment, listening, even though he was painfully aware that the time when he should be with Alness was getting near. There was no sound but the melancholy dripping of the rain from the trees. And then it seemed to him that he caught something else. He listened again, and this time there was certainly something. It was the sound of a woman sobbing, and it was quite close.

From the time when his match lit up her face in the lane there had been only one woman who occupied any prominent place in Tony's thoughts, and, ridiculously, he jumped to conclusions. The sobbing came from his left. He seemed to remember a gap in the hedge there, casually closed by two fir poles instead of a gate. Whoever was sobbing must be making for the gap. He found it in the dimness and fixed his eyes upon it, and a moment later he was rewarded. A shadow moved in the gloom as though someone was mounting the obstacle, then there was a crack of something breaking and a woman's cry.

Tony ran forward. As he did so, he felt there was something wrong about that cry; but the thought in his mind as he felt urgently in his pocket was still that it must be Virginia. He found the torch, and flashed it as he spoke.

"Virg—Miss Blakeney," he said. "You're not—"

The words broke off abruptly. It was not Virginia, and even then he realised his own folly in thinking it must have been. But it was no stranger either. The woman who had just struggled to her feet in the glare of the torch was Newent's daughter.

For a second or two, the realisation left him stunned, and with the torch turned full on her he simply looked. She had certainly been crying, for her eyelids were red and swollen. Her skirt hung heavily with the damp, and the rain glistened on her face and hair. The dark eyes were wide with something very like fear, and Tony remembered the necessity of explaining to her about his own apparition.

"I say, you're not hurt?" he asked. "Mrs.—Miss— It is Miss Newent, isn't it?"

Simultaneously he remembered that the one-sided view given by a torch directed full at a person is hardly an aid to conversation. He turned the beam aside, so that only the reflected light showed on both their faces. His voice seemed to have reassured her. Her eyes studied him for a moment. She drew a deep breath.

"I—I don't know you," she said in a rich, deep contralto which trembled only a little. "I fell—"

"We've never actually met," Tony answered. "But I've just come from your father at the bungalow. We were hoping you'd be back before I left... I think he was getting a little worried—"

A shadow of pain or anxiety seemed to cross her face. It was followed by a desperate resolution.

"I can't—" she broke out. "I can't go back... You must tell him... I am all right. But I cannot be back—tonight."

"But—but Miss Newent—" Tony protested helplessly. "I don't quite see—"

She had drawn herself up to her full height, and she was nearly as tall as he was. In her face there was a strange rapt look.

"I cannot come back tonight," she repeated. Before she had spoken on a sudden impulse, now she spoke with a complete determination, and he felt that her resolution would be unshakable. "You will tell him—please. There is no danger. I shall be with friends. Tell him I know he will have confidence in me. I cannot come—"

"But, Miss Newent—" Tony began helplessly, and stopped, not knowing what to say. It occurred to him oddly that he was really not worried about the girl. He was worried at having to explain, and curious—intensely curious; but there was no real alarm. If it had been Virginia— "But, Miss Newent, consider your father—" he began. "He'll be most fearfully worried. Let me see you home—"

There was a real sacrifice to chivalry in the last words, for he knew only too well that it was already getting late for his appointment with Alness. Then he saw the refusal in her face and anticipated it. "Miss Newent, I don't know what's the matter, and probably it's no business of mine... But you seem to be in trouble of some kind. Now, I know your father. I'd like to help you if I could—"

"I may ask you," she said surprisingly. "I do ask you. Tell my father. I was going to send a message... Tell my father as I ask you... But not yet. In an hour's time... Tell my father. Please—"

She seemed to be taking his consent for granted, and there was a magnetism about her personality which made Tony exasperatedly aware that he probably would do just as he was told, neither more nor less. He made a last effort.

"Well, Miss Newent," he said. "I don't know where you're going. But let me see you on your way—"

"No," she said with firm decision. "Goodbye."

"But—but you can't go like this!" Tony broke out. A sudden annoyance at the unreasonableness of the whole position assailed him. "Miss Newent, think of your father I can't let you go—" He never quite knew whether he meant to restrain her forcibly or not, though it was certainly in his mind. The fact that he had not the smallest right to do so delayed him too long if he ever meant to. Before he could stretch out his hands, she had slipped out of the circle of light into the shadows and was lost to sight. He felt savagely angry, and at that moment he could have smacked her like a child. The torch flashed up and down the lane without result. Then he heard a crackle of a dead twig in the wood which bounded the road towards the lake.

He was up the bank in an instant. The beam of the torch glistened on a wet wall of rhododendron leaves mixed with brambles, which was as near impenetrable as could be. There must be a way, for she had gone there. But if he had to waste time in searching, he could never hope to catch her in a thicket like that, especially as she obviously knew her ground and he did not. And if he did—? A vivid picture of himself dragging a full-grown woman unwillingly back home to her father crossed his mind, and perhaps he blushed. At least he stood for a minute or two in indecision on the bank-top, with the rain dripping from his hat-brim, and swore mildly beneath his breath.

Faint sounds still came from the wood; or he fancied so, for they were hopelessly blended with the dripping of the rain and it was quite impossible to place them. Once he turned quickly at a more definite noise from the other side of the lane, and stood waiting, until a low "moo" brought it home to him that the inhabitants of the country at night are not all human. He switched off his torch and jumping down, started off up the lane again at an increased pace.

After all, he asked himself, what could he do? The answer seemed to be to do just what the girl had asked him—to ring up her father, or call, as soon as possible, and tell him that his daughter had asked him to say that she— He repeated the message over to himself several times, and it did not improve with repetition. But, after all, they were artists. He had known a number of artists, many of whom were as Bohemian as bank-clerks; but others were odd in their attitude. He comforted himself with the thought that it was quite possible Newent Pater would merely say: "Not home? Then I must order less milk," and bent to the rain.

He was opposite the cottage now. A whiff of steam came warm and clammy on the wind, but there was no trace of any flame. In spite of himself he stopped for a moment, felt for his torch and flashed it.

Blackened in patches by the smoke, the rough stone wall in front still stood almost to where the roof had been, and he was just opposite the window from which the policeman had dragged him. The sight of it revived in his mind the glimpse of the interior which he had had through the whirling smoke, and the momentary impression which, in the excitement of the events which followed, he had long since dismissed as fancy. But was it? Before he had quite decided whether to look or not, he found himself through the gateway and opposite the opening.

He flashed the torch through and looked, leaning on the stonework of the sill as he did so, then jumped back hurriedly. The granite slab was nearly red-hot. Obviously there was no getting in that way without being roasted in the process. He tried again more gingerly, keeping away from the wall. The steam prevented any good view, and in one corner a dull-red glow sent a whiff of acrid smoke in his direction which set him coughing. There was a certain amount of charred wreckage and fallen stones, but less than he would have expected. Another glance through his watering eyes showed him something else. He stepped back, tripping over a half-burnt remnant of the roof, and started round the side.

The whole rear of the cottage had fallen out bodily. Deceptively massive in appearance, the masonry was filled with rubble and clay, and had failed to withstand the fierceness of the heat. It had simply toppled outwards, carrying a large part of the roof with it, and lay scattered over the back garden and path.

He had to pick his way carefully over the lumps of fallen stone and charred roof-beams; though luckily these had already cooled a great deal. At last he reached the point for which he had been aiming, the corner in which, from the pile of rubbish, he had seen protruding the old boot which had nearly proved his death.

Here about three feet of wall remained, scalding hot to the touch, and hissing faintly as the rain percolated into the warmer depths. He got as near as he could, leant forward gingerly and flashed the torch.

There was the rubbish, certainly. Some of it had been of a permanent, cast-iron variety which had withstood even the fierce heat to which it had been subjected. In one place there was a burst can; near it some leaden object had simply subsided into a pool of molten metal. And the whole was covered with a thin veil of steam and a carpet of ashes which defied any careful examination. He turned the beam fruitlessly this way and that for a minute or two without result.

For a second the steam blew aside, allowing a clearer view. And then, with an involuntary gasp, he saw it. Outlined against the dark background of charred wood, something stood out white and quite horribly distinct. It was a skeleton hand.

# 15

---

# On the Trail

THE CONSTABLE ON THE cycle was a young man, not old enough in years or experience to conceal his excitement in being the messenger for a piece of news which he obviously thought was important.

"We've found him, sir," he broke out. "A great bit of luck—"

"Who?" Dunster asked a little coldly, and the constable repressed his exuberance.

"We have received a telephone call at the station about a man answering to the description of Mr. Richard Blakeney, sir," he said woodenly. "From Sturminster Newton, sir."

"Sturminster Newton?" Dunster echoed without expression. "Ah. They've detained him?"

"Well, no, sir... You see, he'd gone before they got our message, sir. Just as it happened, he was involved in a bit of an accident there—ran into the back of a lorry. Not much harm done, I understand, sir, but the police took particulars and his name and address... But of course, until they got our message there was no reason for detaining him—"

"So we haven't got him. You should be more accurate in your reports, constable... Sturminster Newton—"

"Narrows things down a bit, anyhow... But what's he doing there?"

"If he were bolting," Dunster said slowly, "it might mean he was making for the coast—"

"But he's going east—"

"I mean to some port or other from which he could get a passage out of the country. Obviously it's no use buzzing down to Seaton or Lyme and asking for a passage to Callao in a hurry. He'd have to go somewhere like Bristol, or Southampton, or—"

"Callao?" Stockton demanded.

"'On no condition is extradition allowed in Callao!'" Dunster quoted. "He might be trying to go abroad to some place where we couldn't get him. But if that's so, he's extraordinarily dumb even as murderers go..." He turned to the farmer who had joined them and was trying to listen. "You might ask William to call at the station sometime, will you?" he asked. "We're going there now—"

He was evidently thinking as they started, and Stockton did not interrupt him. They had almost finished the short trip before he spoke again.

"The interesting thing is to see what he does next," he said. "If he's innocent, I suppose he'll go on and do whatever he meant to do. If he's guilty, he'll presumably try to cover his tracks—"

"I suppose he couldn't help giving his name and address, when once he'd been involved in the accident," Stockton suggested. "They'd want to see his licence and so on."

"Yes. But if he wants to hide, that encounter with the police must bring home to him the fact that he's no hope of getting anywhere by car. In that case—"

It appeared that they had read Richard's mind correctly; for there was another message already waiting for them at the police station.

"Car answering to the description left at a garage near Blandford, sir," the policeman on duty reported, and handed him the pad on which he had scribbled the particulars of the telephone call. Dunster read them.

"Damaged?" he said. "Serious? Did they say?"

"Steering a bit out of order, I understand, sir. Not so bad he couldn't have gone on—"

"And again he seems to have left his full name and address... It's a pleasure to track him. And at a garage—"

"After all, he couldn't know we'd be after him so soon," Stockton pointed out. "He didn't know he was being followed. Besides, the mere fact he bolted shows he lost his head."

"Yes. One reading of the business would be that Richard has acted rashly throughout. He kills his brother—if he has killed his brother, and if his brother's killed at all—in the heat of the moment. He realises that Bere may give him away, and without a second thought gives him the poison. There's something about that cottage which might be incriminating, so he burns it down. It's all very nice, but—"

"Well, that's exactly like him," Stockton pointed out. "He has a violent temper. If he killed his brother at all, it was probably as the result of a quarrel. And then all this, with the anonymous letters and so on, has obviously been getting him down. You couldn't expect him to plan everything cold-bloodedly and properly."

"Maybe not... I'll telephone."

Stockton was scribbling on a pad when he rejoined him a few minutes later. The superintendent had apparently been collecting his thoughts, and he lost no time in coming to the point.

"If Blakeney's found after this, it seems to me we've no option but to arrest him," he said with decision. "Look at it for yourself. Quarrel with his brother—brother missing—Richard last with him and lies about it—probably poisoned Bere—"

"Yes. But all that's supposition. The one concrete fact is the burning of the cottage. And there's one thing which doesn't fit in at all—"

"The graves?"

"Yes. What earthly motive could Richard have had for doing anything like that?"

"But probably they haven't anything to do with the rest of it," Stockton pointed out. "And that reminds me. That latest grave business. There's nothing in it... No, I don't mean there's nothing in the grave. I mean that we've had a look, and whoever did it didn't go down more than a foot or so. In fact, he didn't dig up the grave at all, really. He merely made it look as if he had."

Dunster frowned a little as he thought. "That must mean something," he said. "But I'm hanged if I can see what."

"It can only mean that some fool is playing a joke—though he won't find it one if I get him. No, I'm not worried about the graves—"

"And I am," Dunster said seriously. "It's the thing that worries me more than anything else. Because I believe that one fine day we'll open one of them and find George Blakeney there!"

The superintendent made a gesture. "Then the murderer must be plumb barmy," he said with resignation. "I don't say it isn't a good idea, mind you—for a detective story."

"It's been used," Dunster said. He was a student of crime fiction.

"Has it? Well, it might work even in real life—or it might have worked the first time. If a murderer had wanted to dispose of an odd corpse, he could have dumped it in Lady Blakeney's grave—if he hadn't been such a fool as to leave the rake in when he filled it in. But he didn't. He digs out that grave, leaving an obvious clue to the fact he's done it; he tackles another pretty well next door to it, although he knows he's been seen. And when he's just escaped capture that time, he has another shot later. And in no case does he bury his corpse. It's sheer foolishness. When he's advertised it as he has done, he can't think a grave's a good hiding-place for the body where it won't be found... No. He's just barmy, or playing a trick, and trying to make us think something."

Dunster nodded. "You may be right," he said slowly. "But just to humour me, Superintendent, and to make sure, I'd like you to do what I mentioned—"

"What?"

"Get the local bobbies to have a good look, in company with the local gravediggers, at all the secluded churchyards in the area. Say for ten or twenty miles round. Get a list of recent burials, from, say, a week before this business first started with the disturbance of Lady Blakeney's grave. And, if you can, get some kind of a watch put on the churchyards at night for a bit."

"But, dash it all—" Stockton started to protest, then shrugged his shoulders. "You're in charge of the case," he said. "But it's a tall order... I suppose the first part's easy enough. It'll make some of these village chaps think they're real policemen if nothing else. What exactly do you want 'em to look for?"

"It's too late to look for recently-disturbed graves," Dunster answered. "Because it may have been done three weeks or a month ago. I'd like any grave that could have been dug up in the time. And a list of the persons buried there."

"Right."

"And I'd like enquiries made into the possibility that anyone who could be concerned—so far as we know—could have got out to do it. I mean particularly Richard. Alness, maybe—"

"Alness? Well, he's been in on the business from the start..." Stockton assented reluctantly.

"Stroud, of course. Yes, and da Vargas... Also Crouch and his sister."

"And Doctor Staithes?" Stockton suggested sarcastically.

"Why, yes... As a matter of fact, he's a better chance than most people. He could always plead a serious case in the small hours to account for his going out."

"Well, we'll do it," Stockton assented without enthusiasm. "And now, let's leave this nonsense and get back to business. If we find Richard—"

But he was not to be let off so easily. Sergeant Comfrey entered, still nursing his damaged eye.

"There's a man outside for you, sir," he announced with unconscious plagiarism.

Dunster eyed him. "I didn't know you were a wireless fan, Sergeant," he said. "And by the way, it's no use keeping that beef there now. The damage is done... Who is it? William, about the padlock?"

"No, sir. It's Harry—Harry Shepton... He's seen a ghost, sir!"

"A—a ghost?" Stockton said weakly. "And he wants us to exorcise it?"

Comfrey was impervious to sarcasm. "He didn't say so, sir. He thought it might have something to do with the grave, sir."

"Jolly reasonable," Dunster murmured. "We'd better see him, Sergeant."

He glanced at Stockton not without a trace of triumph. "I'd a feeling that the grave business was going to get a move on," he said. "After all, perhaps someone did see the chap at work—"

"It's a darn sight more likely to be this local cider," Stockton growled. He was not a Somerset man. "Had a pint too much and started seeing things—"

But in that he had apparently done his visitor an injustice. An apple-cheeked countryman who must have passed the normal three-score years and ten, he certainly showed no trace of insobriety; and Dunster's keen eye saw the badge in his button-hole.

"Good evening, Mr. Shepton," Dunster said. "I hear that you've something to tell us?"

"Well, zur, maybe I have," the labourer said cautiously. "Anyway, it be queer, zur... Not that I was coming to 'ee, till I heard tell of what happened in the churchyard, zur. And then I thought, 'Well, maybe they'd like to hear at the station.' And here I am, zur."

"You saw something at the churchyard?" Dunster suggested.

"No, zur. Nor near it. But 'twas queer, and I thought you'd better know... You see, last night I'd been to see my aunt. Getting on, she be, and lives just over the hill. Well, zur, it might have been about half-past ten, zur, when I was coming back through the wood—"

"Just a minute," Dunster interrupted. "Just where is this—"

"Why, you can see it from here, zur." He pointed through the window to where the hill, crowned with a dark patch of firs, raised itself above the village. "See where the road bends there, zur? Well, 'twere as near there as possible."

Dunster followed his pointing finger. The place indicated must have been nearly a mile from the village, and a mile in the wrong direction so far as the village where the grave had been disturbed was concerned. There was no definite link. And yet, whoever it had been might have come from that direction.

"I see," he said encouragingly. "What happened?"

"Maybe you don't know the place, being a stranger? 'Tis before the wood begins, but all hazels, and proper thick. The moon hadn't got up, zur, and I tell 'ee 'twas dark; but I've been that road fifty years or more, and I knew my way well enough. Well, zur, I was just nigh the turn, where the bushes is thickest, and I heard it... And I don't mind saying I felt queer for a moment, because you couldn't say what it was. And coming out of the dark like that—and quite close, too, zur— I stood there for a minute. You see whatever 'twas, 'twas just ahead. I wasn't afeard, but I didn't think I'd go no nearer—"

"What exactly did you hear?"

"Just a second... 'Twere a kind of sobbing, zur, as like as anything."

"Sobbing?"

"Sobbing and moaning, zur... I stood there, and it coming nearer. It was sort of talking, too, mumbling and crying. And then it were quite near, but behind the bushes, you see, and I could hear 'un plain. 'Mother—mother—mother—' it said, and cried—but not a child, zur—"

"What was it then? Like a woman?"

"'Twere kind of deep for a woman, but it might have been; for 'twere kind of high for a man. I wouldn't just say... Just opposite me, zur, there were a gap. They'd cut the hazels for the shooting. And the next minute I seed 'un!"

"It was dark?" Dunster suggested.

"Dark enough, zur, but not proper dark. I could see 'un moving black against the grass, and a white face; and then it were gone. I heard 'un in the bushes. And I heard 'un still crying. And I was a mite scared, but I called out. 'Who be 'ee? What be wrong?' I calls, but it didn't answer. Then the crying, stopped, zur. I waited a bit, and I came along home, zur."

"You didn't go to see what it was?" Dunster asked.

"Well, no, zur... Maybe I ought to have done, and maybe 'twere better I didn't. I wasn't right afeard, mind you, but I came along home."

Dunster rose to his feet. "You wouldn't mind showing us the place now?" he asked.

"No, zur. It be daylight still, zur."

The superintendent followed them unwillingly. He could see little enough point in viewing the spot where a ghost had been twenty hours before, but he still followed, and seated himself in gloomy silence in a corner of the car. Dunster himself only spoke once on the short journey.

"You're a teetotaller, Mr. Shepton, I see," he said.

"Ay, zur. Man and boy these seventy-odd year, and my father before me."

Stockton made an obscure noise, just as the car drew up at the bend.

They got out. Stockton pulled up the collar of his coat. It was getting chilly; a slow drizzle of rain had begun, and the dusk was falling. On the whole, he could think of many better places to be at that time; though on a summer afternoon it would have been a pleasant enough spot for a picnic. On their left the hill rose steeply, thickly covered with a tall growth of neglected hazels, intermingled with bracken and bramble. Mounting the hill direct, a gap cut through the thicket ended in the dark wall of the pinewoods on top.

"Here it were, zur," Shepton said, and pointed. "And it were across there it went, zur."

"How far up?" Dunster asked. "Just show us, will you?"

Trailing through the wet grass, they followed him a few yards up the slope before he stopped again.

"It were by thicky bush, zur," he said. "Come from behind like—"

Dunster was already investigating, and as he pulled aside the branches he saw that the bushes were not quite the impenetrable jungle they appeared. There was a path of sorts, snaking its way under and between the hazels, faintly marked but quite practicable. Probably it was some kind of an unofficial short cut, or it might have been made by the village boys. Shepton joined him.

"Ay, it would be down here it come, zur—" he confirmed and broke off, cocking his ear as if to listen. Then Dunster heard it too.

"Someone's coming now," he said. "Quick. In here."

He dived into a hole in the undergrowth beside the track and the others followed. There was a minute of waiting. Above the irregular dripping of the leaves, Stockton made out the noise of someone steadily coming nearer. Suddenly he found himself wishing that the old man had not so consistently referred to his apparition as "it." In another second or two they would see, anyhow—

A twig cracked quite close. Then a figure emerged round a hazel clump not a dozen feet away. It came towards them slowly, not moaning, or mumbling, or behaving in a ghostlike manner at all; and yet Stockton's hair prickled on his scalp. As it crossed the gap and plunged into the bushes the other side, he could make out the face. It was Jim Bere.

# 16

---

# A Fugitive Comes Back

Tony's view lasted only for a moment; the next the steam drifted back. He leant forward eagerly, recoiling with a burnt hand as he unintentionally touched the hot wall. The haze seemed obstinately determined not to allow him another glimpse, though he strained his eyes in the direction for a minute or two.

But he had seen it; and the question was what he was to do next. There was no getting nearer just yet for further investigation. Even with the rain, the spot would be unapproachable for several hours. But the bones had certainly been there, and where there was a hand it was only reasonable to suppose there was a body. After all, then, it had been more than an old boot which he had seen. It had been a man, and Tony would have given a good deal to know who it was.

George Blakeney was the obvious candidate. Here was the eventuality which both Alness and Virginia had forecast with what had seemed to be undue pessimism—and what was he to do about it?

Certainly he was only wasting his time peering into the ruins. What he wanted was a telephone, and as quickly as possible. He ought, of course, to tell the police; in fact, he would have to, or run the risk of getting himself into trouble. But he need not do that just yet; at least before he had sent a message off to the paper.

His general policy suddenly became quite clear. He wanted the police to know, and to know through his agency so that, in common gratitude, they might give any available information. But by now he would no longer be alone in the field. Probably the village by now, and particularly the inn, was overrun by mixed correspondents seeking whom or what they might devour. It just so happened that his own line of investigation had been that one of them was likely to strike and he had not met them. But they would certainly be there.

The police must know, then, at a time when most decent reporters had called it a day, and retired to rest, or when it was too late to catch the edition. He had a momentary twinge about the ethics of it, but dismissed the thought. Anyhow, he must telephone, and in all probability the handiest place was Alness's house, where he was less likely to be seen or overheard. His immediate point was to get there unobtrusively, without meeting police, reporters, or anyone who could ask inconvenient questions.

He switched off his torch. That advertised his presence too much, and he could do well enough in the dark. And the next minute, as he stumbled along the side of the ruin, he realised that he had only just dispensed with its help in time.

There were voices in the lane. Policemen's voices, he decided after a moment's listening, and one of them at least was excited. For a moment Tony hesitated; then, as a glare of torches showed through the hedge, he made up his mind, and moved silently to one side in the direction where he had noted two or three derelict apple-trees which might offer cover.

He was too late. Three pairs of boots and trouser-legs, illuminated by the downward beam of a torch, were already moving up the path. He did the only thing possible if he were not to show himself, and simply froze where he stood, within a yard or two of them, and absolutely open to view if the light happened to turn that way.

But luck was with him. The police were obviously too intent on their own business to think of anything else. As they passed him, he caught a grumbling word or two.

"—a lot of nonsense. When the inspector comes back—"

"But I did see it, Sergeant. There wasn't any mistake. It was sort of burned a bit, but it was a skull all right—"

Exasperatingly, they passed out of earshot. Tony was almost tempted to follow them; then realised the impossibility of doing so undetected in the passage of the rubble. So the ruin had been guarded, and the guard had found the body, or at least, like himself, seen a portion of it. He puzzled for a moment over why he should only have seen the hand, while the policeman saw the head; but it made no difference. At least all the indications were that a complete skeleton lay somewhere in the ruin, and the need for a telephone was all the more urgent.

By the lane, it was not so far as he had expected to Alness's house, nor was the going so bad. He had previously taken the precaution of locating all the vital points on a largescale ordnance map, and even in the darkness found the drive-gate easily enough. The house itself, from what he could make out of it, was hardly so large as he had expected, though he judged from the silhouetted roof that it must be at least as old as the Hall. It was, in fact, little more than a cottage; though, as the door opened in answer to his knock, he saw that the small hall contained a few pieces of antique furniture of some value.

It was Alness himself who opened, and there was agitation in his manner.

"You've come at last, Mr. Mayfield," was his greeting. "I was wondering what to do... But... but this is awful... And yet, you know, Richard can't have done it—"

"You've heard then?" Tony was startled. From the few words he had caught, he had supposed that the discovery had only just been made. "But your cousin— He's not been arrested?"

"You don't know, then? No. But he's run away... But he couldn't have killed Bere—not poisoned him... It's simply impossible... But what are we to do?"

Tony accepted the chair he offered and lit a cigarette. It had dawned upon him that they were talking completely at cross purposes; and that a good deal had happened that he ought to know about. He thought for a minute, and decided it was perhaps as well not to reveal the extent of his ignorance.

"I know a certain amount of what's happened," he said with limited truthfulness. "But perhaps it would be better if you told me what you've heard... Give me as many details as you can."

Rather to his surprise, Alness obliged without protest, and on the whole his account was reasonably clear. Tony listened with an expressionless face and very mixed emotions. Whatever he might have promised Virginia, it seemed to him all too plain that Richard must be arrested, and was in all probability guilty of at least one murder, if not two. But, heartless though it seemed, there was blended with that thought a certain exultation in having what might be exclusive information of one of the finest crime stories he could have dreamed of. That emotion, in fact, predominated as Alness finished.

"I suppose the Press has got hold of this?" he asked.

"The Press?" Alness echoed bewilderedly.

"I imagine there are other reporters here by now... I've been rather out of touch with things—"

"Oh. Yes. I believe there are four of them at the inn... No. I very much doubt if they have. That inspector chap—Dunster—particularly told us not to talk about it just yet. Though I don't see what good that will do—"

"It's the natural official instinct for withholding information if possible. But in this case I'm afraid we must disappoint them... Look here, Mr. Alness. I expect you can see that I simply must use this... In any case, it will all be out tomorrow—"

For a moment Alness seemed a little taken aback. He frowned slightly as he considered; then his face cleared.

"I don't see that it can do any harm," he said slowly. "In one way it might be a good thing. I mean, the only reason the police could have for keeping quiet is that they want to get Richard. If he saw it was discovered, he'd have more chance... Mr. Mayfield, I don't believe for a moment my cousin can be guilty, but if he is, I still want him to get away."

"I can understand that," Tony agreed. "Well, if you've no objection, then, I'd like to use your telephone. I confess it seems a little cool to ask, but—"

Alness nodded and jerked a hand towards the instrument on the desk beside him.

"I might say," Tony went on, "that there's another reason why the whole business is bound to come out soon... You'll hear as I telephone... Trunks, please—"

Alness merely looked on curiously, and Tony did not notice him. While he waited for the number, he was scribbling on the pad a few guiding lines, and by the time he got the office was ready to dictate.

"Ready?" Alness heard him ask briskly. "All right. Begin: 'The discovery of calcined human bones in the ruins of a burnt-out cottage adds a second inexplicable death to the mystery that broods over the little village of—'"

He heard Alness utter an exclamation behind him, but paid no attention. As a purist in English style in his better moments, he reflected a little sadly that it was certainly journalese; but there are occasions when journalese comes naturally. On the whole, he was feeling distinctly satisfied with himself as he replaced the receiver and turned to face Alness, who had been listening in a stunned silence.

"Good heavens—" he commented helplessly, and paused. "Then—then you actually found this—the bones?" Tony nodded. "And the man you saw leaving the cottage just before the fire broke out—"

"Was certainly Richard? Yes." Necessarily, in view of the law of libel and the risk of prejudicing a case, his account had omitted some points. "Of course, he may have had some perfectly good reason—"

Alness did not seem to have much faith in that. There was a hopeless look on his face.

"And 'the police are anxious to interview Mr. Richard Blakeney'—" he quoted. "I suppose that means arrest?"

Tony hesitated. "I'm afraid it probably does," he admitted. "Apart from the fact that the evidence against him is pretty strong, if he's showing a disposition to run away they obviously can't take any risks—"

"But what are we to do?" Alness demanded with something like desperation in his voice. "He couldn't have done it—"

But there was a lack of conviction in his voice. Tony thought for a moment.

"Look here," he said. "I don't want to pry into family affairs. But exactly what was Richard's account of the whole thing?"

"Well—" Alness hesitated. "Of course, I wasn't in on the beginning of it at all. George had already gone before I even heard anything was happening, and it must have been pretty sudden. It was only when I actually got the letter that I tackled Richard himself."

"The letter—" Tony suddenly remembered. "You said you'd show it to me."

"Yes... Anyhow, I took it to Richard and showed it to him, and asked him what on earth was happening. And from what he said my letter wasn't the first. People were beginning to talk already—"

"How long was this after George was—went?"

"Exactly a week... At first he simply flew out at me, and I thought we were going to come to blows. Then he calmed down a bit and told me. Apparently two days before George left, the old man got a letter—"

"An anonymous letter?"

"I gathered so. Richard himself didn't see it. But the old man sent for George and there was a terrific row. Richard himself wasn't there. He didn't know precisely what the accusation against George was. But it must have been something pretty bad, because the sum total of it was that George would have to leave the country until things could be straightened out."

Tony nodded. There was no particular reason why he should tell Alness about the bigamous marriage; but in all probability that was what the letter had revealed.

"George was ready to go?" he asked.

"From what Richard said, he wasn't at first. He was all in favour of facing it out, whatever it was. But it was all a question of his father's health. The old man was almost mad at the thought of the scandal, and it was he who insisted that George should bolt. And George couldn't argue the point without running a risk of killing his father. So he consented."

"Then his health is very bad?"

"Very. Apparently this business gave him an attack from which he hasn't really recovered. He may go at any time. The news of Richard being arrested—" Alness made a hopeless gesture. "Actually, it was Richard who made all the arrangements—which, of course, doesn't make things any better for him. He had a friend at Southampton who was in the shipping business, and his idea was that George shouldn't travel by any one of the regular liners, but should get a passage on one of the cargo boats—sign on as purser, or supercargo or something under a false name. Richard went to see his friend and fixed it all up. And finally, Richard drove George to the station for the night train, and left him there."

"He didn't see him off?"

"No. George had finally consented to go, but he wasn't in exactly a pleasant temper, and apparently he told Richard to go to the devil and leave him alone. They were a bit early for the train, and there was no one at the halt. The last Richard saw of George was that he was sitting on a seat on the platform lighting a cigarette."

"His luggage?" Tony asked.

"He'd only got a case with him. The idea was that he should buy an entirely new outfit, so that there should be no clue to his identity... Of course, the whole thing seems daft enough. But the trouble was my uncle's health wouldn't permit argument, and it was his scheme."

"And then?"

"That's all, really. Only, unfortunately, Richard didn't go straight home. He wanted to cool off a bit, and so he drove round for about an hour, so he says, and it's quite reasonable. But, you see, what the police might say would be that he was murdering George and getting rid of the corpse."

"Then they never heard anything from George?"

"No. They'd arranged some kind of a code message to let them know he'd got the boat and was on his way, but it never came—"

"So they don't know that George went at all?"

"No. In fact, the worst part of it is that it seems pretty certain he didn't."

"Vir—Miss Blakeney wasn't there at the time?"

"No. Richard sent for her. She was really needed to nurse the old man."

Tony thought. "That grave business—" he said. "What did Richard have to say about that?"

"Nothing, really. He thought it must be some lunatic—and apparently a lunatic with some kind of grudge against the Blakeney family."

"That hardly fits in with the other graves."

"No. But it fits in with the letter. I'll show you." Alness rose to his feet and stepped across to the bureau. "And, personally," he said over his shoulder as he unlocked a drawer, "I don't believe that the digging up of the graves has anything to do with it. After all, it hasn't stopped now that George has gone. And while it might have been a good idea to hide the body in a grave as long as no one thought about it, this tinkering about with graves is plain nonsense."

He closed the drawer again and turned to Tony, holding out a sheet of paper.

"Here you are," he said. "You'd better take it and study it at your leisure... I don't quite know why I kept it, anyhow. I suppose I ought to have taken it to the police, but—"

Tony accepted the letter. It was a single sheet torn off a pad, with a few lines of rough printing standing out very blackly. In fact, the blackness struck Tony so much that even before he read it he stepped across to the light and scrutinised it closely.

"Indian ink," he commented softly. "Now, I wonder—"

"Indian ink?" Alness echoed, and joined him to look over his shoulder. "So it is. I hadn't noticed that... But why?"

"There might be several reasons," Tony said thoughtfully. "For instance, it wouldn't run if it got wet—"

"But there's no point in that... There's another puzzle." He pointed to a group of letters in the top righthand corner. "What d'you make of that? 'NO IF.' Meaning there's no 'if' about the finding of the body?"

For a moment Tony was inclined to agree; then he saw the full stop after the first two letters and shook his head.

"It's not that," he said. "It's 'No. 17,' presumably the number of the letter? That's a foreign way of writing the figure seven."

"Foreign?" Alness echoed. "I wonder—it couldn't—"

He broke off. Tony waited, but he did not continue, or at least he did not finish the incomplete sentence.

"Well, that's two clues you've got out of it already that I missed," he said. "A chap who uses Indian ink, and who writes sevens like a foreigner... By the way, who does use Indian ink?"

"Artists—" Tony began a catalogue, and stopped at the first word as the thought of Newent came into his mind.

Apparently Alness thought of the name too. "Well, the only artist round here is Newent at the bungalow," he said. "And there's never been any question of a row with him or anything like that—"

"I wonder if he's lived abroad," Tony said casually as he read. "Artists often do—"

"He has, as a matter of fact," Alness said. "But that's absurd... I think that chap da Vargas is the only foreigner round here I know of. He's much more likely, I should say, in view of the rows he's had with the family."

"The family," Tony repeated. "And this letter rather hints at that too. 'That Blakeney family that you're so proud of is going to get a shock soon.'"

He broke off as a sharp rapping sounded on the panes of the french window at the far end of the room. Both turned to face it. As Alness stepped forward, there was a click of the latch and the curtains parted. Richard Blakeney plunged into the room.

He looked about him wildly, rather like a trapped animal. In his agitation he did not seem to recognise Tony. He faced Alness with a desperate appeal on his face.

"They're after me!" he burst out. "What am I to do?"

# 17

# Out of the Ashes

STOCKTON MADE A MOVE as if to follow as the gamekeeper disappeared into the bushes on the far side of the gap; but Dunster laid a hand on his arm.

"No good," he said in a whisper. "He couldn't help hearing us... Besides, we've no reason to think—"

He broke off uncertainly. From beside him came a chuckle from the labourer.

"And it were only Jim going home!" he exclaimed. "Well, and for a moment I was proper scared... Jim Bere going home!"

"Going home?" Stockton demanded.

"Why, yes, zur...'Twould be his shortest way if he'd been up to the woods. Though, with his brother lying there dead—"

He shook his head. In fact, as Dunster knew, Joe Bere was not lying in the cottage dead, having been removed for a post-mortem; and it was probably natural enough for his brother to carry on with his normal routine. And yet—

"But was he your ghost?" he demanded.

"Him? No, zur, nor like him. Dressed different, it were, in black... No, it weren't Jim."

"Where would that path lead?" Stockton asked.

"Why, it doesn't properly lead anywhere, zur... 'Tis just a track used now and again... Comes out in the pinewood, near the old hut, zur. But it doesn't lead anywhere—"

The distinction seemed to Dunster a fine one, but he had another question to ask.

"And your ghost?" he enquired. "Was it going the same way as Jim or the opposite direction?"

"Why, no, zur. It were going up the hill, towards the wood, zur... No, it weren't Jim Bere—"

There seemed to be the faintest shadow of doubt in the last words, and Dunster was on the point of pressing him when the headlamp of a motorcycle breasted the hill. It drew to a halt beside the spot where they had left the car.

"Someone for us," Dunster commented, and led the way down towards the road. "Wonder if they've got hold of Richard?"

But the news was more surprising. Dunster and the superintendent listened in silence to the first brief report on the supposed discovery of the skull in the ruins, given not without a certain incredulity by the bearer of the message.

"Hm," he commented. "And the sergeant's gone to have a look? We'll join him."

It was a short drive, though not a pleasant one, with the rain making the mud of the lane more like a quagmire every minute. The superintendent broke the silence once.

"George?" he asked.

"Perhaps," Dunster said non-committally.

"Bet you a dollar it is George," Stockton persisted. "We haven't anyone else likely to be murdered, have we?"

"I'll take you," Dunster rejoined. "Besides, we don't know yet that he's been murdered— We don't know that he isn't a tramp who went in there to sleep and burnt himself to death—"

But that point at least was soon settled. In the short time during which he had been at work, the sergeant had been almost embarrassingly active. With the help of poles cut from the hedge, he had again uncovered the relic which a fall of the rubbish had temporarily buried; and there through the steam the hollow eye-sockets glared at them in the torchlight. And yet, in the first glance, Dunster saw there was something wrong. This skeleton did not grin—for it had no teeth. There was no approaching the bones yet, but here was a point that could be settled perhaps. He turned to the local policeman.

"Do you happen to remember if Mr. George Blakeney had had his teeth out?" he asked.

"He did, sir." The constable gave the reply in an awed voice which showed he realised the significance of the question. "A couple of years ago, sir—just after I came. I remember it seemed queer, him being a fine man, when he opened his mouth. Then after a month or so he got a temporary set, sir."

Dunster caught the superintendent's glance and was moved to the defensive, idle though it seemed.

"He's not the only one, after all," he said.

"You're trying to save your five bob," Stockton rejoined crudely.

"Well, he may have died a natural death—"

The sergeant had been trying to say his piece before. Now he would not be denied.

"Just step round here, sir," he said, "and I'll be surprised if you think so... Mind that beam, sir—"

He led the way round the corner to a spot from which, by mounting precariously on the fallen stones, they could peer over the wall at the side towards the back of the skull. One glance was enough. Practically, there was no back. It seemed to have been blown to pieces, and the surrounding bone was pitted and shattered in an unmistakable way.

"Shotgun at close range," Stockton said unnecessarily. "Of course, he might have fallen and shot himself with his own gun—though it's a queer place to do it. But I don't suppose you'll say that the next thing he did was to get up again and burn the house down."

Dunster admitted defeat. "Looks as though I'm five shillings poorer," he admitted. "But I'm not going to pay you before identity is proved at the inquest... By the way, Sergeant, you'd better stop trying to uncover any more. We'll wait till it cools. It may be a matter of importance just how the bones are lying... Well, there doesn't seem much doubt—"

"You can see the hand, too, sir," Comfrey announced with a melancholy satisfaction. "And there's a ring on it, sir—"

"A ring?" Dunster echoed with a shade of incredulity. "But—"

They moved a little farther along the wall to the point where Tony had stolen his glimpse only a short time before, and the sergeant directed his torch.

"There, sir," he said with a slight suggestion of triumph. "See?"

There was certainly the outline of a band which still encircled one of the calcined finger bones. Apparently it was a signet ring.

"I should have thought the gold would have melted," Stockton suggested a little dubiously. "A fire hot enough to leave just bones like that—"

"It's not gold, anyhow," Dunster said. "You can see the colour a bit there. It's more silvery. Platinum, perhaps. That would stand the heat—"

"Mr. George did wear a ring, sir," the constable supplied. "With his initials. I always thought it was silver, sir—"

"With his initials?" Stockton echoed, and looked meaningly at the inspector. "Couldn't get it out, could we? That needn't disturb much—"

It was the ingenious sergeant who improvised the means, from a long ash-pole and a nail recovered from the ashes of a burnt window frame. The latter, after a few unsuccessful attempts, he hooked under the ring where the burning of the flesh had left it hanging loosely, and, bone and all, triumphantly landed it.

Dunster flashed his torch on it as it hung; then he nodded.

"G. B. or R. B.," he announced. "So that's that... Lend me that pole, Sergeant. There's something else there, I think—"

This time the task proved longer. It took him several minutes before he finally captured the object which had caught his eye during Comfrey's operations. It dropped with a clink on the stones as he got it over the wall, the barrel portion of a shotgun, with a charcoal remnant of the stock still adhering. The metal was still too hot to touch, and Dunster turned it over with a stick. Then he bent forward to look more closely.

"Great Scott!" he exclaimed. "Look there... R.B.—"

Stockton in turn stooped to look at the almost obliterated initials engraved in the metal.

"That's it, all right," he said. "R. B.... Richard Blakeney... Why, what's the matter?"

"That is." Dunster pointed to the gun. "And the ring. It's a bit too good to be true. First of all the murderer leaves a ring—a platinum ring, mark you, which won't melt—on the body just to help us with the job of identification. And then, to make things a bit easier, he leaves the gun with which he has committed the crime still marked with his initials just beside the body... Either it's all wrong, or Richard is a complete idiot."

"Well, he is, isn't he?" Stockton demanded. "I mean, he's certainly an idiot one way or the other, so I don't see why he shouldn't be a guilty idiot... Murderers aren't generally cool and collected; and Richard in particular, if he killed his brother, almost certainly did it in a sudden fit of temper. He probably lost his head—"

"Anyway, it certainly seems to clinch things," Dunster said almost with resignation. "Just look at the case against him now. First of all, he's got a double motive, in the quarrel with his brother and in the fact that he benefits by his death.

Then he seems to have lied about driving his brother to catch the train—or if he didn't lie, his story can't be substantiated in any way. He was missing just about the time when one would expect him to be busy doing something about the body, say, bringing it to the cottage here. He is seen in this neighbourhood, on two occasions, acting suspiciously; he has a key to the cottage and apparently uses it; and the second time the cottage is mysteriously burnt down. And just to cap it all, Richard proceeds to run away, apparently making for the coast... Short of a signed confession or an eye witness, I don't see how the case could be much more solid against him."

"Then, there's Bere—" Stockton suggested. "That's not quite so plain, but—"

"It's plainer against him than anyone else. Admittedly his motive in that case is sheer supposition. One can only imagine that Joe Bere knew something about his brother's alleged going away, and told him he knew. And so he had to poison Bere. But there's a snag there. That would hardly be committed on the spur of the moment, which is what you'd expect."

"Why not?"

"Because, although he might give him the prepared capsules on the spur of the moment, he couldn't be expected to have them ready. And it would take him a little time to get them ready. About that poisoning there's nothing of the quick, violent temper business. It's cold-blooded and deliberate... No. There's nothing about the method in that case which points to Richard—"

Something occurred to the superintendent. "I'm not so sure of that," he said slowly. "Didn't it strike you that that girl—Miss Blakeney, I mean—looked a bit queer when we mentioned belladonna? Said something about liniment, didn't she? Now, I shouldn't be surprised if, on enquiry, we found that there was some belladonna he had access to."

"Neither should I," Dunster admitted, but his tone was still gloomy. "All the same, it's hardly in keeping. I don't see why he should be carrying belladonna capsules when he meets Joe Bere quite by chance—"

"There might be several answers to that," Stockton said briskly. "First of all, he might have prepared the poison for his brother, and then used a gun instead. Secondly, he might have prepared the poison for himself—as a way out, you know, if he got caught. Third, the meeting with Joe Bere might not have been casual at all. We've only secondhand evidence on that."

"It still leaves out three things—the desecration of the graves, the anonymous letters, and this ghost business."

"All of which can quite easily be explained. Richard did mean to get rid of the body by burying it in a grave. The trouble was that he was interrupted every time he tried to dig. And when this journalist chap publishes his little article, he realises that that game won't do, and so he burns it in the cottage instead."

"Yes. That's quite plausible. The letters?"

"Were written by Joe Bere. So far as we know, none have appeared since his death."

"There's not been much time... And the ghost?"

"Was simply someone who'd had a drop too much taking a short cut home. I don't see there's anything wrong with that?"

"There isn't," Dunster confessed. "And yet—"

"Well, I suppose you'll arrest him?"

"I don't see that we've much option—when we catch him."

And in the meantime, it seems to me it wouldn't be a bad idea to make a few more enquiries at the Hall... For example, to find out whether any belladonna is available there. To make quite sure Richard was out that morning. And to find out a bit more about this quarrel."

Dunster assented unwillingly. "We'll have to wait for this to cool down, anyhow," he said. "You'd better stay here, Sergeant, but don't touch anything more. I'll send someone to relieve you later... The old man's ill, I believe. I suppose it means questioning the girl—"

The thought lingered uncomfortably in his mind during the drive there; for years of experience, while they had abundantly proved to him that women could be as vindictive or greedy and quite as ruthless as men, had never quite overcome his preference for dealing with criminals of his own sex. And in this case, so far as he could see, the girl herself was perfectly innocent.

The result defied his expectations. Miss Blakeney, the butler informed them, was out; and he would thereupon have shut the door in their faces: but Stockton insisted. They must see the housekeeper, or the butler himself, or someone; and, in fact, he suggested that it might be a good thing to see all the servants. Finally they were shown into a room and sat waiting for what seemed a very long time. Stockton sniffed around restlessly for a little, apparently searching for traces of belladonna, and he had only just sat down when the door opened. Both men rose at the sight of the white-haired man who entered.

Whatever else might be said of the squire, he looked a gentleman of the old school, and had the manners of one. That was Dunster's first thought, as their unwilling host greeted them courteously, and offered them refreshments which they refused. Dunster's next reflection was that the old man ought certainly to be in bed. What had been a strong, determined face, was lined and grey with worry and pain, and his hands trembled so that he could scarcely control their movements.

Even Stockton seemed to be affected. His tone was quite solicitous.

"You're quite sure, sir, that you feel fit to answer a few questions?" he asked. "We didn't want to disturb you, sir—"

"I will answer anything I can." The voice was weak but quite firm. "What did you want?"

"Well, sir, I believe you know something of these letters," Stockton said a little hesitantly. "A point has arisen about which you might be able to help us. Is there any medicine or substance of any kind in the house which—well, which—"

The superintendent hesitated at the appalling bluntness of his own question. The old man waited for him.

"Which contains belladonna?" he completed the sentence at last quite calmly. "Yes, there is, Superintendent. I myself use it on occasion for poultices when the pain is bad. I'll give instructions for you to inspect the medicine chest... Yes?"

Stockton plunged again, wildly. "Perhaps you could tell us, sir, if you had ever seen this gun before?"

He had been carrying the wreckage of the shotgun; now he held it out, and the other accepted it.

"Yes," he said calmly. "I should say that this gun belonged to my son Richard. You notice that his initials are upon it. All his guns are marked in that way... With regard to this one, I cannot say positively, in view of its condition. But I am inclined to think it is an old one which he gave away."

"Gave away?" Dunster said eagerly. "To whom, sir?"

"I believe to one of the gamekeepers—Jim Bere, or was it Joe? No doubt Jim would be able to tell you."

"Jim Bere?" Dunster echoed, and for a moment found nothing more to say. The name was the last straw on the gradually-accumulating burden of surprises. Did the old man know that every word he spoke might help to hang his son? Was he doing it deliberately? He could find no answer, and was glad when Stockton, who was scarcely less surprised than himself, plunged on in a bulldog way.

"I wonder if you can give us any explanation for your son's absence at the present time, sir?" he demanded.

"I believe so. I understood him to say that he was going to Southampton, to ascertain, in view of some allegations made in these letters, whether his brother George did in fact sail from that port."

Dunster was conscious of a growing feeling of horror at something in the old man's manner. He had the sensation that the man had determined to tell the whole truth at any cost. It was like listening to a death-bed confession. But Stockton, if he felt that, did not let himself be deterred.

"We've never had a chance to question you about that, sir," he said. "I wonder if you could tell us what the original quarrel was, as a result of which Mr. George Blakeney left home?"

"There was no quarrel, exactly. I received a letter alleging that my son had contracted a bigamous marriage with a lady in the village. He admitted the truth of this, but claimed to have done so innocently. I quite accepted his statement. Since there was a threat of proceedings, we thought it better that he should leave the country for a time to save the scandal, and give us a chance of straightening matters out a little. The family name—the family name—" And here for the first time his voice faltered. Momentarily his iron self-control slipped, and he looked a very old and sick man. "The—the family name—" he repeated vaguely, as though he had forgotten what he was going to say.

"We won't trouble you any more, sir—" Stockton said hastily. "I think, sir, if I were you—"

The opening of the door interrupted him. The butler entered, and from the first glance at his face, it was plain that he was the bearer of bad news. He stood looking helplessly from the two officers to his master.

"Well, Johnson?" The old man seemed to have pulled himself together again. "What is it?"

"A message, sir... For the inspector—"

"You had better deliver it to him, then."

The butler hesitated: then blurted it out.

"But—but it's Master Richard, sir... The police say—he's come back—and are they to arrest him or—"

He never finished for the old man rose to his feet, stood swaying for a second, and then toppled limply forward.

# 18

# Warrant for Arrest

ALNESS WAS THE FIRST to recover his presence of mind. He stepped forward and, taking Richard gently by the arm, led him to a chair.

"Sit down," he commanded. "You're all right here... You'd better have a drink."

He poured out three stiff ones, and with his own glass in his hand stood looking down at Richard as he gulped the whisky down.

"Why the devil did you bolt?" he demanded with a suggestion of irritated desperation in his voice. "Anyone but a fool would have known that they'd be after you at once. And, of course, they will assume—"

Whether intentionally or not, this little lecture had a good effect. It made Richard angry, and he sat up and glared at his cousin.

"Don't be a damned idiot!" he broke out. "I didn't bolt. I should have been all right but for that beastly lorry. I had to leave the car—"

"You'd probably have been in gaol if you hadn't," Alness said calmly. "Didn't it occur to you that, under the circumstances, the police would be bound to circulate its description?... But why did you go?"

"I was coming back," Richard said aggrievedly. "After all, no one's charged me with anything. I'm not a criminal just because some imbecile is writing a lot of idiotic letters accusing me of goodness knows what... I didn't think about the car—"

He broke off as for the first time he recognised Tony. A flush came on his face, and he half rose to his feet. Alness gently pushed him back.

"Mr. Mayfield is helping us just now," he said. "And you need all the help you can get... Don't play the fool. Think of your family, if you won't behave sensibly for yourself. You know what this will mean. If—"

The anger died out of Richard's face, leaving a kind of frightened look.

"I know," he said. "That's what made me go, you know. I got worried about it all, and I felt I had to settle it somehow. So I thought I'd run over in the car, and find out if George really had sailed by that boat. You see, when we made the arrangements, we covered his tracks so damned well that that seemed to be the only way. And then I had a bit of an accident, and I had to leave the car at Blandford. Well, I decided to go on by train; but of course there wasn't one: I sat down in the waiting room, just out of sight of anyone on the platform... Of course, I didn't mean to hide, but I was hidden. And then I heard a couple of chaps talking as they passed the door. 'We've had a message that he may leave the car,' one of them was saying. 'He'll probably book to Southampton or London. You've got the description right?' And then he started to describe someone—and I suddenly realised he was talking about me."

He laughed savagely. "It wasn't particularly flattering, either," he said with grim humour. "Well, I looked out, and there was a sergeant of police talking to the station master. Apparently he'd only just arrived. I heard the stationmaster say, 'We'd better ask at the office,' and dodged back just as they turned round. They didn't see me, and then the train came in—"

"The train?" Alness interrupted. "But you didn't go there—you couldn't have got back—?"

"All I know was that it was a train, and that it was leaving. As a matter of fact, it was coming back this way. And I suppose that was the one thing which saved me, because it was what they didn't expect. They were watching the east-bound trains and I was going back west. In fact, no one noticed me at all, until the train was just starting from the station before this. And then I saw the porter chap passing the carriage sort of gape at me and he stepped forward. But before he could do anything, the train had left him standing. I looked out and saw him staring after it. Then he ran down the platform. I suppose to telegraph or something. Of course, it's only a few minutes' run from there, and I suppose they hadn't time to do anything. When I got out, the platform was absolutely deserted—just as it was when—"

He broke off. While telling his story, the excitement of the chase seemed to have made him forget the realities. He sat frowning in silence for a moment.

"Well, I decided to take the field-path," he went on in a more subdued tone. "And I hadn't gone more than a few yards before I saw a couple of cars full of police coming up the ramp to the platform. I bolted for it, and I suppose they didn't tumble to what had happened in time... It was obviously no use going back home. They'd certainly have been watching. So I thought I'd better come here... That's all."

He finished his drink, and sat staring at the glass with a frown growing on his face.

"But I still don't understand it," he broke out. "Why on earth should they be so keen on getting me now?"

On the whole he had impressed Tony favourably; but there was certainly anxiety in the last words. Alness's eyes appealed to the journalist, and Tony stepped into the breach.

"Well, Mr. Blakeney, a good deal has happened that I don't expect you've heard about," he said. "First, Joe Bere was found dead—poisoned. And I gather that they think he was poisoned by some capsules you gave him?"

"Capsules?" Richard's bewilderment seemed perfectly sincere. "I never gave him a capsule in my life. Utter rot!"

"And then," Tony went on, "you were followed when you went to the cottage—"

Richard suddenly whitened. He opened his mouth as if to speak, but no words came.

"The cottage was burnt down, and they thought that you'd set it on fire... So they put a guard on it—"

"Burnt down?" Richard echoed. "But it wasn't burning when I left—"

"It was, about two minutes afterwards," Tony said dryly. "I was there myself. And, since there was no one else there, the choice seems to be between you and me—and I didn't do it."

"You were there?" Richard flushed angrily. "Then you followed me—you damned spy! What—"

"For heaven's sake—" Alness intervened. "Mr. Mayfield is doing all he can to help. And there's worse coming yet—"

"Worse?" Richard echoed, and the horror returned to his face. "Go on," he said quietly.

"Well, the man on guard seems to have been poking about the ruins on his own, and he saw a skull. In fact, there was a human body in the house—"

"But—but that's impossible—"

"It's true enough. I've seen it myself. Now, Mr. Blakeney, you can understand that the police have got some grounds for wondering about you."

Richard drew a deep breath. His eyes studied Tony's face for a moment, and he seemed to make up his mind.

"Well, I may as well tell you what there is," he said. "As you can imagine, all this business has been getting me down. And then I started getting letters. I had one just after George left, and it was about George."

"Anonymous?"

"Yes. Printed, you know, and all that—"

"You kept it?"

"No. It wasn't the kind of thing to leave lying about, because whoever had written it seemed to know all about what was happening—more than I did myself. That was what got me... The letter made an appointment at the cottage, and sent me a key to the back door... Of course, I thought it was blackmail. But at the time, we were desperately anxious to keep the thing quiet, so I went. I let myself in, but there was no sign of anyone. Then I saw a note pinned to the mantelpiece so that I could hardly miss seeing it. It simply said the writer couldn't come, but that he'd write to me again."

"You kept that note?" Tony asked.

"No."

"Just a minute. Perhaps you could describe the notes."

"There wasn't much about them. Just the kind of thing you'd expect. Written on cheap paper—printed, I mean. And rather badly spelt—"

"Did you notice the ink?"

"The ink?" Richard stared.

"It was ordinary ink."

"It wasn't particularly black?"

"No. In fact, it struck me that the second note hadn't been written long. The ink hadn't changed colour—"

"Might have been a chemical ink," Alness suggested. "But for goodness sake, go on."

"Well, I didn't hear from the chap for quite a time. In fact, until this morning. Then I got another note—"

"You kept that?"

"No, I tell you. I burnt the things just as soon as I could. Anyway, it told me to go to the cottage and I should find out everything. So I went."

"Well?" Tony urged.

"Like a fool, I went. And there was no one there again, and not even a note. Nothing at all—" He paused for a moment. "So I came away," he ended lamely. "And the house certainly wasn't alight then. I looked into every room."

"And you saw—nothing?" Tony said slowly.

"I've said so." Blakeney did not meet his eyes. "And so, of course, I came away—"

"Rather hurriedly, and looking as if you'd seen a ghost."

"What do you mean?"

"Exactly what I say. And if I'm called upon to give evidence, it's a point about which I am sure to be asked—"

"Look here," Alness intervened, "it seems to me that this is definitely a situation in which half confidences are worse than none. You'd better understand, Richard, that if you're put into court with the amount of evidence you seem to have collected against yourself, your chances will be pretty poor. Our one hope seems to be to find someone else before you're put on trial, and we must have all the facts. Any fool can tell you saw something in the cottage, so you might as well tell us what it was."

Richard hesitated, glancing from one to the other. On the whole, Tony could not blame him. His own importation into the case on the side of the defence was a little too recent; and he was only surprised that Alness had apparently so completely accepted him. Richard braced himself.

"I suppose I can't expect you to believe me," he said, "but it's quite true. I really didn't see anything, or I don't think I did. It was like this, you see. I'd looked all over the house, and I knew that there was no one there. And I was standing in the room to the left of the front door, wondering whether to wait or not, and all at once I had a queer feeling that there was someone there—that I was being watched. I suppose I was jumpy already. So I had another look round—and I just happened to notice it——"

"Nothing really. It was an old brown boot sticking out of a heap of rubbish. I don't know what the association of ideas was, but it suddenly made me think of George. And I thought—I thought—just suppose it was—"

His voice faltered; but his meaning was unmistakable, and Tony relentlessly put it into words.

"You thought—suppose that it really was George's boot, and that George was hidden there, under the rubbish, or rather his dead body... Is that what you mean?"

Richard nodded dumbly.

"Well?" Tony snapped. "Was it?"

"I didn't look! I couldn't look!" Richard cried out. "I couldn't stand it. I simply ran for it... And yet—and yet it must have been just fancy. It must have been—"

"And yet, there is a body there," Tony said grimly. "And that was why—"

He stopped. In the dead silence, the front door bell was ringing, ringing insistently. Richard rose to his feet.

"They're here," he said, and there was almost relief in his voice. "Let's get it over—"

"Wait—" Alness broke in. "Perhaps I can—"

The door closed behind him. There was a minute or two of waiting. Neither man said a word. Then the door opened again, and there was someone with Alness, but not the expected police. With a little cry Virginia threw her arms round her brother's neck.

"Oh, Richard—"

For a moment neither spoke. Tony suddenly found Alness's eye fixed upon him sardonically, and flushed, without exactly knowing why. Then Richard disengaged himself gently.

"It's all right, Virginia," he said shakily. "I hope it will be—"

"But, Richard, you must get away!" Virginia suddenly returned to realities. "They're after you—going to arrest you.

I was out trying to find where you'd gone— You must get away——"

"It's no earthly use, Virginia," Richard said wearily. "I'm not going to run. I wasn't before... The only thing to do is to face it... In a minute, I'll get on the phone—"

It seemed for a moment as though his wishes had been anticipated. The phone on the desk burred sharply. Alness looked at it as though it was a venomous reptile before he lifted the receiver, but he spoke in a voice which was perfectly normal.

He snapped out the last word in a way which made the listeners jump. There was a long pause before he spoke again.

"I'll be round at once," he said, and hung up; then turned to face the question in their eyes.

"No," he said. "It wasn't the police. That was John-son—your butler, you know... He said—Virginia, you must know it. He said that Uncle is dead. Your father is dead—"

Virginia said nothing. She stood there staring, quite dry-eyed; but the look on her face brought into Tony's mind a line which he had always before dismissed with contempt. "She must weep or she will die—" It needed all his self-control not to clasp her in his arms and comfort her to bring the relief of tears. But there was no time for that. There was a heavy knocking on the outer door, and this time not one of them doubted. Alness only looked questioningly at Richard, who nodded. As Alness went out, Richard's hand stole forward and found his sister's, gripping it fiercely.

The front door opened. Across the hall came a voice of which the ring was unmistakable.

"Good evening, sir... I believe that Mr. Richard Blakeney is here, sir."

It was a statement rather than a question. They did not hear Alness's protest, but he must have made one.

"I'm afraid I must see him, sir," the voice came inexorably. "I hold a warrant for his arrest—"

Richard dropped Virginia's hand and stepped forward.

# 19

---

# A Case for Arrest

IF IT HAD RESTED entirely with Dunster, perhaps the arrest of Richard Blakeney might have been at least postponed; for he liked to have things in order. Since Richard had returned, apparently of his own free will, the chances of his attempting escape were small enough, and those of his succeeding almost negligible. In fact, he would have kept. But chief constables must at least be humoured, and in the present instance Colonel Saltash had taken the bit in his teeth. Once convinced that, however improbably, a member of a county family had actually come under the notice of the police, he had impulsively taken out a warrant for double murder and arson.

That worried both Stockton and Dunster. Any one of the charges would have sufficed for the time being; as it was, it was desirable to present at least a prima facie case for the magistrates on all three, and there were nasty gaps. Richard had not obliged with a confession. In fact, he had acted quite sensibly under the advice of Alness and refused to make any statement whatever except on the advice of his solicitor, who, having heard what he had to say, advised silence for the time being.

In one respect only the arrest had been helpful. A search at the police station revealed a key which was found to fit the padlock which Sergeant Comfrey recovered from the ashes of the back door. That was at least a positive piece of evidence to explain away; and Dunster had hopes that the ruins would provide more.

He had been at work from a very early hour when Stockton joined him at the burnt-out cottage, and had succeeded in uncovering the body with a minimum of disturbance. The superintendent, whose stomach in the early mornings was poor, eyed the grisly remains with disfavour. They were even more unpleasant than he had expected.

"He's not made a good job of it, has he?" was his first comment. "I should have thought, with that heat, there'd only have been the bones. There's quite a lot of flesh left."

"A body takes a lot of burning in a lump." Dunster was unaffected by such things. "Besides, you can see what happened. Some of the rubbish fell on the lower half of the trunk, and protected it from the worst heat... Anyhow, the head and hands take less burning."

"Hm... Might have been an attempt to hide the identity?"

"By destroying the hands and head separately? No, I think not. It all seems just as you'd expect it."

Stockton eyed the position of the body. "Put up a struggle, didn't he?" he suggested.

"Probably not. That's merely the effect of the heat on the tissues... In fact, I'm hoping that the doctors will say that he'd been dead for a few weeks; and that's the beauty of the body's not having been burnt completely. If it were proved that he'd only died recently, the defence might ask where he'd vanished to in the meantime."

Stockton had had enough of the body for the moment. He turned from it and cast an eye over the ruins.

"Anything else?" he asked.

"The teeth." Dunster indicated a little pile on a sheet of paper. "I think we've got them all. Either they fell out before the body was burnt, or when the jaw—"

Stockton made a gesture. "Will they be any use?" he asked.

"We know the dentist who made George Blakeney's set. He may be able to identify them... Luckily the plate is gold... And there are various oddments like buttons, coins, part of a pocket-knife, and two or three considerable pieces of burnt cloth... Yes, we should be able to establish identity all right. At least to the satisfaction of a magistrate. Stockton fancied he detected an undertone of doubt in the last words. He raised his eyebrows.

"Not to yours?" he asked.

"Oh, I suppose so... Only I wish we could have got things a little more settled... Any luck about Bere?"

"Yes. They sat up all night over him. I've the reports here—"

"I'll look at them later. What's the general idea?"

"Quite O.K... Bere died of a large dose of atropine—I gather that is belladonna. The capsules contain a solution of atropine, with certain impurities which are also present in the stomach. In other words, the capsules almost certainly did the business... Oh, and the doctor was right. They had previously contained ammoniated quinine... Also, I went to the Hall—"

Dunster frowned a little. "How are things there?" he asked.

"Better than I expected," Stockton answered. "I saw the girl—not that I wanted to. She doesn't blame us for her father's death... In any case, that was partly his own fault, and partly that idiot of a butler... She's convinced of her brother's innocence, of course, but not awkward... According to her, it's all a mistake, and we shall find the right man eventually."

"I wish it could be," Dunster said with real feeling. "But I don't see how. Unless the whole thing was a plant?"

"You don't think that?" Stockton was startled.

"I'm looking into it, anyway... It's all too easy... And that grave business— Are you doing anything about that by the way?"

Stockton had forgotten all about it. Luckily he had given instructions the day before, and he nodded.

"If it's any comfort to you," he said, "at this moment eight local constables are touring graveyards and bothering eight local vicars for details of interments. You should have a lovely lot of reports by lunch time—and I wish you joy of 'em."

Dunster ignored the sarcasm. "Any luck at the house?" he asked.

"Oh, I was going to tell you. I got a sample of the belladonna the old man used—in fact, I got the lot. Also a gun engraved with initials in the same way... Also a sample of ammunition... You see, it struck me that there might be some shot lodged in that skull, and we might be able to show it was the same kind—"

"Yes. That might be important, as the old man said that he gave the gun to Bere. Especially if Bere used a different kind of ammunition—which he probably doesn't... You've not seen Bere—Jim, I mean?"

"No. But he's at the cottage all right... Wonder what he was doing out last night?"

"That's one thing I'd like to know." Dunster thought for a moment. "I think I'll slip round and see him. The sergeant can carry on here."

The superintendent looked a little curiously towards where Comfrey was directing a group of searchers at the other end of the building.

"You seem to be making a job of it," he commented. "It'll take a year at this rate... What d'you expect to find?"

To his surprise, Dunster coloured a little. "I don't expect to find anything," he rejoined. But there's something I might find—which would make a good deal of difference. Well, I'll get going. So long."

Inspector Dunster was, in fact, more worried than he had been ready to admit about the easy success which had all at once rewarded their efforts. It was too easy. Of course, things sometimes happened that way. But, if it had been arranged, it could scarcely have been more simple and perfect. He racked his brains in vain, however, to find anyone who could conceivably want to get Richard accused of murder; or who could possibly have done it. The only person who occurred to him, even as a vague possibility, was da Vargas; and against him there was hardly an atom of evidence. Nevertheless, he made a mental note to consider the South American from the point of view of a potential murderer just as soon as he had time.

That did not look as though it would happen just yet. As he made his way along the lane, he thought of someone else whom he wished to see, and instead of taking the shortest way to the Beres' cottage, turned up towards the village. He found Tony Mayfield in the inn parlour, talking earnestly to another man who, to Dunster's discerning eye, had all the hallmarks of a reporter.

Tony was a little taken aback at the sight of the inspector. He had begun to hope that the police were satisfied with what they knew already, and would have no need of him as a witness. If they were going to start questioning him, it might hamper his own activities. He had to make up his mind quickly what to do.

"Right, John, then. See you in an hour's time," he said, dismissing his colleague and waiting for him to go before he turned to Dunster. "Good morning, Inspector," he said cheerfully. "I understand we can congratulate you. Good work... Anything for the Press?"

His manner might have irritated Dunster, and was perhaps meant to; but the inspector did not rise.

"Good morning, Mr. Mayfield," he rejoined. "No, I'm afraid there's nothing I can tell you... As we explained last night, all communications will be made by the superintendent or Chief Constable at the local station... But I believe you were not here when we told the others?"

"No, I believe I was out," Tony said sweetly.

"That's why I'm here, sir... I wanted to see you as a possible witness for the prosecution. I have reason to believe you can help us in some vital particulars."

That, Tony reflected, was first blood to the inspector. If there was one thing which he particularly did not want, it was to be called as a witness against Richard Blakeney. He played for time.

"Witness to what?" he asked.

"My sergeant informs me that you were following Mr. Richard Blakeney when he went to the cottage yesterday. Obviously, sir, that is important evidence. But, since your sergeant was also following Mr. Blakeney, I don't quite see why it should be necessary to ask me about it."

"In a serious charge such as murder, Mr. Mayfield, one cannot have too much corroboration... For example, I should like to know whether or not you saw him go inside."

"I did not... Is there any evidence whatever that he went inside at all?"

"Have you any, Mr. Mayfield?" Dunster countered.

Actually, Tony knew from Richard's own story that he had not only entered, but searched the place. But after all, what Richard told him was not, strictly speaking, evidence.

"I'm afraid not, Inspector," he answered.

Dunster tried another tack. "I believe, sir," he said, "that you were talking to Mr. Blakeney for some time before the actual arrest... Did he give any account of his actions to you?"

Tony thought. "If he had done," he said at last, "I don't see that I could repeat a confidence, in view of the fact that he has decided not to make a statement to the police."

"I won't remind you that there is such a thing as withholding material evidence," Dunster said patiently. "But I would point out, Mr. Mayfield, that we can prove all we want from the prosecution side about that visit. By withholding an explanation which we could test for ourselves, Mr. Blakeney is probably doing himself more harm than good."

"And naturally the police are anxious to find all the evidence they can in favour of the man they've just charged with murder."

Dunster faced him squarely. "I don't see why not, Mr. Mayfield," he said. "In fact, if you really are on Mr. Blakeney's side, I believe the biggest service you could do him would be to collaborate a little more with us."

"Really?" Tony smiled. "And how much time are the police likely to devote between now and the prosecution to proving his innocence?"

"Speaking for myself, just as much as I can spare," Dunster said seriously. "Look here, Mr. Mayfield. Admittedly there are reasons why you and the police are a little at cross-purposes in this business. But, in view of the seriousness of the affair, I think it might be as well to forget old grudges and tell us what you know."

"Why?" Tony demanded.

"Because I don't believe you're a fool by any means—" He ignored Tony's murmured thanks and went on: "And I believe you may have found out a certain amount that we don't know. On the other hand, we probably know things you don't. And that's where the danger comes in."

Tony eyed him with a puzzled frown.

"I mean that, if two people know half the truth, the views they form may both be different, and probably both wrong. And if you're convinced of Mr. Blakeney's innocence, all you can desire is that the whole truth shall be known."

Tony considered. He was inclined to like Inspector Dunster, and more than half convinced by what he had said. On the other hand, he scarcely felt justified in telling everything on his own account. He must consult Alness at least.

"Look here," he said after a pause. "I might be able to help— I only say, I might. If, on thinking things over, there's anything that occurs to me, I'll give you a call at the station in an hour or two."

Dunster accepted that. "Very well, Mr. Mayfield," he said. "But don't forget that time may be precious. Supposing someone else is guilty of the murder, it may give him some chance to escape."

That brought Tony up with a jerk. He suddenly remembered that Crouch and his sister had been driving away in a car the night before. Almost certainly they were somehow connected with the business. If they were the murderers? After all, no one had made any confidences to him on that subject.

"There's one thing," he said, and the inspector turned in the doorway. "I don't know if you've heard that a chap called Crouch has been talking rather at large about Mr. George Blakeney. He suggests, at least, that he can reveal some scandal or other, and it's possible that he may have attempted some blackmail—"

"About Mr. George Blakeney's bigamous marriage," Dunster interposed. "Yes, Mr. Mayfield—"

"You know that?" Tony looked surprised. "Well, quite by chance yesterday afternoon, I happened to see the man and his sister. They were driving away in a hired car, and had luggage with them—"

Dunster swore under his breath. He felt himself partly to blame, because in the rush of events he had completely forgotten them. But that did not lessen his anger with Tony.

"You saw them leaving yesterday afternoon—and you tell me now, sir—"

"I'm sorry," Tony said quite humbly. "But of course at the time I didn't know the importance of it. And since then—"

"You could describe the car? You took its number?"

Tony shook his head. "I only know it was a big car, dark-coloured, and it looked hired," he said. "But you might be able to trace it at the garages."

"We might," Dunster said with suppressed exasperation. "And now, before I go, Mr. Mayfield, are you quite sure there's nothing else you've forgotten?"

"One thing, perhaps," Tony said. It was verging on the borderline, but he took the plunge. "I don't know if you're still interested in the anonymous letters? Well, I happened to see a copy of one yesterday— I'm not prepared at the moment to say how—and two possible clues suggested themselves—that the man was an artist and a foreigner—"

"Why?"

"The letter was written in Indian ink, and the number seven was crossed like an F. I think it might be worth your while to consider those possibilities." He saw the question rising on Dunster's lips, and forestalled it. "That's all I'm free to tell you just now, Inspector. Perhaps in an hour or two—"

"I think you will be well-advised to tell me everything," Dunster said grimly. "But you can think—or talk—it over... Good day, Mr. Mayfield."

Dunster was distinctly annoyed as he left the inn, and he was also in a hurry. He brushed by two reporters who emerged from the bar in a very cavalier fashion, which got him a bad word next morning, and set off for the telephone. A message to the station immediately might make up for his own forgetfulness and Tony's delay; and he was not going to make the mistake of neglecting another possible line in Bere. As he finished the call and started off towards the gamekeeper's cottage, he devoted his mind to the other half of the information he had just received.

Whose letter had Tony seen? In all probability it was one written to Alness, Richard or Virginia—since he had been surprised in conference with them, and apparently on excellent terms the night before. Dunster told himself he must see that letter. There were several curious points about it. First, none of the others had been written in Indian ink. Then why had this one? Then the police actually possessed the letter bearing the inscription "No. 7," and on that the figure was written in the ordinary way. Why was it written differently on this? And again Tony had said "Number seven" and not "Figure seven." That suggested that the seven had appeared in an actual number at the top of the letter. But it was not the original "No. 7," and the next possibility was "No. 17." So far as they knew, only eight letters had been written in all, and these they had. The one Tony had seen made nine—leaving eight successive numbers about which no one had reported. Who had got those?

By the time he reached Bere's cottage, he had reached the determination that he would get the information from Tony that morning by peaceful means, or else he would stretch his authority to the utmost to force him. In the meantime, he dismissed it from his mind, and concentrated on the problem of Bere. He was going to need delicate handling on the subject of the gun if he were not to turn obstinate; about his walk up the hill Dunster had very little hope, if there was anything behind it. But he would have to do his best.

There was no smoke coming from the cottage chimney. The whole place looked deserted. Perhaps Bere was out on another mysterious errand. Dunster opened the gate silently and walked in, treading on the grass beside the gravel path as he moved towards the door. Then, as he reached the house, instead of knocking openly, he stepped across the path to the window, and peered in.

Jim Bere was not out. But he had obviously just been going out, or had just come in. He wore his hat, and a stick was lying on the table beside him. His back was towards Dunster, and his body partly obscured whatever it was he was bending over. Then, as some sixth sense apparently warned him, he turned, and Dunster saw the medicine bottle in his hand. And simultaneously the inspector let out a yell of pain and surprise. Something gripped him with painful violence by the right calf.

# 20

---

# Wrong Lady

THE INTERVIEW WITH THE inspector left Tony a prey to mixed feelings. He had woken up that morning with a strong conviction of Richard Blakeney's innocence which did not rest merely on his feelings towards Virginia. Damaging though it had been in its admissions, and difficult to confirm on any vital point, he believed Richard Blakeney's statement, and had been absolutely determined to foil the apparent intention of the police to prove him guilty by any means in his power.

Dunster's arguments had shaken him. The possession of exclusive information dear to any journalist which he had regarded as a possible weapon suddenly seemed very much more of a responsibility. Obviously it was impossible for the police to confide in him; but it was quite conceivable that, as the inspector had pointed out, the combined knowledge of the two parties would indicate the real answer.

By the time he had smoked a cigarette, he had practically decided that the only thing to do was to tell the police everything; and yet he must at least warn Alness of his intention, even if he was not bound to get his assent. And it was with this end in view that he finally left the inn and set off down the street.

Even on so innocent an errand, there were precautions to be observed. By this time the number of reporters permanently stationed in the village had swollen to seven, and among one or two of them he had observed a disposition to dog his footsteps as the simplest method of picking his brains. So far, Alness had been relatively free from their attentions, and he had no intention of setting the hunt in that direction. It was therefore by a circuitous route, and after setting off in entirely the wrong direction, that he finally reached the head of the lane leading past the burnt cottage.

That was his most direct route; but it led past an obvious danger point. Most of his colleagues, including his own reporter, were probably keeping a watchful eye upon the police investigations which were still proceeding among the ruins, and he must somehow dodge them. Instead of turning down the lane, he chose the track which continued along the hillside and, apparently, led only to the farm visible a quarter of a mile ahead. That would take him past the cottage, and he could cut across the fields to Alness's house.

Certainly there was plenty of activity at the scene of the fire. From the vantage point the hill gave him, he could trace the whole course of the lane along the valley bottom, and there was quite a little crowd on the site, with at least three cars. One was just starting back as he drew level, and as he followed it with his eyes towards the tall trees by the bend, a thought suddenly came to him like a thunderclap. He had forgotten all about the message he was to have given to Newent from his daughter.

His first reaction was a feeling of surprised annoyance. Even the rapid course of events immediately afterwards could hardly excuse the complete blackout of so dramatic a meeting, and with a guilty sensation he reflected that, as a result, Newent must have been in complete ignorance of what had happened to his daughter. He reproached himself severely, and tried to find comfort in the fact that the incident had been so far off the main line of happenings. But had it? After all, the Newents were connected most vitally with the whole affair. If either of them had any mysterious errand it was very likely indeed that it was somehow connected with the main problem. It suddenly seemed to him an important question where she had come from, and where she had been going.

The gate over which she had climbed was plainly visible. On the other side of the lane towards the lake, the woods prevented any hint of her direction being gathered. So he thought at first. Then as his eyes studied the lay of the land, he realised that this was not entirely the case. The one reason which he could imagine for anyone to take that particular course was a desire to take as short a cut as possible to the other side of the lake. And beyond the lake, just visible above the woods, he could make out the roof of a cottage which might have been her destination. With a slight shock of surprise he realised that it was Bere's.

The curving of the roads to avoid the lake had misled him. He had thought of the gamekeepers' cottage as being in the park; but the park itself stretched in a half-circle, with da Vargas's house adjoining on one side near Bere's cottage, and Alness's smaller establishment making an indentation on the other. And the gamekeepers, and for that matter da Vargas, had a distinct connection with the problem.

If that was her destination, where had she come from? Not from the bungalow, which lay almost behind him. If she had wanted a short cut from there, she would have turned off to the right of the main road, and not circled round to the left. From the Hall or from Alness's she would have gone round the other side of the lake, and the sole remaining possibility seemed to be the steep hill crowned with pinewoods which rose on his left.

He realised all at once that he must be almost on the very route that she had taken. There was an irregular line of gates, though not a real track, leading from the lane to the farm road;

and the hedges were sufficiently thick to make it very unlikely that she could have deviated from it in the dark. She must have passed only a few yards ahead of him, and it was conceivable that, in the mud which seemed a normal accompaniment of gates in that part, she might have left some traces. With the idea, he started forward; and then suddenly stopped. A woman's figure had shown for a moment in a gap of the hedge just ahead.

It had been the merest glimpse, but it changed his plans completely. Alness and the police must wait. It might, of course, be someone else entirely on some perfectly normal errand; but there was at least a sporting chance. With the enthusiasm of the chase outweighing all other considerations he started to follow.

They regained the farm road and crossed it. Ahead, his quarry showed tantalisingly from time to time, never long enough for a fair view. The actual line of gates stopped; but gave place to a footpath, which plunged down into a little valley to cross a stream before it sidled up a steep slope covered with hazels. For half a minute Tony had a fair view of the girl, and he was conscious of a doubt. Certainly the figure was about the right height and age; there was even something familiar about it; and yet—

As the girl disappeared into the bushes, his thoughts broke off abruptly, as he became aware of the danger of losing touch in the thicker ground ahead.

He started forward again in haste; and as he crossed the brook a faint track leading off to the left suggested a possibility of more than making up lost ground. The path which the girl had chosen curved round the hill to avoid the steepest slope; this went straight up, and at the cost of a scramble would save more than half the distance. He turned off, and for the next few minutes had no time to think of anything but keeping his footing in the slippery sand. The track disappeared completely; it was a matter of pushing himself between the bushes and pulling himself up as best he could. An unusually thick patch of brambles tugged at him viciously. He tore his way through by main force, and unexpectedly found himself on the path.

A quick glance up the slope showed no sign of his quarry. He turned to look the other way; and found himself face to face with Virginia Blakeney.

She had stopped dead at the sight of him; and for a second or two they stood staring at each other. Tony was utterly unprepared for the meeting, or with any explanation of his sudden emergence from a blackberry bush. It was the girl who first managed a rather uncertain smile.

"Good morning, Mr. Mayfield—" she said and hesitated. "I—I didn't expect—"

There was a constraint in her manner which was hardly accounted for by his surprise appearance. Tony coloured, as the horrible suspicion crossed his mind that she had realised that he had been following her. He made an effort to retrieve the situation.

"Neither did I," he said with an assumption of cheerfulness. "In fact, I didn't expect to be here at all… I was trying a short cut, and a blackberry bush didn't like it—"

He suddenly felt his lightness was terribly forced; and in the same instant was conscious of the effect on his appearance of his crawl up the hill and a cheek torn by the thorns. Instinctively he straightened his tie and brushed at his coat.

The smile on the girl's face faded. She eyed him for a moment.

"You were following me," she said simply, but there was an accusation in the words. "I saw you—over by the lake, going in quite a different direction."

A little flush which was not embarrassment came on her cheeks. Tony had been on the point of denial, but her last words deprived him even of that. It was impossible to explain, other than by telling the truth, why he should suddenly have departed from his original direction by some ninety degrees.

"I wasn't—really, I wasn't, Miss Blakeney," he protested. "That is, I didn't know it was you... I thought it was—was someone who might be connected with—with all that's been happening, and I couldn't understand what was the idea of coming up here—"

His obvious embarrassment and sincerity convinced her, and her face showed signs of relenting. Tony hurried on.

"Though, as a matter of fact, I did want to see you... I was on my way to see your cousin when I saw you—I mean, when I thought I saw—"

"I'm sorry, Mr. Mayfield," she said simply, and then a sudden hope showed in her eyes. "You—you've found out something—you've discovered who—?"

"No," Tony admitted. "It was the whole thing I wanted to talk about. Whether we're on the right lines or not. You see, I had a visit from Dunster this morning—"

She glanced at her wristwatch, and there was a little frown of bewilderment on her face.

"I—I can't wait now, Mr. Mayfield," she said. "I have to—to see someone... Perhaps you'd better see my cousin. I must go—"

Whether it was the mention of Dunster's name or not, the constraint had returned to her manner. She turned to resume her way up the hill. Tony made a last effort.

"But, Miss Blakeney, I must talk to you for a few minutes," he began. "You see—"

She had actually turned her back. Now she glanced round, and there was certainly doubt and suspicion in her face.

"I'm sorry," she repeated. "I really can't wait, Mr. Mayfield—good morning."

She had actually gone three or four yards up the hill before Tony found an answer. Certainly there was no encouragement in her manner to continue the conversation. Tony stood staring after her; then a sort of angry desperation came over him. In two or three strides he regained her side.

"I'll walk a little way with you if I may, Miss Blakeney," he said, and saw the refusal on her lips. "I must speak to you," he said grimly. "I've got to see the inspector again soon—"

"Well?"

There was an icy sound about the monosyllable; but Tony's blood was up, and he was prepared to brave any amount of snubbing.

"It's just this," he said. "Dunster knows very well that Richard talked to us last night. He believes that I know a good deal which might help them in the case—"

"Against my brother?"

"No. I didn't mean that. Nor did he. I honestly think he's perfectly willing to investigate other possibilities; and there's no sense in ignoring the simple fact that the police have a far better chance of dealing with a murder than any outsider can have. I think it would probably be much better for me to tell him everything I can."

He waited for some comment, glancing towards the half-averted face, but she would neither look at him nor reply. Only she walked a little more quickly.

"You see," Tony went on a little desperately, "since your brother has made no statement, it doesn't give Dunster much to go on... He told us everything last night, and I believed it. If the police knew, they might be able to prove it true to their own satisfaction. If not, there is a danger that Richard—"

"But Richard is no danger—" she broke out, and stopped. Tony waited for her to continue or explain. But she said nothing.

"I don't understand," he said hopelessly. "Yesterday, when your brother was merely under suspicion, and there wasn't even any evidence of a murder at all, you were worried about him. Now, when he's actually charged, and when there's what seems to be an unbreakable case against him, you say there's no danger... Miss Blakeney, please believe that I want to do all I can to help and that in suggesting this—"

The path suddenly emerged upon a secondary road. She stopped and faced him.

"Mr. Mayfield," she said. "I want no help from you."

"But, Miss Blakeney, what am I to do?" Tony demanded. "The inspector will be asking me again—"

"As to how far you are prepared to respect my brother's confidence, it is a matter for yourself... You will no doubt continue to serve your newspaper... But I and my family want no help from you."

She paused, perhaps to let that sink in, or waiting for a reply; but Tony made none. His own temper was beginning to rise, and he felt that he was being treated with a good deal less than justice. On the other hand, to quarrel would only make things worse. He kept silence, not without an effort.

"And now, Mr. Mayfield, perhaps you would be good enough to leave me." There were no signs of relenting in her voice, or in the face which she turned defiantly upon him. "No doubt, in your occupation, you are often under the necessity of forcing your company where it is not wanted. But I hope that, since I can assure you there is nothing to be gained by it, you will make an exception and leave me alone."

Tony stood looking at her, and he was angry too. At that moment he would have liked to shake her. And then the signs of grief in her face and the reddened eyelids brought a sudden sympathy. If only he could help— But there was plainly no dealing with her in her present mood. He accepted his dismissal.

"Very well, Miss Blakeney," he said. "I'm sorry you feel like this about me... Good morning."

He did not wait for a reply; though he listened for one as he walked away. But none came. He went forward resolutely without turning his head, and had gone about fifty yards before the temptation overcame him. He looked round. Virginia was hurrying up the hill in the opposite direction, and showed no sign of turning. Tony faced right round, and stood gazing after her with a frown of bewilderment on his face. Her whole changed attitude was incomprehensible, and although he could make every allowance for the effect of events of the night before he felt hurt in spite of himself.

Still without a glance behind her, she was nearing a point where the road curved, and in a moment would be hidden from view. She disappeared round the bend, and Tony was in the very act of turning away when a figure slipped from the bushes at the roadside, glanced quickly round, then moved towards the bend, very obviously in pursuit.

# 21

---

# Cain or Abel?

DUNSTER DID NOT SEE how Bere reacted to his shout. He was too much interested in the large dog of indeterminate breed which was firmly clasping his leg in a pair of very well-equipped jaws, and looking, on the whole, quite amiable and pleased about it, with one floppy ear half cocked, and a pair of very bright eyes fixed upon him warily. Only as he made a move the lips rose in a snarl, and the pressure increased painfully. On the whole, the best thing to do seemed to be to stay still. Then the door opened, and Bere emerged. He eyed the inspector expressionlessly for a moment.

"Off, Towser," he said in a conversational tone.

The dog released his grip, jumped a couple of yards away, and sat eyeing Dunster speculatively, lolling out a long red tongue with every appearance of satisfaction. Dunster rubbed his leg. So far as he could make out, there was no great harm done. He looked up to see something approaching a grim smile on the gamekeeper's face.

"Towser doesn't like strangers snooping round, sir," he commented. "Lucky you stood still—"

"I was just trying to find out if you were in—" Dunster said defensively. "I wanted a word with you—"

"I generally knock at the door myself, sir," the gamekeeper said dryly. "Come in, sir... Good dog, Towser."

Dunster followed him inside. It could only have been a minute between the time Dunster had seen him and the opening of the door, but the table was empty. That was interesting, Dunster thought. Whatever Bere had been doing, it was something he wanted to conceal. He glanced casually round as he accepted the offer of a seat, but there was no clue to what it might have been.

"Well, sir?" Bere demanded.

"I shan't keep you more than a few minutes," Dunster said with a suggestion of apology. "I'm afraid you were going out?"

Bere did not rise to that one way or the other. He simply waited.

"There are one or two things I wanted to ask you," Dunster went on. "I expect you've heard about the body in the cottage. Well, I think we can say that the identity is established. I'm afraid that there's no doubt it was Mr. George Blakeney—" That produced an effect. A kind of flicker passed over the gamekeeper's impassive features, leaving them almost as blank as ever. But not quite. There was a subdued gleam in his eyes which Dunster wished he could understand as he answered:

"No doubt, sir?"

"Very little, I'm afraid. Of course, it's badly burnt, but there's enough to identify it... But we found something else. A gun, or what was left of one."

Bere had a great capacity for silence. He continued to say nothing.

"I should like you to have a look at it later," Dunster went on. "We understand that it belonged to Mr. Richard Blakeney, and that it was given by him to your brother... Is that correct? I mean, that Mr. Richard Blakeney gave your brother a gun?"

"Ay," Bere assented slowly. "He gave him one, sir. But poor Joe didn't have it long, sir. It were lost."

"Lost?"

"Well, sir, stolen, Joe always said. You see, he'd just put it down against a tree, sir, and he weren't away two minutes, and it had gone."

"When was this? Where did it happen?"

"Last autumn, sir. There was just a little family shooting party up by the pinewoods there. And 'tis a mystery who had it, for Joe searched the wood properly, but it were gone, and he never saw 'un again."

"The pinewood?" Dunster echoed. He felt that that ought to fit in somehow, but he could not see where. In the meantime it provided a handy opening. He left the gun for the moment. "By the way, you were up there last night, weren't you?"

Obviously that question told somehow, but Dunster wished that Bere's face registered his emotions more adequately. The gamekeeper considered.

"Might have been," he said dubiously.

"Well, I saw you," Dunster said.

"Ay... Come to think of it, I came back that way You saw me, sir? I didn't notice you?"

Dunster had no intention of revealing that he had been hiding behind a bush. He changed the subject.

"By the way," he said. "It's a funny thing... we had a chap come into the station yesterday, who swore he'd seen a ghost up there... Did you ever hear it was haunted?"

"Haunted?" There was derision in Bere's voice. "No, sir. First I've heard tell of it. And I've been up there all times of the day and night and all weathers."

"And you never saw anything?"

"There be nothing to see, sir."

"At any rate, you didn't see anything last night?" Dunster returned to the charge.

Bere shook his head.

"You said you were coming back? Might I ask where you'd been?"

Bere received the question with perfect calm. But then by that time he might have been ready for it.

"Just from my cousin's. I'd looked in, you see, to tell him about Joe."

Dunster thought he would enquire about that, but it was likely enough. He wanted to ask Bere a few more things; but he also wanted to prepare his ground a little first. He got up.

Bere seemed oddly reluctant to let him go, though Dunster had seen him steal glances at the clock. He came to the point as Dunster moved towards the door.

"About them things, sir," he said hesitantly. "The capsules, I mean... I were muddled, sir. What Joe—what Joe said to me were that a gentleman had given him them, and I thought in my mind it must have been Mr. Richard or Mr. George. Of course, I was wrong, sir. Mr. George couldn't have done it, for he'd gone, hadn't he, sir? And Mr. Richard—Mr. Richard—"

He broke off. His face was working under what must have been strong emotion.

"Well?" Dunster asked coldly.

"Well, sir, neither of them wouldn't have given them, not if they'd known what was in them. That's all I've got to say, sir."

Dunster considered him. This latest improvement upon what he had said in the first instance must have some significance. Equally, it must be a lie. And a lie, presumably, to shield both Richard and the dead George.

"You said a gentleman gave them to him," he repeated. "But what gentleman was he likely to meet up there?"

Bere frowned with the effort of thought; then his face cleared.

"There's that foreigner chap, sir," he said. "It might have been him, sir. He be often up that way, sir—"

"On the Blakeneys' land?"

"Well, no, sir... But the parks run adjoining just there. Now, I wouldn't be surprised if it weren't he, sir."

"Mr. da Vargas?" Dunster asked. He was not inclined to believe a word of it, but the particular form the lie had taken was interesting. "But why should he give your brother anything?"

"Ah, why should he?" the gamekeeper repeated with bent brows; then he looked up quickly. "Mind you, sir, I'm not saying he did give them. Only that he might have done—"

Dunster fancied he detected a belated repentance at the false accusation; in any case, he decided to leave it at that for the present. There was still another point, which had, in fact, been the main reason for his coming.

"Perhaps you could tell me whether your brother used the same type of cartridge as those at the Hall?" he asked. "I mean, for the gun he lost?"

"He would, sir... Mr. Richard used to order all the cartridges, sir, and we brought down what we wanted." He glanced at the clock. "If that's all sir—?"

"Ah. You were going out?" Dunster asked, but got no answer. "Well, I won't keep you any longer just now... Good day."

As a liar, Dunster reflected as he got into the car, Bere had the qualification of a poker face, but otherwise showed a regrettable lack of finesse—for example, in being so obviously eager to get rid of his visitor as soon as he had said his piece. As he let in the clutch, aware of the gamekeeper's stare, he found himself wondering what the exact significance of the interview might be. There were several curious points. For one thing, there was something about the pinewood which made Bere uncomfortable. There had been a distinct reaction to his mention of the identification of George Blakeney's body; and finally there was the lie which the gamekeeper had gone out of his way to tell.

At the moment, however, he had no time to reflect on all that; for he drove only until the car was out of sight round the first corner before he stopped and jumped out. A few steps back brought him within view of the cottage, and of Bere himself. The gamekeeper had evidently been standing there until the car was out of sight; for after a moment he turned and entered the cottage. When he emerged a minute later, he was carrying a basket in his hand, and instead of coming out into the lane, he moved round to the back of the house, opened a small gate into the field, and crossed towards the wood.

That was precisely what Dunster had been hoping for. He waited only until the other had a fair start before he himself pushed his way through the hedge, and started along the side of a hedge which gave him cover as far as the wood. The track which Bere must have followed was plain enough, apparently leading in the direction of the lake. In a more open patch he had a glimpse of the other for a moment, and, satisfied that Bere was unsuspicious, started after him. Then as he rounded the trunk of a large tree he came to a full stop.

The dog was sitting in the path immediately in front of him, looking at him quizzically with his head on one side. No doubt he looked harmless enough, and normally Dunster was fond of dogs; but he was not so sure. With an assumption of confidence he did not feel he took a couple of steps forward. Towser rose to his feet and stood waiting. At the next step, he seemed to tense a little, and his lip rose the merest fraction. Dunster stopped again, and swore under his breath; then he laughed.

There was no getting past the dog. Bere had obviously suspected his intention, and had left this rear-guard behind him. It was annoying, but he could not see what was to be done about it.

"All right, Towser," he said. "I'll give you best... Good dog."

Towser acknowledged the compliment with a conciliating wag of his tail, but his eye was unwavering. Dunster turned in ignominious retreat, and made his way towards the car, making a mental note to put someone on to watch Bere's comings and goings—though how anyone was to do it was another matter.

The clock on the dashboard told him that it was nearly lunchtime, and he was feeling distinctly hungry. There was just time, he decided, to go round by the ruin and see how the work there was progressing. And, after that, he had a good deal he wanted to talk over with the superintendent...

Stockton had not waited for his colleague. He was already busily engaged upon a cold pie, and though he cast a curious glance at the brown-paper parcel which Dunster placed on the sideboard, at the precise moment his jaws were too busily engaged upon a particularly durable piece of crust to put the question. Instead, he waved a hand invitingly to the pie, and then pointed to the pile of papers beside the second plate. Dunster picked them up.

"Oh. The reports from the graveyards... I was just wanting them—"

He sat down, and forgetful of the meal, started to skim through them. Stockton recovered his power of speech.

"Most of 'em," he said. "There's a couple still to come in... What have you got there?"

Apparently Dunster did not hear him. He was going through the reports with a systematic care which seemed to the superintendent worthy of a better cause. Two or three he sorted out to one side, and apparently these were the cream of the collection, for he read and re-read them before they were finally reduced to one. Only then he looked up to see Stockton eyeing him sardonically.

"Nice lot, aren't they?" he asked. "I told 'em they were important, and you wanted 'em particularly... And you've got a detailed life-and-death history of everyone who's died recently for ten miles round... What's your little exhibit?"

"It may not be important," Dunster said slowly. "But I think it is. It's what I hoped to find at the cottage. And I think it's the first real flaw."

"Flaw?" Stockton echoed. "In what?"

"Well, I've an idea that, up till now, everything has gone exactly according to plan—the murderer's plan. Everything has gone exactly as he calculated—"

"Except for the minor detail that we've arrested him," Stockton suggested.

Dunster looked at him for a moment. "Have we?" he asked quietly.

The superintendent's eyebrows rose. "Good heavens," he said. "You don't mean to say that Richard is innocent?"

"I'd hardly go so far. But I can see quite a possibility that he might be—"

"But, dash it all, you could hardly ask for a clearer case than there is against him," Stockton protested.

"That's it. It's too clear. It's so clear that I'm more than half inclined to suspect a plant." He saw the objection rising to the superintendent's lips, and went on determinedly. "In fact, I suspect that up to date we've found out precisely what we were meant to find out; and that we're mistaken in thinking the murder of Bere or of George was the main fact in all this."

"Really?" Stockton asked. "Then, brushing aside an unimportant detail like a couple of corpses, what is the main point?"

Dunster ignored the sarcasm. "The murder of Richard Blakeney," he answered.

The superintendent stared at him for a moment; then he exploded.

"But, damn it, Richard hasn't been murdered! And what's more, no one can murder him in gaol—"

"Except the hangman." Dunster was very serious. "Suppose the main plot is to make us the instruments of the murder—by getting an innocent man convicted and executed."

"It's utter rot," Stockton rejoined. "If you're going to commit a couple of murders, in order to get someone hanged, why not just murder him right off?"

"That's one thing I don't understand," Dunster admitted. "I mean the second murder—the poisoning... The rest would all fit in."

"But it does fit in at the moment," Stockton said hopelessly. "It all fits in neatly with Richard's being the murderer."

"There's something that doesn't." Dunster jerked a thumb towards the parcel. "And I've an idea that this"—he held up the selected report—"I've an idea that this is something else."

"I don't know what you're talking about," Stockton said with something like desperation in his voice. "What have you got?"

"Let me just ask you something. Why did Richard go to the cottage that morning?"

"To set fire to it, of course."

"Exactly... But he might have been induced to go there somehow. Anyhow, it was working on that assumption that I found that—or rather Comfrey did." He rose and picked up the parcel. "Granting you believe Richard is innocent, what would you expect this to be?"

Stockton only shrugged.

"Well, as a precautionary measure, I did suppose him innocent; I told them what to look for, and they found it. That's a first check. Now, we can get another one. If I'm right, I can tell you what we'll find when we dig up this grave—"

"Dig—it—up?" Stockton said weakly. "But you've read the report. There's not the faintest indication that it's ever been disturbed at all."

"But we've got to dig it up," Dunster said firmly. "And as soon as possible."

"There'll be trouble," Stockton prophesied with deep gloom. "They're very funny about exhumations... And we've had three—none of which showed a thing."

"It's got to be done. I'll get on the phone and see if I can hurry it up a bit... And in the meantime, I'll write down the answer and give it you. You can look at it afterwards—or now if you like."

He scribbled a few lines on a leaf of his notebook, produced an envelope, and was on the point of sealing it when Stockton stretched out his hand and took it.

"I'll buy it," he said. "Never was much use at guessing games— Great Scott!"

He stared at the sheet; then looked at Dunster.

"But why?" he demanded.

"It's obvious enough," Dunster said tantalisingly, and cut the string of the parcel.

"And anyway, what's all that rubbish?" Stockton scowled at the fused heap of brass and iron that the unfolding paper revealed.

"Just a clock," Dunster answered.

# 22

## Tony Makes a Capture

IT WAS WITH NO thought of shadowing that Tony started off up the hill. Even in his present temper and to save his life, he would never have spied upon Virginia Blakeney. He was equally determined that no one else should. Possibly it was one of Dunster's men. That made no difference. Whoever the shadower might be, Tony proposed to invite him, very politely, to go somewhere else rather quickly. If it came to a fight, so much the better.

But he had his work cut out. The man, whoever it might be, had got a good start, and just round the bend Tony almost missed him completely. The man, and presumably Virginia, had left the road, and was going straight up the hill towards the wood, and it was by the merest chance Tony saw him.

After that it was simply a matter of speed, and Tony had it. He was not trying to conceal himself, and the other man was. But he was much too intent on what was ahead to look round. By the time they reached the top, Tony was hardly a dozen yards away. Then he caught a glimpse of Virginia.

Inside the wood itself there was practically no under-growth, and the trees were planted regularly, allowing long vistas between the lines of trunks. She was at the far end, where the light filtered through the thinning boughs, and just at the moment he saw her was disappearing behind a shed which stood at the edge of the plantation. Then she had gone, and though he waited for her to reappear there was no sign of her. It looked as if she had gone inside.

Momentarily he had forgotten all about the stranger. He looked round to find him. There he was, apparently giving a ludicrous impersonation of a Boy Scout on the warpath, peering cautiously, dodging from tree to tree, and occasionally crawling. It seemed fairly certain that he was not a policeman, though who he might be was a complete mystery.

Apparently his object was to make a circuit of the hut and take up a position at one side that would command the entrance. With his bloodthirsty intentions momentarily forgotten in the mere excitement of the game, Tony stood watching him until he finally gained a clump of bracken in a suitable position, and, since he did not emerge, had apparently decided to stay there.

It was time to make a move. Tony did not particularly mind being seen by Virginia or anyone who might be in the hut. In fact on more sober reflection he was disposed to think it would be better to find out what was happening first, and perhaps warn her, before proceeding to more violent extremes. By keeping the hut itself between him and the watcher he could get there without any trouble, and the sight of a door on the side nearest to him made him hopeful about actually obtaining an entrance unobserved.

There was no sign that anyone had noticed him as he gained the back of the building. He moved along to investigate the entrance which he had noticed.

Before he reached it he realised that he was in all likelihood doomed to disappointment. That part of the place was a lean-to, built on to the main structure, and in all probability there was no communication between the two. Still, there was an outside chance. The door was only secured by a drop bar without padlock, and he opened it cautiously.

It looked pitch black inside at first. He stepped inside and the door swung to behind him. As his eyes became accustomed to the gloom, he saw that his fears had been justified. It was the merest box of a place, without an opening that he could see in its four walls, except the door by which he had entered, and it contained nothing more interesting than a few planks against the wall at one side. Obviously he could do nothing there. He was on the point of going out again, when he caught the sound of voices.

He listened. There were no intelligible words. It was a queer, mumbling kind of sound, apparently a man's voice; though he would not have sworn to that. Obviously it came somehow through the wall of the main building.

Tony had no intention of eavesdropping any more than of spying on Virginia, but for the moment he did not know what to do. The puzzle was to know who was with her on the other side of the wall. He could only think of Alness. Although it was ridiculous, he was conscious of a faint twinge of jealousy. And then Virginia's voice reached him. It was raised as if under the impulse of some strong emotion, and the words reached him quite clearly.

"But he's my brother... We can't give him up... There must be somewhere where we could hide him—"

Another voice, and he fancied this time it was a feminine voice, answered, apparently arguing the matter. Then Virginia spoke again, and he caught the name "Richard" with just after it the word "escape".

They brought a sudden illumination. That must be it. By some means or other, Richard had contrived to escape from the police, though how he could have done was a mystery. Perhaps he had been hurt. That would account for the mumbling, delirious tones of the male speaker. And Virginia was determined to hide him.

It was absurd, of course. The police were bound to search in the neighbourhood of the village, and undoubtedly they would watch the activities of the Blakeney family. And even as he decided that the whole thing was utterly idiotic, he made up his mind that he would help. With that one idea in his mind, he pushed the door open and stepped out.

He had forgotten the watcher. Now, while he was still blinking in the sunlight, he saw him. He seemed to be doing another of his scouting acts, and this time had circled the building again, and was coming up from behind. At the precise instant that Tony emerged, he had made one of his dramatic pauses to look behind him, and was turned the other way. Tony had about a second to make up his mind. He slipped round the corner to the front of the house.

He listened. All at once he was aware of stealthy footsteps approaching the side which he had just left. There was a pause; then a faint creaking of the door. Tony could resist the temptation no longer. He peered round just in time to see the door closing, apparently behind the stranger, for there was no one visible.

The idea came to him so suddenly that he had no time to reflect upon it or on its possible consequences. In an instant he had covered the yard or two between him and the door, and noiselessly slipped the bar into place.

There was a moment's pause. Presumably the man inside was satisfying himself that that part of the place was empty. Or perhaps he was listening. Tony himself stood there, momentarily astonished by the brilliance of his own manoeuvre. And then came the sound of someone trying the door.

Tony watched the woodwork move with a kind of detached fascination. The door, like the rest of the shed, was a good, stout piece of work, and not likely to succumb easily. From the inside, there was no shifting the bar. In fact, so far as he could see, there was no reason why his prisoner should not remain there as long as they wanted. And in the meantime, he could see Virginia, and perhaps they could get Richard away—

The shed door was tried again, this time regardless of any noise. Evidently the man inside was using all his strength. He must have realised his position. Tony had just satisfied himself that this latest effort was in vain, when there was a terrific outcry from inside the shed. Tony decided he had better make a move. He darted round the corner of the shed, and came face to face with Virginia.

Her face was pale with fear and bewilderment, but she held her ground in spite of the suddenness of his appearance. Then, as she saw who it was, a sudden flush which might have been anger reddened her cheeks. Tony spoke hurriedly.

"Look here, Vir—Miss Blakeney. I didn't mean to follow you or anything like that. But there was a chap going after you, and I thought I'd better stop him... He's in there now."

Their prisoner, in fact, was making no secret of his presence. A perfect hail of blows was resounding on the door, punctuated at intervals by shouts which grew more and more incoherent. Virginia stared with frightened eyes, then looked desperately at Tony.

"He'll get tired of that," Tony commented heartlessly. "If no one hears him— But, I say, we must do something... Please let me help. I know what the position is more or less. Your brother—"

"You know—? But then—"

"It's all right. I don't think anyone else does." With the fear that an accusation of eavesdropping might shatter what seemed to be a reconciliation, Tony did not particularise. "Well, I'm not sure that the best thing wouldn't be to give himself up and make a clean breast of it, but I'm ready to do anything you want. But we must do something quickly. We must get him away from here—"

"But—but we can't... He—he's ill. He doesn't know what he's saying. If they heard—"

"All the more reason for getting him out of the way," Tony said firmly. "The question is where can he go to?"

"I—I don't know... I don't know what to do. Oh—"

She buried her face in her hands and burst into the sobbing that comes from a hopelessly overtired mind. Tony moved to her side.

"Virginia," he said. "It's all right... We'll move him somewhere... And I believe the police are on another track, anyway. If we can just keep him dark for a bit. He was suddenly aware of another figure standing in the doorway and looked up to see a woman who for a moment he could not place. Then he recognised Newent's daughter.

"Good afternoon, Mr. Mayfield," she said in her deep, musical voice, and for the first time he noticed a trace of foreign accent in it. "You did not deliver my message."

Tony abruptly realised that his arm had somehow gone comfortingly round Virginia's shoulders, though until that moment neither of them seemed to have noticed the fact. He removed it hurriedly, and blushed scarlet.

"I—I'm afraid I forgot," Tony stammered. "You see—"

"It did not matter... My father does not worry about me... But who is there?"

After an interval the shouts broke out with redoubled violence. They listened.

"I don't know," Tony answered. "Some foreign-looking chap who was following Virginia... He went in there, and I shut him up."

"It is Mr. da Vargas... He cannot know. He must have seen Virginia and suspected." She took Virginia by the arm. "Come," she said firmly. "Wait, Mr. Mayfield. I will send out my father. You will decide what to do."

Virginia obeyed meekly. So did Tony, though not without a certain surprise at his own submissiveness. For a minute or two nothing happened, and Tony had leisure to reflect upon the extraordinary position in which he somehow found himself. He was committed, apparently, to helping an escaped prisoner; he had shut up someone who, so far as he knew, had done nothing particularly illegal—who, in fact, was probably helping the law. A more surprising fact occurred to him a moment later, just as Newent emerged from the hut. He had called Virginia by her Christian name, and she had not appeared to mind.

Newent, apparently, shared his daughter's magnificent calm in an emergency. He nodded to Tony almost casually.

"Good morning, Mr. Mayfield," he said. "We're partners in crime again, apparently... The question is, what's to be done."

"Well," Tony said, and paused. "You're sure the best thing wouldn't be for him to go to the police... I'm quite ready, of course, to help in anything you may decide; but it seems to me there's a risk of making things worse."

"They couldn't be very much," Newent answered. "If you'd heard what he's been saying... No, Mr. Mayfield. I admit he'd be better in hospital from a medical point of view. From a legal point of view, I think having a policeman taking notes by his bedside would be fatal... We've got to keep him for the present."

"You mean—?" Tony asked, and broke off. He looked at Newent for a second or two in horrified amazement. "You don't mean to say that he is the murderer?"

"I'm not interested in that, just now," Newent answered with perfect calm. "The point is that he can't walk. So it's a question of carrying him. I expect we could manage that between us. Only I don't quite see where to take him. I'd suggest my house, but there's no way of smuggling him in through the village. The Hall is out of the question, as the police are certain to be there—"

"There is one place." The girl had apparently left Virginia inside, and now she rejoined the conference, speaking with her customary certainty. "The boathouse by the lake. No one goes there... You will carry him."

"But—" Tony protested. "I suppose we could—if we didn't meet anyone. But it must be a good mile, and we're almost certain to be spotted. And besides, they'll search the whole district—certainly as soon as he gets loose." He jerked his head in the direction of the shouting.

"He must not get loose... Let us see."

She led the way, Tony and her father following meekly. It occurred to Tony that he had never met a more masterful woman. Perhaps da Vargas heard their footsteps. He had been silent again for a space, but the battering on the door recommenced as they reached it. So far as Tony could understand the shouts at all, he seemed to be either swearing or praying in Spanish. The girl eyed the shaking door with a calmly-speculative scrutiny.

"He will not get out," she said positively. "But perhaps it would be better to tie him up? Or could you stun him?"

She was looking at her father as she made the last suggestion, but Tony intervened hastily.

"It would be better if he didn't see us at all," he suggested. "So far, he's seen no one but Miss Blakeney. He can't swear to anything—"

She inclined her head. "Yes. He can stay there. He will stay there until tonight, or tomorrow. After a little, he will be sore and hoarse. Then there is less likelihood that he will be heard. Come."

Tony duly obeyed, but was moved to a horrified protest.

"But look here, we can't leave him shut up like this indefinitely... If anything happened to him, it would be murder. He's nothing to eat or drink—"

"Nothing will happen. When we are ready, we can arrange for Bere to find him by accident—"

"Bere's working with you?" Tony asked in surprise. "But—"

She paid no attention to his remarks. She was standing looking thoughtfully down the hill, and there somehow came into Tony's mind the comparison of Napoleon planning a campaign. Both men waited for her to speak, but when the words finally came they did not seem to be particularly helpful.

"It will rain," she said. "Look."

Tony looked. The further hills were already veiled in a white mist which was slowly spreading towards them.

"Yes," he agreed, without comprehension. "It'll be beastly wet in a few minutes."

"Good. If it is wet, people will be indoors. No one will see us... Over there—" She pointed. "There is a hurdle. We can use it as a stretcher. If you will get it, I will see that he is ready."

"But are you sure—?" Tony ventured. "If he's a sick man, and delirious, carrying him all that way—even if we're not seen—to a boathouse which is probably damp—"

"We shall meet no one. We shall reach the boathouse. He will take no harm. The hurdle, please."

She did not wait for an answer, but entered the hut. Newent was already moving off, and Tony joined him unwillingly.

"My daughter is a fatalist," the artist observed conversationally. "And sometimes she has second sight... I expect you are surprised at the way she is taking this. But, you see, she has definite knowledge that all will be well."

"That's good," Tony said without conviction. "Personally, he had no such assurance. In the absence of Virginia, the whole business seemed to him to be as risky as it was idiotic. It was one thing to try to prove a man innocent of a crime which he might not have committed. It was quite another to carry an escaped prisoner who apparently admitted to being a murderer all over the countryside with the police looking for them, and a man forcibly detained who would have to be accounted for sooner or later. They picked up the hurdle in silence and retraced their steps. Tony noticed that it was an old and rather decayed specimen of its kind. Perhaps Miss

Newent or Mrs. Blakeney, or whatever she should be called, knew by second sight that it would hold out, but he himself was far from sure. They dumped the hurdle on the ground outside, and Newent pushed the door open and led the way in.

The place was dark, except for a single night light in one corner, which lit up a pile of bracken on which a man was sitting, holding his head between his hands, and swaying to and fro as if in pain. Newent's daughter was kneeling beside him, and Tony caught a flash of something bright in her hands. Then the man spoke.

"I could end it all if I had the capsules," he said, and the tone startled the journalist. It was so calmly reasonable. "But, you see, I gave them to Bere—"

Tony could quite understand the undesirability of letting Inspector Dunster overhear the man's conversation if he had much to say on those lines. He heard Virginia give a gasp, and only then became aware of her standing in the shadow beside him.

Miss Newent, on the other hand, was perfectly unmoved. She raised the bright object in her hand, and Tony saw that it was a hypodermic syringe.

"This will stop the pain," she said. "Your wrist—"

"No—no—no!" The voice of the man on the bracken bed rose to a shriek, and he backed from the outstretched hands. In the half-light the Newent girl bending over him had a horribly sinister look, which somehow brought to Tony's mind a performance of Sybil Thorndike as Medea. She turned to Tony.

"We must," she said briefly. "Hold him."

Tony obeyed in spite of himself. The sick man struggled violently, but his strength had gone. Tony winced as the needle went home in the wrist. Little by little, the man relaxed, and Tony laid him gently down on the bed. As he did so, for the first time he saw the man's face clearly, and started back in surprise.

"But—but—" he said, and sought for words. "It—it isn't Richard at all."

# 23

# Drunkard's Doom

APART FROM WHAT HE was inclined to regard as the fantastic theories of his colleague, Superintendent Stockton would have said that the case against Richard Blakeney was progressing well. Technical details, which so often cause delay, had given them very little trouble, and by late afternoon he had at his disposal several reports which made the charges at least distinctly plausible.

The doctor's report on the remains from the cottage showed that they were those of a man of approximately George's age and build, who had certainly been dead for something over a fortnight. One fragment of cloth had been positively identified as a suit which had disappeared at the right time, and last and most clinching, the local dentist was positive that the false teeth were a set which he had made for George Blakeney.

To Stockton, that settled the question of identity, and in view of all the circumstances he was not prepared to consider very seriously anyone but Richard as the murderer. In the case of Bere, he had been less fortunate, and he was frowning over the analysis of the belladonna when Dunster, who had been busy on some mysterious errands of his own, returned to the station just before five o'clock.

Dunster was looking tired and dispirited, and he shook his head in answer to the superintendent's look of enquiry.

"Not much luck," he admitted. "Possibilities, that's all. And I can't find anyone I want."

"Can't find them?" Stockton asked. "Not bolted?"

"Shouldn't think so. Can't see why most of 'em should bolt, anyway. All the same, Newent and his daughter have gone off sketching; Alness is out for the day; Stroud has gone to see his old mother—"

"Stroud? He can't have an old mother. Besides, what d' you want him for?"

"She's ninety-eight... Oh, just exploring possibilities... da Vargas went out sleuthing and hasn't come back to lunch—"

"Sleuthing? Why on earth—?"

"I gather he doesn't think we're competent to hang Richard Blakeney without help."

"Well, he's starting right by missing lunch," grunted Stockton. "Anyone else?"

"The vicar and Doctor Staithes. But I caught them."

"You seem to have had a good time... Still chasing your own mare's nest?"

"I don't believe one could... I was just taking a general run round to see if there's anything else that doesn't fit."

"Then here's something that'll suit you." He tapped the report he had been reading. "It's the belladonna. Apparently there is a little difference between the stuff in the capsules and the sample I took from Blakeney's. More impurities, or something. Probably they got in while he was filling the things. I don't expect it matters."

"Let's have a look." Dunster took the paper and studied it. His eyebrows rose a little. "I don't know," he said slowly. "No, it would hardly be that."

"Why not?"

"Well, I'm not a whale on pharmacology, but I looked it up in the Encyclopaedia. The interesting thing is that the 'impurities' here are drugs associated with the atropine in the plant itself. In other words, it looks a little as if one is a home-made product, and the other from a laboratory."

"Could anyone make it?" Stockton asked dubiously.

"I don't see why not. If the deadly nightshade plants were available... Pity I didn't think of asking the vicar. I gather he's the local botanist... However, it strengthens my case—"

Stockton grunted disagreement.

"You're seriously suggesting that the whole thing is a plant against Richard?" he demanded.

"I am."

"By whom?"

"Well," Dunster said very slowly. "On the whole, the likeliest seems to be George."

"What?"

"You see, it's someone who knows him quite well—knows the family secrets, has heard of the belladonna and so on. Now, if I'm right, that body we've found isn't George's at all. That is the reason for the digging up of graves. He wants a body that he can pretend is his own—"

"Just a minute," Stockton interrupted. "Take a look at those."

He pushed over the reports on the remains from the ruins. Dunster read them through carefully.

"Well," he said. "There's nothing really to identify the body itself, except that it's about the right age. Might I point out that the clothes, the teeth, the ring and so on are all movable articles?"

"What is your theory, then?"

"At present, my most plausible idea is this. Richard and George had quarrelled, about this bigamy and blackmail business. George decides to kill Richard, and at the same time he wants to disappear himself. The best way of disappearing is to die. He arranges to go off to the station with Richard under circumstances which will be suspicious; doesn't travel by the train but goes into hiding somewhere. He gets a body—that one from the grave which I want dug up—of about the right age and so on, puts it in the cottage, with enough articles to identify it, leaves an automatic timing device to start a fire, and induces Richard to go there at a certain time. And there it is. He's covered his tracks, and Richard is duly tried and murdered judicially."

"You've ignored Bere altogether."

"That's actually another point in my favour. You remember in his first statement Bere said that Joe had met 'the young master' a day after he was supposed to have gone? Well, he did. George was hiding somewhere in the neighbourhood and had gone out for a breather or something, and he realised it would be fatal if Bere said he'd met him. He decided to poison Bere. He had the capsules ready prepared in his pocket—"

"Why?"

"Originally he had intended to poison his brother, or perhaps to leave evidence that he himself had been poisoned. He may have kept them so as to commit suicide if he were to be caught. He simply gives them to Bere, with instructions to take them when required and, incidentally, provides more evidence against his brother."

Stockton thought it over. Unwillingly he had to admit that the theory had some advantages.

"Why make his own belladonna if there was some available in the house?" he asked.

"Hm... That's certainly a point... In that case, perhaps—" His voice trailed away into silence. Stockton saw his advantage, and pressed his objections.

"You've got to show he could get out to do all this gravedigging stuff; that he'd have opportunities to make the belladonna—in fact, that he knew the plant by sight. I don't."

"Might I point out that most of the grave business occurred after George had disappeared?"

Stockton digested that. "Why dig up Lady Blakeney's grave? He must have known that a woman's body wouldn't do. And, well—his own mother—"

"He made a mistake. In fact, he tried to remedy it the following night when Mayfield caught him."

"He couldn't make a mistake. He'd attended the funeral only a few days before and stood by the graveside. It was fairly bright moonlight. It's absolutely impossible for him to have gone wrong."

That made Dunster think longer than ever. He sighed. "Anything else happened?" he asked.

Stockton felt he had won at least a moral victory. "Not yet... Oh, we may be on the track of Crouch. There's a garage that had a booking out this way, but they can't be sure till the driver comes back. I'm expecting them to ring any time now... Anyhow, how does Crouch come into this picture?"

"Only incidentally into any picture that I can see. I mean, he and his sister had the knowledge of George's bigamy and caused the original fuss. No doubt they blackmailed him, and he kicked."

"Who was the woman? I mean, the bigamous wife?"

"I'm inclined to think it was Miss Newent. From something that journalist chap dropped... I've an idea that Crouch's sister may be the original Number One, and Miss Newent is Number Two... After all, there aren't many suitable candidates in this place... By the way, Mayfield hasn't been here yet?"

"No. You expecting him?"

"I'd have sworn that he'd come clean. That's another of them missing. I wonder— Good heavens! But that's impossible—"

He jumped to his feet and ran out of the room. Stockton heard him calling for the sergeant, but he did not catch what was said. In a minute Dunster returned.

"I've sent Comfrey on a wild goose chase," he said. "Just as a precautionary measure... And now—"

"Just a minute," Stockton said. "I've one or two theories for you myself. Miss Newent is responsible for the whole thing. She had the necessary knowledge. She had motive, first to kill her 'husband' and then his brother... Or it was Stroud. The Rural Council have recently lowered the gravedigging fees, and he couldn't make ends meet. So— Going out again?"

Dunster reached the door. "To pay a call on the vicar," he said, and went out.

He was gone barely twenty minutes, but he found the superintendent waiting for him in a fever of impatience.

"We've got 'em," he announced. "Crouch and the woman. The driver phoned through five minutes ago. He can take us to the very house— Come on. We've a twenty-mile drive to do."

There was very little conversation on the way. Dunster, at the beginning, volunteered only one remark.

"D'you know," he said, "there might really be something in one of your theories? At any rate, I've an idea—"

That, and the fact that he did not communicate the idea, so disgusted Stockton that he lapsed into a grim silence which remained unbroken until they finally pulled up at the police station of the neighbouring town from which the message came.

The hired driver was waiting for them. Taking a couple of local police, as Stockton put it sotto voce, "for ballast," they set off under his guidance for the far side of the town, and at last pulled up outside a detached house which stood rather alone, with the high wall and wide grounds of a hospital on one side, and the canal on the other.

"Secluded spot," Stockton observed. "Wonder why they chose it? It's best to hide in a crowd."

Dunster had a good idea. Personally, he would have preferred a less direct approach, but he had left it in Stockton's hands. A minute later, his fears were justified. The superintendent was just raising his hand to the knocker, having sent the two local men round to the back, when the inspector saw the window curtains twitch. He had a momentary glimpse of a woman's face behind the glass.

Stockton's effort could hardly have remained unheard, but the door remained unopened. He was on the point of trying again, when from inside there came the shrill sound of a woman's scream ending horribly in a choking gurgle.

"Quick!" Stockton shouted, and threw his weight against the door. It was locked. As he gathered himself for a second attempt, Dunster picked up a piece of stone from an ornamental rockery beside him, and in three good blows smashed the whole of the lower window sash. The next minute, at the cost of a few minor cuts, he was inside.

Crouch stood facing him, his eyes blazing with the light of madness, and he was bending over the woman on her knees before him, gripping her throat between his two hands. As Dunster crossed the room at a bound, he threw her from him.

"I've killed her!" he shouted wildly. "I'm the killer! I've killed them all—all! And I'll get you—"

Dunster had been in some tough struggles in his time, but he never remembered a worse one. The man's strength seemed positively superhuman, and either by luck or skill he seemed to counter every attempt to throw him. The detective was only dimly aware that Stockton was climbing through the window. Then, as his colleague joined him, quite suddenly, with a horrible choking scream, Crouch went limp in his arms, pulling him down with his weight.

Dunster was prepared for a trick; but the man made no move. As the inspector struggled free, and gained his feet, the stertorous breathing suddenly ceased. Stockton knelt down beside him as Dunster wiped the perspiration out of his eyes.

"He's gone," the superintendent announced. "Nasty one, eh? They sometimes go that way... How's the woman?"

The red marks of the choking fingers stood out startlingly against her throat, but she was still breathing. Stockton turned to the two local constables who had followed them.

"A doctor?" he suggested. "Or wait a bit, that hospital? They'll take her there? Good... We'd better just have a look round here... I say, what was that he said? Could it have been true?"

"I don't think so," Dunster answered. "But I think that's why she brought him here... What's that?"

A mobile policeman was standing beside the car talking to the driver, and as he turned to the house Dunster crossed to the window, and through the broken pane took the message. He smiled at Stockton a little wryly.

"Well," he said. "We shall soon know who's right. They've fixed up the exhumation for tonight."

# 24

# Night Pursuit

SITTING UNCOMFORTABLY ON A locker in the boathouse, with a view of a yard or two of lead-grey water lashed by the rain, and an expanse of sky which was scarcely brighter, Tony Mayfield was conscious of an acute depression. Beside him the invalid moaned and muttered in his sleep at intervals, and that was one thing that worried him. Although he might accept Newent's assurance that his daughter had been trained as a nurse, he was far from certain how what seemed to have been a fairly stiff dose of morphia would affect a man in a poor state of health and suffering from a nervous breakdown. If he died, it seemed to Tony that at the least he and Miss Newent would face a charge of manslaughter, and be lucky to get off with a term of months.

That, however, was only one possibility out of several. They were all, he supposed, accessories after the fact to a murder; he himself could certainly be charged with something like wrongful imprisonment so far as da Vargas was concerned, and the horrible thought kept recurring to his mind that the man might die there shut up in the shed. Any suggestions on his part that something ought to be done about his release had been treated with contempt, and Miss Newent had pointed out that it was possible to go for weeks without food, and several days without water.

As long as Virginia had been there he had managed to keep his spirits up. Now that he was left to hold the fort alone, it was only by remembering the last glimpse he had had of her as she looked back in the doorway that he managed to stop himself from going to the police.

Miss Newent had organised everything marvellously. The journey carrying the sick man from the hut to the boathouse had been an agony that lasted a full hour, and on three separate occasions they had almost been caught—twice by wandering farmworkers, and once, crossing the lane, by the police. But, as Miss Newent had prophesied, they had duly gained the boathouse, and the invalid was still alive.

His lonely sentry-go was part of her organisation. They could not, she pointed out, all disappear indefinitely for a long period without some suspicion being excited. It was necessary for them to show themselves to reassure the village in general, and the police in particular, that all was well with them. Tony had been left holding the baby on the ground that no one expected a journalist to be punctual for meals, anyhow. Certainly Tony had already missed lunch, and she met that by the present of four very dry and hard biscuits. His timid suggestion that he had already promised to meet the inspector was countered by the production of writing materials for him to scribble a note of apology saying that he would be back later that evening, and, in one way or another, the woman had demonstrated conclusively that he was the one person to stay there, and that was the one place where he should be.

Alness, summoned by Bere, had been called into council soon after their arrival there; and it gave Tony something of a fellow feeling that, apparently, he was just as much taken aback by the general situation as he himself was. He had been allotted the more active part of arranging a conveyance to carry their charge to a place of safety, first by boat across the lake, and then by his car which was to be waiting in a suitably lonely spot on the other side. Unfortunately, Tony was scheduled to help in both operations.

It was getting darker and darker outside. Certainly no one would be able to see them crossing the lake; the only doubt was whether they would be able to see to cross. He peered out into the gloom, trying to make out any sensible object to test the visibility, and right in his face the heavy shutter outside slammed into place.

He jumped back and almost cried out. For a moment he had a feeling like a trapped animal, as he remembered that the door had a padlock outside. It could not have been the wind. To make that absolutely certain, next second he heard the bolt shoot into its socket. He waited no longer, but made a dash for the door. As he reached it, a timid knock sounded.

"Tat-tat. Tat-tat-tat-tat."

It was only then he remembered that the Newent girl had said something silly about a code and the initials of his name in Morse. Presumably that was an attempt at T. M. It sounded again, a little more loudly. He drew back the bolt and opened. On the threshold was a slight form which even in the inadequate light he recognised, before a voice which trembled a little said, with doubtful grammar:

"It—it's me."

He wiped the perspiration from his face as Virginia Blakeney entered, glad of the darkness which concealed his confusion.

"There's nothing wrong?" he whispered, and closed the door.

"No. But I was worried. I had to come—"

"You shouldn't have done," Tony protested, all at once remembering the black, muddy lane and the tangled wood. Strangely enough, he felt all at once large and protective; and ready to meet the world—if he had had a cigarette. And her next words proved her to be not only an angel from heaven, but a ministering one.

"I've brought you some things—tea, and a few sandwiches and cigarettes... Athene said—"

"Who?" Tony demanded.

"Miss—Miss Newent—or ought it to be Mrs. Blakeney? Anyway she said we were sisters-in-law morally and I had to call her that, you see—"

"It's a fine point," Tony murmured. "But appropriate... The goddess of wisdom who sprang fully armed from the head of Zeus. A formidable lady—"

He was suddenly aware that he was giving rein to the nonsense which seemed to be bubbling up inside him. Then he remembered.

"I say. The shutter. Was that you?"

"Yes. Athene said"—Tony groaned—"that if I insisted on coming I'd better make myself useful; and that you'd probably like a light which would be quite safe if we put the shutter up. If you've a match—"

She was holding out a night light as the flame flared up, and the sight of her upturned face brought a sudden memory of their meeting in the lane. But she was terribly pale, and the raindrops glistened in her hair like diamonds. She smiled faintly as her eyes met his.

"We seem to meet by matchlight," she said. "It seems a long time ago—"

There was a world of tragedy in the last few words, and Tony was reminded of a line from an old play: "Long, long ago, a great long time ago!" In fact, it seemed as if they had known each other for years. Then he saw her lips trembling a little. He took the night light from her, and pointed to the locker.

"Sit down," he said firmly. "Where's that tea? You need some."

She bent over to look at the sleeping man as he took the basket from her and found the thermos flask; then, with more irritation than gratitude, he saw that there were two cups.

Second sight again, he supposed. He poured it out and offered it. She hesitated.

"But that was for you," she said. "I've had some—"

"You'd better have some more... Athene said—"

She was startled. "How did you know?"

"Second sight," said Tony darkly, and was rewarded by a rather tremulous smile as she took the cup. He lit a cigarette, and began to feel better even about Miss Newent.

"She—she is wonderful, isn't she?" Virginia said a little doubtfully.

"She is," Tony assented grimly.

"She's arranged everything—she and my cousin."

Tony made no comment on that. Perhaps it was the mention of Alness that aroused a little spark of jealousy. Mentally he said rather savagely: "Whereas I, like a mug, have been sitting in a damp boathouse playing sick-nurse—" Perhaps she sensed a certain antagonism.

"You—you don't agree with what we're doing?" she said after a pause.

"I—I didn't," Tony prevaricated. "You see, it seems to me that we've no hope of dodging the police indefinitely, and it will only make things look worse. But, of course, when he was talking like that—"

"But he hasn't done it. He couldn't have done anything like that—"

Tony tried to find something to say, but failed to find the words in time.

"You don't think he's innocent, do you?"

"I—" Tony began, and then jibbed at the lie. "I don't know."

"Then why are you helping? Of course, your paper—"

"Damn the paper," Tony burst out rudely. "Sorry... In any case, it isn't doing the paper much good sitting here waiting to do something I can't possibly print without getting gaoled for it." His irritation subsided as rapidly as it had arisen at the sight of her stricken expression; but it left him somehow with enough courage to say what he wanted. He looked her full in the face. "I wanted to help you," he said. "I've wanted to from the first minute I saw you in the lane... And on the whole, a fine mess I make of it," he added bitterly.

"But—but you have done... You're helping me more than anyone. Because, although of course you can't be expected to think about my brothers as I do, you seem to understand more how I feel. Of course, Athene is so terribly fond of George—"

Tony nearly damned Athene. Silence was the most he could achieve.

"I should think she would make him a marvellous wife. I can understand anyone admiring her, can't you?"

"No," said Tony rebelliously.

She ignored that. "I wonder how he came to ask her—to marry him, I mean," she speculated.

"I expect she organised it," Tony said brutally. Then his better feelings asserted themselves. "I say, I'm sorry. But I can't stand the woman. I suppose she'll make a perfect wife, and her husband won't be able to call his soul his own for two minutes... I'd hate to marry a woman like that. I don't mean to say I'd like a wife who was a patient Griselda saying 'Yes, darling. How wonderful you are' all the time. But I'd like someone who, though she had a will of her own, didn't try to boss me about, because I wouldn't stand it, you know. In fact—"

He saw that she was actually smiling at the outburst, and it emboldened him to go on.

"In fact, I'd like someone like you... I mean, I'd like you... In fact, I don't think I'd care if—Virginia—"

"Tony—" she began, "and I think I'd like—" Then she broke off and turned with a start. "What—?"

Tony had heard the knock too. He scowled at the door.

"It's all right," he said. "Dot-dash. That's A. A for Athene or Alness or abominable, or awful—" He saw astonishment turn to amusement in her eyes, and rose with resignation. "I'll let 'em in," he said.

It was Alness who entered, dripping and glistening in oilskins and gumboots, and his face was unusually white and set, as if he liked the business as little as Tony.

"I've got the boat," he said briefly. "It's a beast of a night. Had a job getting here... The boat's outside. If you'd put the light out and open the doors—"

He nodded towards the big double doors which shut the entrance to the dock. Tony glanced at the motor boat which lay there. "You're not using that, then?"

"Noisy," Alness explained. "He'll be all right. I've got something to cover him, and it won't be five minutes... Don't forget the light before you open the doors—"

He had gone. Tony caught a glimpse of a puzzled frown on the girl's face, but he had no time to ask what it meant. He picked up the night light, undid the great bar, and pinched the flame between his fingers before he pulled the door open.

Virginia was at his side. He felt her hand upon his arm, and it was trembling a little. The opening showed as a faint grey patch, and through it came the lapping of the waves and the driving of the rain. Then there was the creak of rowlocks. A dark shadow glided in. They heard Alness whisper, as the boat grated alongside the landing place:

"Where are you?... Oh, there." He pulled himself up. "Just give a hand to make fast, will you? Hold this rope—"

Tony advanced to receive it, and as he did, something struck him sickeningly right on the solar plexus, paralysing every muscle in his body. He simply crumpled up and fell without a cry. Then, as he lay there, trying desperately to rise, he heard Virginia's scream, suddenly muffled.

# 25

## Unburial Party

THE RAIN HAD SET in and was falling steadily by the time Dunster and the superintendent left the car at the churchyard gates and started up the path. Stockton switched on his torch.

"It's always wet for exhumations," he said gloomily.

"Like wash days," Dunster agreed. "Better switch off the torch."

"Why?"

"Reporters. We've dodged them so far. It would be a pity if they spotted us now—all the more if this is a mare's nest."

"Hm." The superintendent put out the light with the words "which it is" trembling on his tongue. "The others should be there now. And the Chief... The doctor will be along later—"

"Doctor? If I'm right, there won't even be a corpse for him—"

"All the same, I think we should have a doctor," Stockton persisted.

"Like the Sea Lady and the stockings," Dunster said flippantly; but the allusion escaped his colleague. "If I'm right, he won't thank—"

"And if you're wrong, no one will," Stockton pointed out cruelly. "The Chief, for example. He suffers from rheumatism, lumbago and bronchitis, and a night like this is just the thing to make the best of 'em. He'll be in a sweet temper tomorrow if—"

He left the words unsaid, and for a few paces they walked in silence. Dunster was, in fact, a little worried himself about the result of the exhumation. He had had to put the case very strongly in order to force it through at all, and there was certainly trouble ahead if nothing came of it. All at once he stopped, and laid a hand on the superintendent's arm.

"Ssh," he said warningly.

But the superintendent's own thoughts had made him a little surly.

"What d'you mean—'Ssh?'" he demanded. "I wasn't saying anything—"

"I heard something," Dunster whispered. "Over there—"

Stockton listened. From ahead, where some half-concealed lights gleamed, came a steady sound of digging which showed that work had already started, but at first he heard nothing else. Then he caught it, the grating of boots on gravel. Someone was coming towards them down one of the little side paths on the left.

"Nab him?" he whispered.

"We'd better."

"Reporter, probably."

"Show a light and stop him. I'll stand by."

He stepped on to the grass verge and vanished into the shadows. The footsteps drew nearer. Stockton flashed his torch.

"Hullo, what d' you want?" he demanded.

The man gave something like a squeal, and turned to run. Dunster stepped forward and grabbed him. And then Stockton saw the face.

"Great Scott, it's Stroud!" he exclaimed. "Now, what are you doing here?"

In the same moment, apparently, Stroud recognised his captor. He broke into excited speech.

"They be at it again, zur—a-digging up Tom Watkins. Near a dozen of 'em, there be, and a girt, ugly chap with a moustache—"

Stockton struggled with mirth as he recognised this description of the Chief Constable.

"That's all right, my man. It's an exhumation, under proper authority... What are you doing here?"

Stroud ignored the question. "I'd ought to ha' been asked," he growled. "A terrible strong digger, I be, zur—"

"That's not the point," Stockton said sternly. "You've no business here—"

"That I have, zur. 'Tis worth a pound note to me... That newspaper chap, he says to me, 'Stroud,' he says, 'if you see anyone a-digging in the churchyard, or any digging that's been done and didn't ought to have been, you come and tell me,' he says, 'and 'tis worth a pound to 'ee, Stroud.' And it were, for he paid up as if he'd been a gentleman."

Dunster ignored the slight upon the Press. "Oh, did he?" he said grimly. "Well, you can't go to him now—"

"It be worth a pound to me," Stroud repeated obstinately. "And I'd ought to ha' been asked—"

Dunster thought. No doubt under the circumstances they were justified in detaining him, but he did not want it to come to that. He saw a way out.

"We'll talk about that later," he said. "Now, I expect they could do with a bit of extra help from an expert... Suppose you come along and lend a hand."

Stroud looked at him shrewdly. "Special rate, zur?" he asked.

"Of course."

"Ay, I'll show 'em, zur. Terrible strong digger, I be—"

Work had apparently been in progress for some little time when they reached the graveside. The Chief Constable, an impressive figure in the half-light, greeted them gruffly.

"'Evening, Superintendent. Thought we'd better get going... 'Evening, Inspector. Hope this idea of yours is going to work out all right. Expense to the Board."

Stockton detected a warning in that. First, if the Chief Constable had had much hope, he would have said "our idea"; secondly, there was the reference to the Board, that body which, unknown to the ordinary public, keeps a watchful eye on county forces' activities in general and their expenses in particular. Dunster faced the storm.

"I am convinced I am right, sir," he said. "But if I were not, it would be anticipating an obvious point for the defence, sir."

"Hope so," the Chief Constable said. "Hope so."

Silence fell. The nature of the proceedings did not encourage much conversation, except for some whispered criticisms on the part of Stroud, which eventually secured him a turn at excavating in the grave. Dunster watched him. He certainly was a good digger, and there was something fascinating in the rhythmical movements of his body and spade. Was he really all right? After all, he had given no explanation of his presence at the churchyard—

"I say, where's the sergeant?" Stockton's voice broke in on his thoughts. "Not here, is he?"

"Good heavens, I forgot!" Dunster exclaimed. "I meant to have relieved him—"

"But what's he doing?"

"Swearing at me, I expect... I sent him out to keep a general eye on Alness, six hours ago—and he hasn't got a coat even."

"'The boy stood on the burning deck—'" Stockton quoted. "But Alness? Why?"

Dunster hesitated. "It was just a damn silly intuition, really," he admitted. "You see, I'd an idea that Mayfield had gone to see him, and he seemed to have vanished. And then da Vargas had apparently been sleuthing round the Blakeney family, and he was missing. Well, I thought that they wouldn't come to any harm with the girl, but if Alness was the murderer, it might be a good thing as a precautionary measure to keep an eye on him—"

"But we've had that note from Mayfield—"

"Yes. And I expect da Vargas is back home eating his dinner. I didn't really think of Alness. He's nothing to gain by killing Richard—"

"No. If you stick to Richard as the murderee, and not the murderer. But, if we're going to move in the higher realm of supposition, supposing he'd murdered George, and Richard got hung for it, he'd get the entailed estate."

Dunster made no reply for a full minute. "He would," he said at last, and was silent again.

But Stockton, once started, was in a talkative mood.

"Seems a queer thing, doesn't it," he said reflectively, "that all this has come about nothing?"

"About nothing?" Dunster said absently.

"Yes. I mean, it all started with Crouch's little attempt at blackmail. They were trying to get money from George to keep quiet about his being a bigamist, and all the time they knew he wasn't. I mean, since Crouch was that woman's first husband and not her brother, it follows George's marriage with her wasn't legal; and, I suppose, that his second one is all right. So Miss Newent is Mrs. Blakeney, and Mrs. Crouch never was, if you follow me."

Dunster at least made no comment. He seemed to be thinking.

"Wonder why Crouch kept all that stuff—marriage certificate, papers, and so on?" went on the superintendent. The strain of waiting seemed to be making him loquacious, whereas it had an opposite effect on Dunster. "Just providing evidence against themselves—"

"Oh, that?" Dunster said absently. "I think that's plain. Crouch wanted to keep a hold on Mrs. Crouch so as to get his share. She was fed up with him, but she couldn't get rid of him, so she reckoned her best way out was to help him to drink himself to death. And that nearly did for her—first, because he started to go off his head, and talk blue murder, and secondly, because he damn near throttled her."

They stood in silence for a moment, watching the flicker of the spade in the lamplight, and the glistening of the rain on the wet earth. Then Stockton asked:

"But why write to the old man? Killing the goose—eh?"

"No. He was so terrified of a scandal that he was the most likely of the three. What seems to have happened was that they were getting on nicely with George, but put the screw on too hard. Either he told his wife, or they did. And suddenly everything changes. There are threats of the police, and conspiracy and so on. Looks as if the woman might not be as meek as she seems—"

"Meek?" Stockton said thoughtfully. "I shouldn't have said she was meek. That voice— Hullo! What's that?"

Stroud's spade had struck something hollow-sounding. He straightened his back and looked up at the circle of faces which all at once craned over the graveside.

"It be the lid, zur," he announced, "and that be queer, too, zur."

"What's queer, my man?" the Chief Constable demanded gruffly. "You'd expect the lid on top, wouldn't you?"

"If 'ee could let me have a bit more light, zur—" Stroud said in unconscious echo of Diogenes, and the Chief Constable stood meekly back.

Stroud bent to his work again. This time he was not digging but scooping gingerly with the spade edge. In the dead silence, every least clink and scraping could be heard. Stroud was muttering as he worked, and his whispers grew louder.

"—Ay, it be the lid... And lid be broken—" The words came in a crescendo which grew to a shout. "And coffin be empty!... Poor young Tom! They got 'un!"

Stockton jumped into the pit. There was no room for Dunster anyhow, and in his triumph it was more dignified to display an outward calm. Even in that moment, he found himself questioning the epithet "young." Probably, to Stroud, anything under fifty was rather boyish.

The Chief Constable, prepared for failure, was only temporarily blinded by success. He made a brilliant recovery.

"Well, Dunster, we were right, then!" he said, doing a *volte-face* in a single word. But what's the meaning of it, eh? What's been happening?"

"Now, zur, if 'ee'll just mind, I'll tell 'ee, zur," Stroud said irritably to Stockton. "Just 'ee jump out, zur, and stop worrying a man, and I'll show 'ee, zur—"

Stockton obeyed, at least in scrambling, rather at the expense of his trousers, over the grave edge. Stroud proceeded with his exposition.

"Well, zur, they buried 'un all right," he said. "And someone dug 'un up again. That be plain."

"Now, my man," the Chief Constable interrupted, "what we want to know is—"

"And I'm telling 'ee what 'ee wants to know, zur... Now, see here—" And he dug his spade into the vertical side of the pit. "And see here," and he dug it into the earth above the unexcavated end. "And see here!"

The last words, spoken triumphantly, were as he dug along the coffin edge to one side. The police looked on blankly.

"Now, the edge here be firm," Stroud elaborated. "Hasn't been dug—not since church were built, maybe... This we've been digging, it be loose, but not so loose. Hasn't settled, like, but it has, if you see, zur... That be so, eh, John?"

John, one of the earlier diggers whom Stroud had displaced, was too embarrassed to assent to so ambiguous a proposition.

"Ah," he said simply, and backed into the crowd a little.

"I see," the Chief Constable said firmly. "Then—"

"Wait, zur, and I'll tell 'ee... Now, here by the coffin, it be firmer, but not so firm, so 'tis easy to see, zur."

To Stockton, whom he had chosen for the appeal, it was not easy at all. He nodded.

"Quite plain," he said. "So, what's happened is—?"

"They buried poor Tom regular, zur, and I helped fill 'un in myself, Bert being ill... And there he lay so quiet and peaceful, with the earth settling over 'un, maybe a week or so. And then they dug 'un up again. But they didn't dig the coffin out proper, zur, for 'twere only poor young Tom they wanted. So, here at the side, it's settled a bit, zur... Poor young Tom, and him dead... 'Tis dreadful to think where he be."

"He were a good man," one of the gravediggers commented. It seemed to Dunster that he had misunderstood, and there was something defensive in the tone.

"Ah, but where be his corpse? Who took 'un? What got 'un?"

There was a sudden queer hush, as momentarily an eerie, superstitious feeling asserted itself even over the group hardened by use to the circumstances of death. Dunster was all at once certain he could answer all three questions. Then, as the Chief Constable shifted and cleared his throat, from the churchyard gate came the sound of a confused outcry.

"Eh? What's that?" Colonel Saltash demanded.

"Someone coming," Stockton said. "Perhaps the doctor, sir—"

"Doctor? Nonsense!... He wouldn't make a row like that—"

And yet, in fact, it was the doctor, but not alone; nor was he responsible for the noise. The more picturesque figures of the trio that entered the circle of light within the screens were Sergeant Comfrey and da Vargas, both in poor condition.

# 26

## Last Voyage

SERGEANT COMFREY, DRIPPING FROM head to foot, and with a streak of dye from his soaked hat making an odd patch on his face, had plainly been in the wars; and Mr. da Vargas, muddy, wild-eyed, and with dank locks of dark hair plastered over his hatless forehead, was even worse. It was from the latter that the shouting proceeded, and he started again, in an odd mixture of Spanish and English, as he recognised Inspector Dunster.

"Just a moment, sir... Just a moment!" Dunster pleaded, and then commanded, "I'll hear what you have to say, sir, in a moment. Well, Sergeant? What's happened?"

The sergeant pushed his hat back and wiped his brow, transferring a streak of dye across it.

"I hardly know, sir," he said lugubriously. "I waited where you sent me, sir, but he didn't come back. It seemed a long time. Then the rain started, sir, and I waited a bit longer. Then he came, and he seemed worried about something. Well, I could see him through the window, sir, and he was having tea— There was a hungry note in the sergeant's voice. I wondered if I'd better slip off—to report, sir—or if you'd send someone. There was no sign of the other parties—"

"But you must listen! The murderer— He has attacked me... He left me, shut up, imprisoned, incarcerated—to die, to starve, to—"

"Just a minute, sir," Dunster pleaded. "Yes, Comfrey... Where is he now?"

"Well, sir, I thought you wouldn't have sent me there on a night like this if it hadn't been urgent, so I held on. He finished tea, and then he collected a bundle of stuff, sir—"

"Stuff?"

"Scarves, so far as I could see, sir," was the surprising reply. "And he put his coat and hat on, and a pair of mackintosh leggings and gumboots. So I says to myself, 'Hullo, you're going out then,' and I wished I'd got my own coat, sir—"

"Where is he now?" snapped Dunster.

"I don't know, sir—"

"The murderer— I know where you will find him—I hear—I listen. It is a woman! It is two woman! It is a man! I hear them say—"

Dunster could make nothing of it. "How did you find Mr. Vargas?" he asked.

"I didn't, sir. He found me... You see, as I was saying, he put on his things and went to the garage, carrying the bundle. And I thought to myself, 'If he takes the car, I'm done,' but I took its number, sir. However, outside the garage, it stopped for a minute. He got out to shut the garage doors. It came to me in a flash. I nipped up behind, and clung to the carrier, sir. Then we were off. It was awful, sir, with the mud, and the rain, and the exhaust fumes—"

"Where did he go?" Dunster asked wearily.

"I know! I will tell you! He went to the boathouse. They were carrying him. I hear it all. And then I dig! I burrow—"

It sounded like raving to Dunster. "Did he go to the boathouse?" he asked. "And what's this about carrying?"

"Well, he did—but no one carried him. He just walked. The car only went about a quarter of a mile, to a place where the road goes near the lake. Then he pulled it in to the shadow of the trees and we walked back to the house. He didn't go in, though. He went through the garden to the boathouse, still carrying the bundle, and I thought he was going to hide it. But instead, he just got into a boat, and rowed off, sir... So I thought I'd better come and report, sir... I couldn't swim after him, sir, and there wasn't another boat."

There was a note of pathos in Comfrey's voice. Dunster nodded.

"And then you met Mr. Vargas?"

"Da Vargas! da Vargas! You insult—and you will not listen—"

"Yes, sir," the sergeant went on. "I thought I'd just make sure about the car, and I'd just left it, when he bounds out of the wood on top of me, sir, and I thought it was a ghost or something. He was simply quivering with fright and blubbing like a baby, and I couldn't understand one word in ten of his gabble— I mean, sir, he was in an agitated condition, sir—but I got his story out of him, more or less—"

"I tell him. I tell you, but you will not understand. There is need for haste, yes? He escape! He go! He evade!"

Dunster decided that on the whole the sergeant was preferable.

"What did he say?" he asked.

"It appears, sir, he couldn't trust the police to find the murderer, so he was doing a bit of sleuthing on his own account. He followed Miss Blakeney to a shed in the pinewood, and went inside a little lean-to at one end of it. Either the door banged, or someone shut him in. He didn't see anyone but Miss Blakeney. But there was a sort of opening in the wall between the two parts of the hut, and he heard them talking. There was a sick man there who he says was the murderer, and they were talking of carrying him to the boathouse. Then they did, and left Mr. Var—Mr. da Vargas alone. That was this afternoon, sir. He burrowed his way out under the door eventually, sir; but lost his way in the woods, and stumbled on me, sir. And as we were coming along, the doctor picked us up."

"You saw nothing of all this?"

"No, sir. They didn't come near the boathouse. And they aren't at the boathouse, I searched it—"

"There's another boathouse on the lake—near the cottage where we found the body—" Stockton broke in. "Could they have gone—?"

"He is going! He is gone—" da Vargas was almost weeping. "By boat—by car! He escape—"

"Quick!" Dunster suddenly saw the situation. "Comfrey, go to where Alness left the car. If it's still there, watch by it and grab whoever comes. Take a couple of men—"

"Oh, it'll still be there, sir. I plugged the exhaust pretty well solid with mud!"

"Thank Heaven for that... You and you—" he turned to two of the constables—"go to Mr. Alness's house. Detain him if he's there, or if he returns... Now—" He suddenly remembered the Chief Constable. "Sorry, sir. It's very important—may be a matter of seconds. Could you arrange for a cordon and a description—"

Colonel Saltash was by no means the fool he sometimes appeared. He did not argue.

"Right, Inspector," he assented. "And perhaps—"

"Quick, Stockton!"

Dunster raced down the path with the superintendent after him. Almost before the Chief Constable had finished his sentence, the car started with a jerk down the lane.

Dunster was at the wheel himself, and he was utterly reckless. Rain made visibility nil; he had only a nodding acquaintance with the twisting lanes, and he drove like a demon. Stockton dare not ask any questions. He sat there hoping for the best, bracing himself against the jerks and lurches of the car, and trying to puzzle out what was happening. Once, on a clearer bit of road, Dunster spoke, and helped to clarify the situation a little.

"Alness is the murderer all right. The sick man must be George. Apparently his sister—and maybe the Newent girl—are trying to get him away. Helped by Alness!... And the scarves—? Oh, Great Heavens!"

The statement was a little obscure, but the accent of the last words conjured up sinister possibilities. They plunged into the lane leading to the cottage.

Luckily the point nearest the boathouse was only a few hundred yards along. It seemed to Stockton that they were on two wheels more often than not, and sometimes on one. He was resigned to their overturning. The car stopped suddenly opposite a gate.

Dunster was over the bank beside it before the superintendent had found it was locked. Stockton was at his heels. They felt grass under their feet, probably a track leading from the gate. And just ahead showed two streaks of light. In a few yards they saw the loom of a building, and as they reached it, it became plain that the light filtered through the cracks at the sides of a door. Dunster bent and peered through.

At first he thought that the place was empty. The big doors at the far end were closed, and two boats lay in the small dock into which they led, a motor-launch and an ordinary fair-sized rowing boat. And then he saw that the second one was not empty. Something moved in the bottom of it, just as a black figure passing across inside momentarily blotted out the view. As the figure receded and the light fell upon it, he saw that it was Alness, and he was carrying the body of a man in his arms.

For a moment Dunster thought the man was dead. Then one hand moved feebly, and his head turned a little towards the peephole. Dunster had never seen the man before, but, wasted as the face was, the family likeness told him that it must be George Blakeney.

Carrying his burden, Alness moved along to the side of the dock by which the boat was lying, and again the inspector had a clear view of its interior. In it were a woman and a man, both of them bound and gagged with the scarves which Comfrey had seen Alness collecting. Dunster had guessed the reason for the scarves. If the murderer aimed at producing the appearance of natural death, or accident, ropes might have left marks which would excite suspicion; the scarves properly used would not. As Alness lowered his burden into the boat, Dunster tried the door gently.

Even before he did so, he realised it was useless, for he could see the two dark patches across the crack which showed the latch and a bolt. Stockton, from the other side, turned a horrified face towards him, oddly illuminated by the vertical streak of light.

"What—what's he doing?" he breathed.

"Drown them," Dunster answered no more audibly, and he was convinced that it was the simple truth. "We must get in—"

"Going round to front," Stockton whispered, and disappeared.

Alness did not get into the boat. Instead, he came back towards them, and for an instant Dunster had a clear view of his face. It was completely unmoved, with just the trace of a frown about the eyebrows, showing the effort of concentration a man makes when he is trying to be particularly careful about some moderately important business. He seemed to be looking round generally to make sure he had forgotten nothing; and he stooped to pick up some small object out of range of Dunster's vision. Then he moved to the far end of the shed, and as he started to open the big double doors the inspector was aware that Stockton was again at his side.

"Can't get through—fence—" he heard a desperate whisper. "In the dark—"

Dunster reckoned they had something like two minutes. Once in the boat and through the doors, there would be no finding Alness on a night like that. They had to do something. The door did not feel very strong. Perhaps the bolt—

"Smash the door!" he said. "Together—now!"

Twenty-odd stone struck the door, and something yielded, but the door still held. They flung themselves at it again and the next moment fell forward inside as both hinges gave simultaneously.

Dunster was on his feet in a second, and dashed towards the dock, but he was too late. He saw Alness glance back at them over his shoulder as the boat's stern passed through the entrance; then it was lost to view in the driving rain.

"The car—" Stockton gasped. "He can't get away—"

"He'll never reach the car—or they won't," Dunster said drearily. "That launch—if—"

He was moving forward as a sudden hope struck him when something darted past. He fell into the launch with Stockton on top of him, and as the engine fired he looked up into the face of Athene Newent seated at the controls.

"Mr. Alness," she said as the boat started forward. "He is the murderer?"

It was as much a statement as a question. Dunster nodded.

"Miss Blakeney—George—Mayfield—" he stammered out.

"I know," she said, and bending forward switched on a powerful headlamp which Dunster had not even noticed. "I was there—when you broke in—"

Dunster tried to pierce the driving rain.

"We'll never find him," he groaned. "He may go any way—"

"He must go this way—a point— There!"

The lamp had picked up something, but lost it immediately, only to find it again at a touch of the rudder. He could see Alness clearly. The murderer had stopped rowing and was bending down in the boat. For a second a horrible idea crossed the inspector's mind that he was actually killing his captives. Then, as the launch drew alongside, Alness rose to his feet, and, before Dunster could jump, had dived over the side with scarcely a splash.

Dunster waited, staring down at the black water as Stockton seized the rowing boat and pulled it in. But Alness did not rise. He was aware all at once that Stockton had clambered into the boat, which Athene Newent had engaged with a boat hook, miraculously produced from nowhere.

"All right," the superintendent announced; then glanced over the side. "That means dragging the lake," he growled.

# 27

## Nemesis at Work

IT WAS NOT UNTIL late afternoon of the next day that the lake mud parted with the body of Alness. A search of the clothes revealed, in the weights Alness had apparently placed in his pockets when he stooped in the boat, the reason why he had never come to the surface, and it also produced from the breast pocket a sheaf of papers covered in black, fine writing. Dunster pulled the sodden sheets apart gingerly, glancing at a sentence here and there, and his eyebrows rose.

"It's a confession," he said. "That's odd, isn't it?"

"Why?"

"Didn't seem to me the kind of man who'd write one."

"Probably it can't be read, anyhow," Stockton suggested pessimistically.

"Written in Indian ink. That doesn't run in water, you know. Clear as print... Shall we—?"

"Get it over," Stockton suggested, and felt for his pipe. "Give us a rest, anyhow."

He settled himself as comfortably as he could and felt for his pipe as Dunster carefully peeled off the first sheet, which was blank.

"'I suppose I am abnormal,'" he read. "'I have just, as I hope, successfully compassed the death of two men, my own relations, and perfectly worthy, honest citizens, and I feel not the slightest qualm whatever.

"'I am not afraid of discovery; for I am convinced that I shall not be found out. I am not afraid of future punishment, for I believe in none. My conscience—whatever the word means—has never troubled me, and I have felt no compunction. In fact, even in the details of the business, some of them physically unpleasant, I have experienced principally a fascinated interest combined with a certain amusement.

"'The fact is, I have never in my life either hated, or been particularly fond of, any person. The passionate part of me seems to be completely wanting. I am not immoral, but amoral. I simply do not understand the attitude of the great bulk of humanity.

"'I am an Epicurean. I believe the aim of human life is the pursuit of moderate happiness, by simple pleasures, and the avoidance of pain and excess which brings it. And on these lines until a few months ago, I had successfully organised my life. Of course, one had to compromise a little.'"

Stockton shifted uneasily, and took his pipe from his mouth.

"Is there much more of this?" he grunted.

"He's coming to the point almost at once. He's trying, I think, to explain his motives."

"They generally do," said Stockton. "All right—"

"'The ultimate responsibility for the deaths of George and Richard Blakeney should be placed upon the heads of certain company directors, the Chancellor of the Exchequer, and His Majesty's Commissioners for Inland Revenue—'"

"What?" Stockton exclaimed. "The man's mad—"

"Not legally." Dunster smiled. "Only severely logical... 'As a result of their combined activities I found myself, nearly a year ago, suffering from a diminution of income. I was not in financial difficulties. I was not what anyone could call poor. But I should have to curtail expenditure, and therefore re-adjust my life.

"'I was not prepared to do this. I looked round for some means of acquiring money without risk or excessive trouble, and I came to the conclusion that my best course was to inherit the Blakeney estate.

"'My uncle, of course, presented no obstacle; since he was likely to die at any time. Virginia, as a woman, was excluded by the entail. There remained George and Richard, and the fact that there were two of them, while it made it highly unlikely I should ever inherit by fair means, made it more possible to succeed by foul. For, if there had only been George and I had murdered him, the police would have been bound to say "Cui bono?" and find the answer in me. But if I murdered George, leaving Richard untouched, no one would perceive that motive.

"'My scheme was, therefore, to kill George under such circumstances that Richard would certainly be hanged for the murder. Justice would be satisfied, and not a breath of suspicion raised against me when I inherited.

"'I gave the matter a great deal of thought, and made a number of preparations. For example, while on a shooting party I acquired a gun which had formerly belonged to Richard. I also prepared, from the deadly nightshade plant, some capsules containing a concoction of belladonna, which I knew to be in use in my uncle's house.

"'These were actually prepared for quite a different set of circumstances from those which actually occurred. George had planned a holiday on the Continent, and it was certain that he would be seasick. I proposed to give him the capsules as a remedy, and, since he was sensitive on the subject, he could be relied upon not to mention them. In fact, when it came to actually giving them, I had to offer them as a general headache cure for fear of hurting his feelings.

"'In the end, things turned out very differently. I had noticed that George was looking worried, but though we were on good terms he had told me nothing. It was entirely by chance that I saw him, on the night that he was supposed to have gone away, sitting alone on the station platform.

"'I went up and spoke to him, and immediately he poured out the whole story. I realised that it was a great opportunity, but, at that precise moment, was entirely unprepared. I had no weapon; the capsules were at my house; and the train was actually visible a couple of miles down the line.

"'I pointed out to him that going off that way was ridiculous; that the police could easily trace him; that he'd better come to my house for the night and think it over, and if he was still determined, I would help him next morning. The beauty of it was that it was all perfectly true, and it persuaded him.

"'We went by the field path, and met no one. I have always objected to servants, and my man, who does the bulk of the work, sleeps in a separate cottage. We were quite alone, and no one saw us. No one, going that way, was likely to.

"'I was still uncertain what to do. I thought of killing him then and there, and leaving the body somewhere in circumstances which would suggest Richard's guilt. But I was reluctant to do the murder actually in my own house. In these days of scientific detection, it is hard to be sure that one leaves no traces at all. I decided, in fact, to proceed with the original plan. So far as I could see, it was perfectly safe; but in case of accidents, I suggested to him that his tracks could best be covered by staging a suicide.

"'With that end in view, he left me various articles, including the suit he was wearing when he left home, to establish his identity with the help of a skeleton.

"'In the morning, to avoid being seen by my servant, he left the house and walked through the woods to a point where I was to pick him up in the car. I had already given him the capsules. By doing this, I established the fact that I left in the car alone, in case I should need to. I duly picked him up, drove him to a station on another line, and saw him off.

"'I believed that my work was finished. George would die at sea, apparently of a poison administered by his brother, who gained by his death, and with whom he had quarrelled. I thought that, when the police came to investigate the death, they could hardly avoid discovering about the liniment; but, if necessary, I was prepared to tell them.

"'He had hardly gone when two great weaknesses of my scheme occurred to me. First, the police might not think it was murder at all, but suicide. I tried to tell myself that they would appreciate the fact that no one would go to the trouble of preparing the capsules in order to poison himself; but the police can be singularly obtuse. Besides, George's manner—he was practically on the verge of a nervous breakdown—would support that theory.

"'The other was that, if George died at sea, the family might say nothing about it, at least until my uncle's death raised the question of inheritance; and while that might happen at any time, it might be postponed for years. In either case, the crime might never be brought home to Richard at all.

"'Evidently my precaution about the clothes and teeth—for, though George had had a permanent set made, the original temporary set was more comfortable, and he had left me the other—had been a wise one. I began to investigate the possibility of using a skeleton.

"'There were all sorts of difficulties. I read up the matter thoroughly, in books of forensic medicine, and I was very doubtful if it would be practicable. For example, it was going to be difficult to arrange circumstances in which the flesh would be entirely consumed, and not the various articles to prove identity. I learnt that experts can tell all kinds of things about age, time of death, height, and so on from the most meagre remnants, and my ignorance frightened me. Finally, it would be hard for me to buy a skeleton, of the right kind, under circumstances which would make it impossible for it to be traced.

"'It was a paragraph in the local paper which gave me the idea. I had been studying the matter all day since George left, and had practically given it up. Then I saw the obituary of a local man and the coincidence struck me.

"'He was within a year or two of George's age; very like him in height and build; had even lost all his teeth. If I could obtain possession of that body, things could hardly go wrong. I determined to dig it up.

"'By chatting to Stroud, I discovered the whereabouts of the grave. That night, I disguised myself so as to frighten anyone who might interrupt me, and as I had some luminous paint the result was really terrifying, drove the car round to a place across the fields and hid it, and then went to the churchyard and started work.

"'It took longer than I expected. However, at last I reached the coffin, and actually laid bare the name plate. I glanced at it quite idly—and to my utter amazement read the name of my aunt, Lady Blakeney.

"'For a moment, I honestly believed that it was some judgment of Heaven. Of course, that body was quite useless to me. For the first time in my life I was conscious of a blind rage against myself and everything else. Then I realised that the mistake was quite natural. I had simply reckoned from the wrong side of the path. Stroud, in his directions, was the reverse of clear. I had just decided to fill in the grave and try again some other time when I heard a cry.

"'It was a woman's voice, and I thought I could probably frighten her. I ran towards her, and she disappeared. Now, perhaps, my safest course would have been to make a bolt for it myself; but perhaps my brain was not so cool as usual. I reckoned that it would take some time before she could possibly induce anyone to return to see what was happening—if she managed to persuade them that night at all. I decided to remove all traces of my work. Then, it was highly improbable that any story she told would be accepted, or at least given a natural explanation.

"'I filled in the grave undiscovered, working like a madman. Of course, it did not take so long as it had done to dig out. It was too late, and too dangerous, to do any more that night, and I was forced to go home.

"'To try again next night may seem foolhardy. But I discovered that the woman whom I had frightened was my cousin, Virginia, and that all the people who knew about it were prepared to hush it up. Except Mr. Mayfield. And he was an argument in favour of doing it immediately; for if he were going to publish an account of it, it would be out next morning, and the churchyard would become an object of interest to the world in general. If any investigation was made, I doubted if it would extend to the other grave. What I had not reckoned upon was Mr. Mayfield's spending the night in the churchyard.

"'I was lucky to escape at all, and it would certainly be quite useless to take that body and pretend it was George's within any reasonable time. I filled in what I had done, and gave it up for the time being.

"'It would have been useless to my main object to kill Mr. Mayfield. I thought of that.

"'The whole matter passed off much more quietly than I had expected. I was able to exert my influence to some extent in hushing the matter up. But I still had no body. The question was, whether I dare acquire one in that way any more, or whether the police would associate the desecration of the graves with the finding of the body.

"'I determined to confuse the issue, and tampered with, but did not dig up, several other graves. Unfortunately, the negligence of the police was such that only one was discovered. Before that happened, from a churchyard some few miles away, I had actually secured a body without much trouble. It was not quite what I wanted. For example, the jaws still held a number of teeth. It was not a particularly pleasant task removing them, and I was afraid it might be noticed, in spite of the burning, at the post-mortem—'"

"And it ought to have been," Stockton snorted.

"Pathologists are almost human," Dunster answered. "I suppose the false teeth fooled them." He went on:

"'I hid the body near the cottage. I had already got to work with the anonymous letters. By means of them I contrived that Richard should make a preliminary visit there, in the hope he would provide some evidence against himself. Then I put the body in the cottage, arranged a simple device to start a fire by means of an alarm clock, and fixed an appointment with Richard for the critical time.

"'Actually, it nearly went wrong. The clock was fast. I had meant the fire to start about a quarter of an hour after he left. It happened immediately; but that did not matter.

"'Of course, the body has not yet been found. But I have taken the energetic and well-intentioned Mr. Mayfield into my confidence—more or less. If no one else finds it, I have little doubt I can induce him to do so. He is coming tonight. I believe I can congratulate myself upon a sound piece of work. George must be dead by now. Richard will probably be arrested tomorrow or the day after, and so far as I can determine, no one has any ground of suspicion against me whatever.'"

The writing ended at the top of a sheet. Stockton had grinned at the reference to Mayfield.

"That's not all?" he asked.

"No," Dunster answered, and peeled off another sheet. "This is a serial confession. Here's Instalment Two:

"'Something has gone wrong. I am almost inclined to believe in some kind of Nemesis. Bere has been poisoned by the capsules. Of course, it is easy enough to see what happened. George must have met him that morning on his way to the car and, very unwisely, stopped to talk. It is absolutely certain that Joe Bere would dilate upon his headaches—he'd had one the day before—and George was the kind of sympathetic fool who would give him the whole box.

"'But I don't know what is going to happen. For George is officially dead. Mayfield has found the body, and they will identify it tomorrow. So, with any luck, Richard will be hanged, if not for the murder of George, for the murder of Bere.

"'But George isn't dead—unless he kept a capsule or two. He may be hiding in some spot so remote from the world that he never hears what has happened. But the danger is that he will come back, and say that I gave him the capsules... I must try and trace him.'"

There was another gap in the manuscript. This time, Dunster had some little difficulty in separating the sheets, and Stockton had time to comment.

"I'm not surprised if he began to feel fate was against him," he said. "And maybe it was—?"

Dunster shrugged his shoulders and went on. "'I can find no trace of George. I have made the most exhaustive enquiries, and it seems absolutely certain that he did not leave by any boat from Southampton. I am getting a little worried.

"'If he should turn up—? It would, of course, be his word against mine, but still—'"

"'I am employing the aid of Mr. Mayfield, a very industrious and well-intentioned young man, who can be relied upon to give publicity to anything I want.'"

Dunster turned to the last sheet. It contained only a line or two.

"'George is here. My cousin and the woman he married, helped very magnanimously by Jim Bere, are looking after him. He seems to be off his head, but I am afraid it is only temporary, in the nature of a nervous breakdown. On the whole, I am inclined to think I have one chance. I must somehow kill George and, if necessary— Well, we shall see.

"'I wonder why I have written this? The truth is that I want to talk to someone about it, and there isn't anyone. Can it be that I have the glimmerings of a conscience after all, and that confession is good for the soul? But that is absurd.'"

Dunster stopped. On the back of the last sheet Stockton noticed that something had been written.

"There's something else," he pointed out.

"It's only poetry," Dunster said. "One might say, his epitaph."

And, not without expression, he read the lines:
"From too much love of living,
From hope and fear set free,
We thank with brief thanksgiving
Whatever gods may be.
That no man lives for ever,
That dead men rise up never,
That even the weariest river
Runs somewhere safe to sea."

# 28

## Conclusion

THERE WAS QUITE A long silence as he finished. Stockton scowled at the paper with an air of great distaste.

"I don't like it at all," he said at last. "Here was this chap, as mad as they make them, and a churchwarden and a J.P."

"But he wasn't mad in the ordinary sense," Dunster answered. "And if there hadn't been such a thing as income tax, perhaps he would have gone on being a churchwarden and a J.P. After all, the extent to which people feel things varies enormously. It just happened in his case, that he simply didn't feel things that happened to other people at all. If one grants the supposition that one's own comfort is the only important thing in the universe, his conduct was perfectly logical."

"But that is madness," Stockton insisted. "And what puts me in a cold sweat is to think how nearly he got away with it. If George Blakeney hadn't come back, or if he'd managed to kill George—"

"I'm inclined to think that we should have had him in the end," Dunster said thoughtfully. "Once one starts to look at him, he is suspicious all right."

"We'd really nothing against him—"

"Oh yes, we had. First of all, there was that alarm clock. That was what started me off. I confess I hadn't much hope when I told them to look for something of the kind; but it had occurred to me that the case against Richard might have been arranged. The clock made it fairly certain that it had; because no one was going to keep a clock in a place like that. When we opened the grave and found it empty, it became certain... I admit that at one time I was inclined to think it meant that George was trying to get Richard murdered. But I was beginning to have my doubts about Alness, otherwise I should never have sent Comfrey to watch him. And at the graveside, when you explained about the inheritance, it became absolutely obvious. We should have got him. Or, at least, we should have known he was responsible."

"We'd nothing definite, all the same."

"One thing, perhaps. The anonymous letter he showed to Mayfield. That was a bit too clever. Using Indian ink might have cast suspicion on Newent, but his real reason was that ordinary ink would have shown he'd only just written it."

"What about the missing letters?"

"There weren't any. He used that to cast suspicion on da Vargas, and numbering it seventeen was the easiest way to use a seven... All the same, it's as well he killed himself. The charge might have been difficult. He didn't mean to kill Bere—and he didn't kill anyone he meant to!"

"George is recovering," Stockton said, changing the subject. "I suppose he lost his head and wandered back by instinct?... And he's not guilty of bigamy after all, but married to that Newent girl—"

"Maybe he'll regret that." Dunster grinned. "He was a fool over that bigamy business. It seems certain that Mrs. Crouch had deliberately faked her death notice to trap him."

"Well, that's one good point about a nasty business," Stockton commented. "Good heavens! Five deaths, because of income tax!"

"Aren't you exaggerating?" Dunster smiled. "Old Blakeney would have died very soon, anyhow. Crouch couldn't last long, and in any case what happened there can't really be attributed to Alness—to give the devil his due. In fact—"

To Stockton's utter disgust, he lapsed into some unintelligible foreign language. He deliberately forbore to put the question, but curiosity got the better of him.

"Meaning?" he said coldly.

"'But they were destroyed by their own folly'... No, the income tax was only to blame for Alness himself and Bere... It seems pretty rough on Bere, but otherwise Nemesis has worked pretty thoroughly. Alness's perfect crime, in fact, failed to kill either of the people he had made sure of getting... Instead, it causes one of them to come into a fortune, clears George's marriage and abolishes a couple of blackmailers."

"Well, I suppose that settles up everything," Stockton said doubtfully. "Presumably the ghost was George?"

"Almost certainly, I think... Oh, and there's another person who benefits. A young, but energetic and deserving editor—"

Stockton sniffed.

"—at present walking in full view on the other side of the lake with a lady, would appear to have every chance of putting something into his paper other than the crime of the past few days."

Possibly recent events had left Stockton a little dense.

"Something else?" he queried.

"In the Births, Marriages and Deaths column. 'The marriage is announced—'"

## THE END

Visit our website to explore the list of great Golden Age books and sign up to our new titles newsletter:*

oleanderpress.com/collections/oreon-golden-age-detective-fiction

## Latest OREON titles in this series

*Casual Slaughters*
James Quince – 9781915475336

*The Doodled Asterisk*
R.A.J. Walling – 9781915475312

*The Mill House Murder*
J.S. Fletcher – 9781915475275

*Q.E.D.*
Lynn Brock – 9781915475268

*There's Death in the Churchyard*
William Gore – 9781915475251

*Murder of the Ninth Baronet*
J.S. Fletcher – 9781915475244

*Dead Man Manor*
Valentine Williams – 9781915475237

*The Man in the Dark*
John Ferguson – 9781915475220

*The Dressing Room Murder*
J.S. Fletcher – 9781915475213

**\* Free ePub & PDF on sign-up to the OREON newsletter**

Printed in Great Britain
by Amazon